BEVERLY LEWIS'
The SHUNNING

BEVERLY LEWIS'
The SHUNNING

BETHANY HOUSE PUBLISHERS

Minneapolis, Minnesota

The Shunning
Copyright © 1997
Beverly Lewis

Cover by design by Dan Thornberg, Design Source Creative Services.

Published by Bethany House Publishers
11400 Hampshire Avenue South
Bloomington, Minnesota 55438

Bethany House Publishers is a division of
Baker Publishing Group, Grand Rapids, Michigan

Printed in the United States of America.

ISBN 978-0-7642-0960-4

The Library of Congress has cataloged the original edition as follows:

Lewis, Beverly, date.
    The shunning / by Beverly Lewis.
        p.   cm. — (The heritage of Lancaster County ; 1)
    ISBN 1-55661-866-2
    1. Amish—Fiction. 2. Lancaster County (Pa.)—Fiction. I. Title. II. Series: Lewis, Beverly, Heritage of Lancaster County ; 1.
PS3562.E9383 S48   1997
813'.54—dc21   97–4648
                                                       CIP

DEDICATION

To the memory of

Ada Ranck Buchwalter (1886–1954),
who left her Plain community and
married the man who would
become my grandfather.

ABOUT THE AUTHOR

BEVERLY LEWIS, born in the heart of Pennsylvania Dutch country, is the *New York Times* bestselling author of more than eighty books. Her stories have been published in eleven languages worldwide. A keen interest in her mother's Plain heritage has inspired Beverly to write many Amish-related novels, beginning with *The Shunning*, which has sold more than one million copies. *The Brethren* was honored with a 2007 Christy Award.

Beverly lives with her husband, David, in Colorado.

I was *born* to other things.

Tennyson—*In Memoriam*

No living man can send me to the shades
Before my time; no man of woman born,
Coward or brave, can shun his destiny.

Homer—*Iliad*

PROLOGUE: KATIE

If the truth be known, I was more conniving than all three of my brothers put together. Hardheaded, too.

All in all, *Dat* must've given me his "whatcha-do-today-you'll-sleep-with-tonight" lecture every other day while I was growing up. But I wasn't proud of it, and by the time I turned nineteen, I was ready to put my wicked ways behind me and walk the "straight and narrow." So with a heart filled with good intentions, I had my kneeling baptism right after the two-hour Preaching on a bright September Sunday.

The barn was filled with my Amish kinfolk and friends that day three years ago when five girls and six boys were baptized. One of the girls was Mary Stoltzfus—as close as any real sister could be. She was only seventeen then, younger than most Plain girls receiving the ordinance, but as honest and sweet as they come. She saw no need in putting off what she'd always intended to do.

After the third hymn, there was the sound of sniffling. I, being the youngest member of my family and the only daughter, shouldn't have been too surprised to find that it was Mamma.

When the deacon's wife untied my *kapp*, some pigeons flapped their wings in the barn rafters overhead. I wondered if it might be some sort of sign.

Then it came time for the bishop's familiar words: "Upon your faith, which you have confessed before God and these many witnesses, you are baptized in the name of the Father, the Son, and the Holy Spirit. Amen." He cupped his hands over my head as the deacon poured water from a tin cup. I remained motionless as the water ran down my hair and over my face.

After being greeted by the bishop, I was told to "rise up." A Holy Kiss was given me by the deacon's wife, and with renewed hope, I believed this public act of submission would turn me into an honest-to-goodness Amishwoman. Just like Mamma.

Dear *Mam*.

Her hazel eyes held all the light of heaven. Heavenly hazel, I always called them. And they were, especially when she was in the midst of one of her hilarious stories. We'd be out snapping peas or husking corn, and in a blink, her stories would come rolling off her tongue.

They were always the same—no stretching the truth with Mam, as far as I could tell. She was a stickler for honesty; fairness, too, right down to the way she never overcharged tourists for the mouth-watering jellies and jams she loved to make. Her stories, *ach*, how she loved to tell them—for the telling's sake. And the womenfolk—gathered for a quilting frolic or a canning bee—always hung on every word, no matter how often they were repeated.

There were stories from her childhood and after—how the horses ran off with her one day, how clumsy she was at needlework, and how it was raising three rambunctious boys, one after another. Soon her voice would grow soft as velvet and she'd say, "That was all back before little Katie came along"—as though my coming was a wondrous thing. And it seemed to me, listening to her weave her stories for all the rest of the women, that this must be how it'd be when the Lord God above welcomed you into His Kingdom. Mamma's love was heavenly, all right. It just seemed to pour right out of her and into me.

Then long after the women had hitched their horses to the family buggies and headed home, I'd trudge out to the barn and sit in the hayloft, thinking. Thinking long and hard about the way Mamma always put things. There was probably nothing to ponder, really, about the way she spoke of me—at least that's what Mary Stoltzfus always said. And she should know.

From my earliest memories, Mary was usually right. I was never one to lean hard on her opinion, though. Still, we did everything together. Even liked the same boys sometimes. She was very bright, got the highest marks through all eight grades at the one-room schoolhouse where all us Amish kids attended.

After eighth grade, Mary finished up with book learning and turned her attention toward becoming a wife and mother someday. Being older by two years, I had a head start on her. So we turned our backs on childhood, leaving it all behind—staying home with our mammas, making soap and cleaning house, tending charity gardens, and going to Singing every other Sunday night. Always together. That was how things had been with us, and I hoped always would be.

Mary and Katie.

Sometimes my brother Eli would tease us. "*Torment* is more like it," Mary would say, which was the honest truth. Eli would be out in the barn scrubbing down the cows, getting ready for milking. Hollering to get our attention, he'd run the words together as if we shared a single name. "Mary 'n Katie, get yourselves in here and help! Mary 'n Katie!"

We never complained about it; people knew we weren't just alike. *Jah*, we liked to wear our good purple dresses to suppers and

Singing, but when it came right down to it, Mary and I were as different as a potato and a sugar pea.

Even Mamma said so. Thing is, she never put Mary in any of her storytelling. Guess you had to be family to hear your name mentioned in the stories Mam told, because family meant the world to her.

Still, no girl should have been made over the way Mamma carried on about me. Being Mam's favorite was both a blessing and a curse, I decided.

In their younger years, my brothers—Elam, Eli, and Benjamin— were more ornery than all the wicked kings in the Bible combined— a regular trio of tricksters. Especially Eli and Benjamin. Elam got himself straightened out some last year around Thanksgiving, about the time he married Annie Fisher down Hickory Lane. The responsibilities of farming and caring for a wife, and a baby here before long, would settle most any fellow down.

If ever I had to pick a favorite brother, though, most likely Benjamin would've been it. Which isn't saying much, except that he was the least of my troubles. He and that softhearted way he has about him sometimes.

Take last Sunday, for instance—the way he sat looking so forlorn at dinner after the Preaching, when Bishop Beiler and all five of his children came over to eat with us. The bishop had announced our upcoming wedding—his and mine—that day right after service. So now we were officially published. Our courting secret was out, and the People could start spreading the news in our church district, the way things had been done for three hundred years.

The rumors about all the celery Mamma and I had planted last May would stop. I'd be marrying John Beiler on Thursday, November twenty-first, and become stepmother to his five young children. And, jah, we'd have hundreds of celery sticks at my wedding feast—enough for two-hundred-some guests.

Days after the wedding was announced, Benjamin put on his softer face. Today, he'd even helped hoist me up to the attic to look for Mam's wedding dress, which I just had to see for myself before I finished stitching up my own. Ben stayed there, hovering over me like I was a little child, while I pulled the long dress out of the big black trunk. Deep blue, with a white apron and cape for purity, the dress was as pretty as an Amish wedding dress could be.

Without warning, Ben's words came at me—tumbled right out into the musty, cold air. "Didja ever think twice about marrying a widower with a ready-made family?"

I stared at him. "Well, Benjamin Lapp, that's the most ridiculous thing I've ever heard."

He nodded his head in short little jerks. "It's because of Daniel Fisher, ain't?" His voice grew softer. "Because Daniel went and got himself drowned."

The way he said it—gentle-like—made me want to cry. Maybe he was right. Maybe I was marrying John because Dan Fisher was dead—because there could never be another love for me like Dan. Still, I was stunned that Ben had brought it up.

Here was the brother who'd sat behind me in school, yanking my hair every chance he got, making me clean out the barn more times than I could count . . . and siding against me the night Dat caught me playing Daniel's old guitar in the haymow.

But now Ben's eyes were full of questions. He was worrying out loud about my future happiness, of all things.

I reached up and touched his ruddy face. "You don't have to worry, brother," I whispered. "Not one little bit."

"Katie . . . for certain?" His voice echoed in the stillness.

I turned away and reached into the trunk, avoiding his gaze. "John's a *gut* man," I said firmly. "He'll make a right fine husband."

I felt Ben's eyes boring a hole into the back of my head, and for a long, awkward moment he was silent. Then he replied, "Jah, right fine he'll be."

The subject was dropped. My brother and everyone else would just have to keep their thoughts to themselves about me and the forty-year-old man I was soon to marry. I knew well and good that John Beiler had one important thing on his mind: He needed a mamma for his children. And I, having been blessed with lavish mother-love, was just the person to give it.

Respect for a husband, after all, was honorable. In time, perhaps something more would come of our union—John's and mine. Perhaps even . . . love.

I could only hope and pray that my Dan had gone to his eternal reward, and that someday I'd be found worthy to join him there.

Thoughts of Dan and the streets of gold were still flitting through my mind long after Ben left. The attic was mighty cold now and I refolded Mamma's dress, trying to find the spot where it had been packed away, when I stumbled upon a tiny rose-colored dress. A satin baby dress. In the middle of our family treasures was the loveliest infant gown I'd ever seen, all tucked away in tissue paper.

I removed the covering and began to stroke the fabric. Amish babies wore plain dresses in pale hues. Never patterns or plaids. And never, never satin. Where in all the world had Mamma gotten such a fancy thing?

Carefully, I inspected the bodice, letting my fingers linger on its creamy smoothness. Suddenly I felt like dancing. And—unruly idea that it was—I succumbed to the impulse. Stood right up and began twirling around the attic, a whisper of satin pressed against my cheek.

I was lost in a world of my vivid imagination—colorful silk, gleaming jewels, golden mirrors. Turning and swirling, I flew, light as a summer cloud, over the wooden floorboards. But with my dancing came the old struggles, my personal tug-of-war between plain and fancy. How I longed for beautiful things! Here I was twenty-two years old, published to marry the bishop—and fighting the same old battles.

In my frustration, I started humming a sad song—a tune Dan Fisher and I had made up on his guitar, the one Dat had forbidden me to play. The one I'd hidden away from his stern eyes all these years.

Time and again, I'd offered up my music and my tendency toward fancy things on the altar of repentance. Long and hard I prayed, but in spite of everything, I'd find myself sneaking glances in a hand mirror, asking myself: *How would my hair look without the bun or the ever-widening middle part?*

Sometimes, as a child, I would pull off my white organdy kapp and let the auburn locks fall free, down past my shoulders. It was most tempting when I was supposed to be dusting or cleaning the upstairs. At least the Lord God had done me a favor and put a right nice color in my hair—reddish brown hues—and when the sun from my window shone on it just right, there were streaks like golden ribbons in it. At times like these, I hated having to wrap my hair back up in a bun, hiding it away under my head covering.

And there was the problem of music—my special tunes. Some fast, some slow; all forbidden. My church taught that music was meant to come from hymnbooks for the purpose of worshiping God. Anything else was sinful.

I'd tried to follow the *Ordnung*, the unwritten rules of our church district. With every ounce of me, I'd tried to be a submissive young woman. Yet finding the fancy dress had stirred it all up again—my stubborn streak and the conflict with Dat over the music. Did I dare marry Bishop John with these sins gnawing away at my soul?

I glanced at the trunk where Mamma's wedding dress lay. Thoughtfully, I went to it, touching the heavy fabric with one hand and holding the satin dress in the other—comparing the two. I'd heard there were modern brides, outsiders in the non-Amish *English* world, who wore such things as satin and lace and gauzy veils.

Mamma's blue wedding dress was far from being truly beautiful, really. Except for its white cape and apron, it looked identical to her other church dresses. I held the dress up to me, tucking my chin over the high neckline, wondering what it would be like to try it on. But Mam had been much stockier than I when she married Dat. I knew I'd probably swim in it, so big it was.

Wear your mamma's clothing, get your mamma's life.

Dan Fisher had said that once, after I'd confessed my silly whim. "You know, it's just for fun," I'd insisted, surprised at what he'd said about my mamma's life—as if there were something wrong with it. I didn't ask him about it, though. Just let it be.

Dan must not have realized it, but what I'd meant to say was: What would it be like to wear "English" clothes—not Mamma's or another Plain woman's clothes, but fancy, modern clothes?

I put the wrinkled wedding dress away and reached for the satin baby garment. Glancing down, I saw a name hand stitched into the back facing.

Katherine Mayfield.

Instantly, I felt envy stir up in me toward this baby, this Katherine, whoever she was. What was *her* dress doing in *our* attic?

Thou shalt not covet.

I could hear the words from Dat's lips. He'd drilled them into me and many others like them from my childhood on. Words like, "If you don't kindle a little fire to begin with, you'll never have to worry about snuffin' out a big one."

My father was like that. Always chiding me about one thing or another growing up. But now . . . now that I was a grown woman, my wicked ways were still very much alive. It seemed I'd never measure up, at least not for Dat. Probably not for God, either.

A half hour later, my brothers found me sobbing beside the attic trunk, still clutching the little rose-colored gown. And from that moment on, nothing was ever the same for me. Not for a single one of us here in Hickory Hollow.

CHAPTER ONE

November days, being what they were in southeastern Pennsylvania, held an icy grip all their own. The wind, keen and cold, whipped at Rebecca Lapp's black wool shawl. Her long apron was heavy with logs for the cookstove as she headed up the snowy back steps of the stone farmhouse.

The sprawling house had been built in 1840 by her husband's ancestor, Joseph Lapp, and his stonemason friend. Now, over a century and a half later, the house was little changed. It stood—stately and tall—untouched by the outside world and its gadgets and gimmickry. Here, things went on as they always had—slow and tranquil—pacing out the days like an Amish *Grossmutter*, with serenity and grace.

Some time after, as was Amish custom, an addition called the *Grossdawdi Haus*—a grandfather house for aging relatives—had been built onto the east side.

The sky had deepened to purple as the sun prepared to slip down out of the sky, and Rebecca made her way into the warm kitchen to slide the chopped wood into the grate on top of her large black-metal stove. That done, she removed her full-length shawl and hung it over one of the wooden pegs in the utility room, just inside the back door.

Potatoes, now at a rolling boil, teased the sides of the black kettle as she tested them with a fork—done to perfection. Turning, she noticed the table still unset and craned her neck toward the front room. "Katie, supper!" she called to her daughter.

Then with the expertise of one who had cooked and baked an array of farm produce for as long as she could remember, Rebecca reached for a potholder and leaned down to inspect the home-cured ham in the oven. "Jah, gut," she whispered, smiling in approval as she breathed in its sweet aroma.

Minutes later, as though on cue, Eli, Benjamin, and their father came inside, removed their wide-brimmed, black felt hats, heavy sack coats, and work boots, and headed for the polished black woodstove near the center of the enormous kitchen.

"Startin' to sleet out," Samuel said, rubbing his hands together. He pulled a chair up close to the old range and stuck out his stock-inged feet, warming them.

"We're in for a cold snap, all right," Rebecca replied, glancing at the long sawbuck table adorned with a simple green-checkered oilcloth. "Katie-e-e!" she called again.

When there was still no answer, concern creased Rebecca's brow. Her worried expression must have baffled Samuel Lapp, for he spoke right up. "*Ach*, what's-a-matter? Do ya think daughter's ill?"

Rebecca gazed at the gas lamp hanging over the table and wondered what could be keeping Katie. It wasn't like her to be late.

From his spot near the warm stove, Samuel began to call, "Katie, supper! Come now, don't delay!"

When their daughter did not come bounding down the steps at his summons, he glowered. Rebecca felt her cheeks grow pale.

Apparently Eli noticed, too. "Mam?"

She stood there, stock still, as though waiting for an answer to drop from heaven. "Where could Katie be?" she managed at last, gripping the platter of steaming sliced ham with both hands.

Samuel shrugged, pulling on his bushy beard. "Wasn't she here in the house?"

Quickly Rebecca turned, fixing her sons with an inquiring stare. "You boys seen her?"

"Don't know that I seen her most the afternoon," Eli spoke up.

"Benjamin? When did *you* see your sister last?"

He ran his fingers through a shock of thick blond hair. "I don't—"

"Well, did you see her or not?" Rebecca demanded, almost immediately regretting the sharp tone she'd taken with her youngest son.

Samuel went to the sink and turned on the spigot, facing the window as the water rushed over his red, callused hands. "Eli and Benjamin were out shreddin' cornstalks with me," he explained over his shoulder. "No need to be pointing fingers just yet."

His words stung, but Rebecca clamped her jaw shut. A submissive wife was to fear the Lord and respect her husband, which meant letting Samuel have the last word. She turned slowly, placing the platter of meat on the stovetop.

Still in his stocking feet, Samuel strode into the living room and called up the steps. "Katie . . . supper!"

It was at that moment that Benjamin appeared to remember. "Oh, she might still be in the attic. I helped her up there a while back."

Rebecca's heart gave a great leap. *The attic?*

"What's she want up there?" Samuel mumbled, obviously annoyed at the delay, and marched back into the kitchen.

"To have a look at Mam's wedding dress, I guess."

Rebecca studied her son. "Well, go on up and fetch her down, will you?" she asked, careful not to betray her growing desperation.

Following Eli, who steadied the oil lantern, Benjamin scrambled up the stairs, his hollow stomach growling as he went.

"Whatcha think's wrong?" Eli asked as they came to the landing.

Benjamin glanced up at his brother on the rung above him. "With Katie?"

"No." Eli snorted. "With Mamma."

Benjamin had a pretty good notion. "Katie's gettin' married next week—Mam's losin' her only daughter. That's all there is to it."

"Jah." It was pretty clear that Eli wasn't exactly certain what Ben meant. But they both knew one thing for sure: Getting married was a way of life in Hickory Hollow. You found a nice honest girl among the People and got yourself hitched up. Mam ought to be mighty happy about Bishop John; Katie, too—with the widower coming to her rescue, so to speak. At twenty-two, an Amish girl—no matter how headstrong and feisty—wouldn't be smart to be too picky. His sister had scared more than one boy away on that basis alone.

Eli continued his climb up the attic ladder but stopped halfway.

"Keep on going," Ben muttered, thinking about the tender, juicy ham downstairs. "Time's a-wastin'."

Eli put out his hand, shushing him. "Wait . . . listen."

"What is it?" Ben cocked his head.

"Hear that?"

Ben strained his ears, staring hard at the attic door above them. "Well, I'll be . . . sounds like Katie's cryin' up there."

Without warning, he charged past Eli—crawled right over the

top of him and up the ladder—nearly knocking the lantern out of his brother's hand.

Downstairs, while Samuel read the public auction notices in *Die Botschaft*, Rebecca pulled out the drawer nearest the sink and gathered up five sets of utensils—one for each of the Lapp family members who would be present around her table this night.

Jah, this was a daughter's chore, but it didn't much matter who placed the dishes on the old table. Katie had been busy, after all, caught up with wedding plans.

Of all things, her daughter—ending up with Bishop Beiler and his young brood. The Lord God sure had a way of looking out for His own. And after what happened to Katie's first love—poor Daniel Fisher, who'd gotten himself drowned in that sailing accident. Yes, Rebecca felt mighty blessed the way things were turning out.

She sat down, recalling the first time Katie's pudgy little hands had set this table. The memory was soothing—a vision of days long past.

Katie's first table setting had been a surprise of sorts. At only three and a half, the little girl was mighty pleased with herself, knowing she'd be winning her mamma's approval. Eventually, though, the years would show that when it came down to it, what people thought of her had little to do with what made Katie Lapp tick.

Rebecca's sweet reminiscence served to push back the secret fear, push it deep into the inner sanctuary of her mind. That place where she'd learned to carry it, sequestered from all conscious thought.

The secret.

She sighed, trying not to think of the consequences of its discovery. Katie . . . in the attic? The thought sent a shiver tingling down her spine. Rebecca rose and touched her kapp, letting her hand trail along the narrow white ties as she went to the back door and stood inside the utility room.

Lord God of heaven, forgive me. She'd prayed the words silently each and every day for the past twenty-two years, wondering if God had heard. Maybe, observing her dedication and contrite heart, He had forgiven her. But if so, what was God doing now? What was He allowing to happen?

Rebecca's gaze swept the wide yard and beyond, toward the barn. Layers of sleet covered the sloping bank of earth that led to the two-story haymow. The ice storm had brought fierce wind, its shrill voice whistling ominously in her ears. She felt it pound against the door like an intruder and was grateful for the reliable woodstove in the center of the kitchen, warming the spacious room.

Rebecca turned away from the cold window and glanced at the day clock, wishing Katie would hurry and come. Supper was getting cold.

Upstairs, a blast of arctic air greeted Benjamin as he shoved open the hatchlike attic door. With little effort, he pulled himself up the ladder and into the storage room. There he was met by a strange sight. Draped halfway over a rectangular trunk, his sister sat crumpled in a heap on the cold floor, her head buried in her arms.

The trunk lid was down now, and Benjamin saw no sign of his Mam's wedding dress. But there was an unusual-looking piece of fabric—he couldn't quite make out what—in his sister's hand. Was it a scrap for a quilt? No, from where he stood, it seemed almost shiny—too fussy for the bed coverings Katie often made with Mary Stoltzfus and their many girl cousins and friends down Hickory Lane.

Unsure as to what to do, he stood there watching as Katie whimpered within arms' reach. As far as he could remember, he'd never touched his sister except when they'd played together as youngsters. He wasn't sure he ought to now. Besides—all bent over that way—she wasn't looking at him, hadn't seen him come up. She'd probably jump right out of her skin if he touched her.

While Benjamin was still wondering what to do, Eli peeked over the opening in the floor, his blue eyes wide. "Psst, Ben," he whispered. "What's-a-matter with her?"

About that time, Katie began to stir. Wiping her tear-streaked face with her long apron, she seemed oblivious for a moment. Then she turned toward them, and in the lantern's glow, Ben could tell that she was trembling. "Mam's waitin' supper," he said, eyeing her carefully.

Katie leaned on the trunk, pushing herself to a standing position, and Ben put out a hand to help her. "It's freezin' cold up here," he said. "Why'dja stay so long?"

Katie ignored his outstretched hand along with his question and adjusted her kapp. Then slowly, she straightened until she stood tall and erect, her jawline rigid. "I'm coming down, so scram, both of you!"

Ben and Eli did as they were told and scuffled down the ladder—Ben, still thinking about Katie's tears. He'd heard about women getting all weepy-eyed before a wedding. His oldest brother, Elam, had said something like that just last year, several days before he and his bride tied the knot.

He scratched his head, puzzled. *Tears must mean Katie'll be missin' us come next week*, he decided. He broke into a grin. Wouldn't do to let on to Katie what he was thinking, though. The way she was acting, there was no telling what she'd say. Or do.

CHAPTER TWO

Katie took her time leaving the attic room. She waited until her brothers were out of sight, then reopened the trunk and returned the baby garment to its original spot.

Downstairs, after washing her face and hands repeatedly, Katie took her usual place at the supper table—to the right of her mother. "Sorry, Dat . . . Mamma." Her face felt flushed, her eyes puffy.

Of course, she wouldn't lie. But she had no intention of explaining the *real* reason for her delay. No one must ever know of her dreadful obsession. Known sin required confession—she knew that. Good for the soul, maybe, but impossible under the circumstances. Confession would mean turning away, never again repeating the transgression. . . .

The fact that Katie hadn't looked either of them in the eye troubled Rebecca. Samuel didn't seem to notice, though. He bowed his head for the silent blessing without the slightest reference to Katie's tardiness.

After the "Amen," Samuel served himself first, then Eli and Benjamin wasted no time digging in to the heaping bowl of buttered potatoes. When the ham platter was passed, everyone took hearty portions. Next came lima beans, and chow-chow—a sweet bean relish—cut creamed corn, and bread with apple butter. A fat slice of raisin spice cake topped off the meal.

An occasional belch from Eli and Samuel signaled that Rebecca's efforts had been a success. Aside from that, there was only the scrape of cutlery against plastic plates, the satisfied grunts of the men, the homey sound of a fire crackling in the woodstove.

From time to time, Rebecca risked a sidelong glance at Katie. The girl hadn't spoken a word since she sat down. *What's ailin' her?* Rebecca wondered, thoughts churning. But it was the fear gnawing at her stomach that brought on the indigestion.

Eventually, Samuel leaned back and folded his arms across his chest, his gesture indicating that he was finished eating. At first, Rebecca wasn't certain he was going to speak. Finally, in measured tones, he asked the question hanging heavy on all their minds. "Did you find your mamma's weddin' dress, then?"

Katie reached for her glass. Slowly, deliberately, she drank from it.

Silence draped itself like a shawl over the barren gray walls. Seconds lagged.

Rebecca could take it no longer. "Katie, are you ill?" She slipped her arm around her daughter's trim waist, and Katie stiffened without speaking.

Samuel was not one to tolerate disrespect, and Rebecca knew what was coming. As sure as a brush fire in a windstorm. "Both your Mam and I have spoken to ya," he scolded without raising his voice.

Still no response from the girl with autumn brown eyes and reddish hair, wound tightly into a bun under the solemn white netting. Katie refused to look up until Eli kicked her under the table. A hefty, swift kick to the shinbone.

"Ach!" She glared across the table at the culprit.

Eli sneered, "Don't you have nothin' to say for yourself?"

"Eli!" his father cut in. "That'll do!"

Rebecca's grasp tightened on Katie's waist. Now the fire was sure to come. She braced herself for the heat.

"I . . . uh, Dat," Katie began at last, "there's something I have to say. . . ."

Rebecca felt the tension draining out of muscles coiled tight as a garden snake. Her daughter—only nine days before her wedding—had averted a near disaster. The kindling of her father's wrath.

"There is something I must tell you—both of you," Katie went on. She looked first at Samuel, then at Rebecca, who had folded her hands as if in prayer. "Ever since I was little, being Plain has been burdensome to me." She took a deep breath. "More burdensome for me than most, it seems."

"Bein' Amish is who you are through and through." Her father's voice was unemotional yet definitive. "Plain is how the Lord God meant you to be. You ought to be ashamed, saying things such as that after bein' baptized . . . taking the kneeling vow and all."

Rebecca clasped her hands tighter in a wordless plea.

"I best be speaking to Bishop John." Katie could feel her eyes filling with tears. "I have to speak to him . . . about . . ." She paused, drawing in another thready breath. "About the wedding."

"Now, Katie," her mother intervened. "Just wait a day or two, won't ya? This'll pass, you'll see."

Katie stared at her mother. "But I've sinned against Dat . . . and . . . the church."

Samuel's expression darkened. "Daughter?"

"It's the music—all those songs in my head. I can't make them go away," she blurted. "I've tried, but the music keeps tempting me." She bit her tongue and kept silent about the other temptings, the never-ending yearning for beautiful things.

Rebecca patted her hand. "Maybe a talk with Bishop Beiler would do us all some good."

"Alone, Mamma. I must see John alone."

Samuel's green shirt and tan suspenders accentuated the red flush creeping up his neck and into his face. "Maybe if you'd destroyed that instrument of evil when I first caught you at it, that guitar wouldn't be destroyin' you now."

He continued to restrain her with a piercing gaze. "You'll be confessing this before the next Preaching. If you're serious about turning away from sin and crucifying the flesh, you'll find a way."

"I've tried all these years, Dat. I wish I could shut off the music." But even as she spoke, a stubborn defiance surged in her, demanding its way. She did not *want* to stop the music—not her beloved music. Not the precious thing she and Daniel Fisher had so joyously shared.

Stubbornness gave way to guilt. She had just lied to her own father. One sin had given birth to another, and penance was long overdue. If she ever wanted to see Daniel in the courts of glory, Katie knew what was expected of her. A private confession in front of their elderly deacon and preacher Yoder. Her first ever.

Samuel adjusted his metal-rim glasses and scrutinized Katie across the table. "I forbade you to play music many years ago, and I forbid you now," he said. " 'Doth a fountain send forth at the same place sweet water and bitter?' "

He pushed his chair away from the table, causing it to screech against the linoleum floor. Significant in its absence was the silent table grace that always followed the meal. With a grunt, he shuffled into the living room. Eli and Benjamin disappeared into a far corner of the house, as if grateful to escape the shameful scene.

Under a ring of light, mother and daughter sat worlds apart. Rebecca willed her trembling to cease, relieved that her daughter's outburst had nothing whatever to do with the past—that dreadful secret that could swallow them up. Every last one of them.

Still, as she sat beside her only daughter—the child of her dreams—there was one consolation. *This* predicament could be remedied easily enough. A sigh escaped her lips, and with eyes closed, she breathed a prayer of thanks—for Katie's confession of sin. For having had twenty-two blessed years with this precious child.

She looked into Katie's eyes and wiped tears from her cheeks, resolving to pay a visit to the attic just as soon as the dishes were done.

Quietly, with Katie's help, Rebecca set to work clearing the table. She heated the water brought up by the battery-operated well pump and began rinsing the dishes. Then into the same hot water she added the dish detergent. Swishing it around, she lowered a fistful of silverware into the foamy suds, allowing the warmth to soothe her. *Things'll be fine*, she told herself, *once the wedding's behind us.*

The two women made quick work of the dishes, rinsing then drying each plate and cup, without their usual lighthearted conversation. Deliberately, Rebecca put away the few remaining leftovers before finding the courage to speak. "So you'll be thinking things over, then . . . about talking to the bishop?"

Katie swept the crumbs from the floor. "Don't you understand, Mamma?" She turned to face her. "I don't want to back out on the wedding. I'm just wondering if I'm the best choice for a bishop's wife."

Rebecca's eyes searched her daughter's. "The time for wondering is long past, Katie. Your wedding day's nearly here."

Katie's lip quivered uncontrollably.

"What's really bothering ya, child?" She reached for Katie and drew the slender form into her arms.

Long, deep sobs shook Katie's body as Rebecca tried to console her. "There, there," she whispered. "It's just the jitters. We women-folk all get them, but as time passes, you'll get better at hiding them." She paused for a moment. Then, attempting to lighten the mood, she added, "Why, I 'spect you'll feel this way before the birth of your first little one, most likely."

Rebecca felt Katie pull away, a curious expression on her face replacing her tears. "What, Katie? What is it?"

Katie straightened, adjusting her long apron and dress. "I almost forgot to ask you something."

"Jah?"

"Mamma, who is Katherine Mayfield?"

Rebecca felt weak, as if her limbs might no longer support her. *This cannot be*, she thought.

"I saw the name stitched on a baby dress . . . up in the attic. Ach, it was so pretty. But where did you come by such a thing, Mam?"

Without warning, the strength left Rebecca's legs entirely. She stumbled across the kitchen toward the long table bench.

Katie reached out to steady her. "Mamma!"

Rebecca dropped onto the bench and tugged at her apron. Then she pulled out a white hankie and with short, jerky motions began to fan herself. Everything came home to her at that moment—the worry of the years, the long-kept secret. . . .

Katie ran to open the back door a crack. "There, Mamma," she called as frigid air pushed through the utility room and into the kitchen. "That's better, ain't?"

In spite of the draft, Rebecca felt heat rush to engulf her head. She tried to look up, to catch one more glimpse of the beloved face.

Only a deep sigh emerged. *Katie, my girl. My precious girl* . . .

Through blurred vision, she could see Katie closing the door, shoving back the wintry blast, then hurrying toward her, all concerned and flustered. But try as she might, Rebecca Lapp could not will away the peculiar, prickly sensation creeping up her neck and into her dizzy head.

She slumped forward, aware of nothing more. . . .

CHAPTER THREE

"Dat, come quick!"

At the sound of Katie's frantic voice, Samuel, along with Benjamin and Eli, rushed into the kitchen.

"I don't know what on earth happened!" Katie's heart was pounding. "We were just talking—Mam and me—and—" Her mother was as physically fit as any farmer's wife in Hickory Hollow, certainly plump and hearty enough to ward off a mere fainting spell. "I'll get some tea leaves."

Reluctant to leave her mother, Katie hurried downstairs to the cold cellar, where neat rows of cabinets stored canned fruits and vegetables. She found the dried mint leaves in a jar and quickly pinched some into her hand, still puzzled over what had caused her mamma to faint.

Katie had mentioned speaking to the bishop. Had the idea of not going through with the marriage troubled her mother enough to make her ill?

She returned the jar of mint to its spot on the shelf and closed the cabinet door, pondering the strange circumstances. "Katie, are ya coming?" Benjamin called out.

"On my way," she answered, running up the steep cellar steps.

In the kitchen, Katie brewed some mint tea, glancing repeatedly at her mother, who had come to and was leaning her head on one hand, while Eli fanned her with the hankie.

Dat stood at Mam's side, pensive and silent. He seemed shorter now, his wiry frame bent over his wife. Katie wondered if he was still vexed over her awkward yet truthful admission at the table. Still, she was glad she'd told on herself. At least one aspect of her sinfulness would be dealt with. And if she was to go through with the wedding, she'd be offering her first private confession tomorrow or the next day.

Katie stirred the hot water, hoping to hurry the tea-making process. She stared at Rebecca apprehensively. Spouting off those careless words—that she'd better have a talk with Bishop John—had wreaked such havoc! She hadn't meant to upset anyone unduly; now she wished she'd kept her thoughts to herself.

"Hurry it up, Katie," Benjamin said, coming over to see what was taking so long.

She moved quickly, spooning honey into the hot water. But by the time the leaves had steeped long enough to embrace the soothing mint taste, Rebecca had gone upstairs to lie down.

When Katie stepped into the room a bit later, she found her mother still fully dressed but covered with the warmest quilts from the handmade cedar chest at the foot of the double bed. She held out the teacup on its matching saucer, and her father took it from her with a curt nod of his head.

"Is there anything else you need, Mamma?"

Dat answered for her. "That'll do."

Katie left without another word.

Rebecca settled back against the bed pillows with a slight smile on her face as she accepted the cup from Samuel and took a sip. "Des gut."

He reached for the kerosene lamp on the bedside table. "I'll go on down and stoke up the stove a bit. Can't let ya catch a chill, not with daughter's weddin' day a-comin'."

"No need to worry."

Samuel shook his head thoughtfully. "A body could get right sick in a cold snap like this."

Rebecca forced a chuckle. It caught in her throat, and she began to cough—as if in fulfillment of his prophecy.

Samuel Lapp was a dear and caring husband. A good provider of the basic needs—an abundance of food from their own land, a solid roof over their heads. . . . Gas furnaces, electricity, telephones, and such luxuries were for the English. Amish folk relied on horses and buggies for transportation, propane gas to run their camper-sized refrigerators, and a battery-operated well pump in the cellar for the household water. In fact, the Lapp family held tenaciously to all the Old Order traditions without complaint, just as generations before them.

"How can ya miss whatcha never had?" Samuel often asked his English friends at Central Market in downtown Lancaster.

Rebecca watched her husband, expecting him to slip out of the room without further comment. She was a bit surprised when he hesitated at the door, then returned to her bedside.

"Are you in poor health, then? Shall I be fetchin' a doctor?" His concern was genuine. "Wouldn't take but a minute to hitch up ol' Molasses and run him over to the Millers' place."

Peter and Lydia Miller—Mennonites who indulged in the "English" lifestyle—lived about a mile down Hickory Lane and had offered their telephone in case of emergency. On several occasions, Samuel had taken them up on it. After all, they were kin—second cousins on Rebecca's side—and modern as the day was long.

"Won't be needing any doctor. I'm wore out, that's all," she said softly, to put his mind at ease. "And it'd be a shame if Cousin Lydia had to worry over me for nothing."

"Jah, right ya be."

Shadows flickered on the wall opposite the simple wood-framed bed. Rebecca stared at the elongated silhouettes as she sipped her tea. She sighed, then whispered the thought that tormented her soul night and day. "Our Katie . . . she's been asking questions."

A muscle twitched in Samuel's jaw. "Jah? What questions?"

Rebecca pulled a pillow from behind her back and hugged it to her. "I have to get up to the attic. Tonight."

"You're not goin' up there tonight. Just put it out of your mind. Rest now, you hear?"

Rebecca shook her head. "You're forgetting about the little rose-colored dress," she said, her words barely audible. "A right fine baby dress . . . made of satin. Katie must've found it."

"Well, it'll just have to wait. Tomorrow's another day."

"We daresn't wait," Rebecca insisted, still speaking in hushed tones, reluctant to argue with her husband. "Our daughter mustn't know . . . she's better off *never* knowing."

Samuel leaned down and gave her a peck on her forehead. "Katie is and always will be our daughter. Now just you try 'n rest."

"But the dress . . ."

"The girl can't tell nothin' from one little dress," Samuel insisted. He took the pillow Rebecca had been clutching and placed it beside her, where he would lay his head later. "I best be seein' to the children."

He carried the lamp out into the hallway, then closed the door, leaving Rebecca in the thick darkness . . . to think and dream.

The children . . .

There had been a time when Rebecca had longed for more children. *Many* more. But after Benjamin was born, two miscarriages and a stillbirth had taken a toll on her body. Although her family was complete enough now, she wondered what life would've been like with more than three . . . or four children growing up here. All her relatives and nearly every family in the church district had at least eight children. Some had more—as many as fifteen.

It was a good thing to nurture young lives into the fold. Didn't the Good Book say, "Children are an heritage of the Lord; and the fruit of the womb is his reward"? Children brought joy and laughter into the home and helped turn work into play.

And there was plenty of work in an Amish household, she thought with a low chuckle. Cutting hay, planting potatoes, sowing alfalfa or clover. Families in Hickory Hollow always worked together. They *had* to. Without the convenience of tractors and other modern farm equipment, everything took longer. But it was the accepted way of parents, grandparents, and great-grandparents before them.

In the early 1700s, William Penn had made all this possible for Samuel and Rebecca Lapp's ancestors. Close-knit Amish communities were promised good land and began to form settlements in Pennsylvania. She thought again of Samuel's great-great-grandfather who had built the very house where Rebecca lay shivering in the dark, cold bedroom.

After a time, she felt the warmth rising through the floorboards, from the woodburning stove directly below. Samuel's doing, most likely. Ever kind and thoughtful Samuel. He'd been a good husband all these years. A bit outspoken at times, but solid and hardworking. A godly man, who held to the teachings of the Amish church, who loved his neighbor as himself . . . and who had long ago agreed to keep her secret for the rest of his life.

"How's Mamma?" Katie asked as Samuel emerged from the bedroom, holding the oil lamp aloft. Evidently, she'd been hovering there at the landing, waiting for some word of her mother's condition.

"Go on about your duties." Samuel gave no hint of a smile, but his words were intended to reassure. "Nothin' to worry over. Nothin' at all."

He headed for his straight-backed rocking chair, pulled it up nearer the woodstove, and dropped into it with a mutter. Pretending to be scanning a column in the weekly Amish newspaper, Samuel allowed his thoughts to roam.

What had Rebecca said upstairs—something about Katie finding the infant dress? He'd always wanted to get rid of that fancy thing. No sense having the evidence in the house. 'Twasn't wise—too risky—especially with that English name sewed into it the way it was.

But he'd never been able to bring himself to force Rebecca to part with it—not with her feeling the way she did. As for himself, the grand memory of that day was enough, though he hadn't laid eyes on the infant gown even once since their daughter had worn it home from the Lancaster hospital.

Minutes ago, it had come to his attention that Katie had stumbled onto the tiny garment—had found it in the attic. How, on God's earth, after all these years? Had Rebecca ignored his bidding? She was a good and faithful wife, his Rebecca, but when it came to Katie, there was no reasoning with the woman. She had a soft place holed up in her heart for the girl. Surely Rebecca had obeyed him and at least done her best to hide the dress away. Surely she had.

Now that Katie had discovered the dress, though, he would remind Rebecca to find another hiding place. First thing tomorrow. Jah, that's what he'd do.

Eli and Benjamin weren't too worried over their mother, Katie observed as she wandered into the kitchen. They'd started a rousing game of checkers on the toasty floor near the woodstove and had barely glanced up at her approach.

She went to the cupboard where the German *Biewel* and other books were kept. Reverently, she carried the old, worn Bible to Dat and set it down in front of him, then seated herself on the wooden bench beside the table. She picked up her sewing needle and some dark thread.

Would Mam mind having company? Katie wondered as she threaded the needle. She'd feel better if she saw with her own eyes how her mamma was doing after the fainting spell a few minutes ago.

With threaded needle poised near the hemline of her wedding dress, Katie gazed at her brothers, unseeing. She'd always insisted on knowing things firsthand. And that stubborn streak in her had caused more grief than she dared admit.

For a good five minutes she sat there, sewing the fine stitches, hearing the steady purr of the gas lantern while a forbidden melody droned in her head. She suppressed the urge to hum.

Looking up from her work, she got up the courage to speak to Dat. "I want to go up and see Mamma, jah?"

Samuel lifted his eyes from his reading corner. "Not just now."

"Tomorrow, then?"

"Jah, tomorrow." With an audible sigh, he picked up the Bible for the evening Scripture reading and prayer.

Without having to be told, Eli and Benjamin put aside their game and faced their father as he leafed through the pages. He knew the Good Book like the back of his hand, and from the firm set of his jaw, Katie suspected he had something definite in mind for tonight's reading.

He read first in High German, then translated into English out of habit—and, probably, for emphasis. Katie put down her sewing needle and tried to concentrate on the verses being read. But with Mam upstairs recovering from who knows what, it was mighty difficult.

"Romans, Chapter twelve, verses one and two." Dat's voice held the ring of authority they had all come to respect. He began reading: " 'I beseech you therefore, brethren, by the mercies of God, that ye present your bodies a living sacrifice, holy, acceptable unto God, which is your reasonable service.

" 'And be not conformed to this world: but be ye transformed by the renewing of your mind, that ye may prove what is that good, and acceptable, and perfect, will of God.' "

The perfect will of God. The words pricked Katie's conscience. How could God's good and perfect will be at work in her? She was harboring sin—continual sin—and with little regret at that, even dragging her feet about the required repenting.

After the incident in the attic, she knew without a doubt that she was spiritually unfit to nurture John Beiler's innocent children . . . or, for that matter, to bear him future offspring. What had she been thinking? How could she stand beside him on their wedding day and for all the years to come as a godly, submissive wife, an example of obedience to the People?

The questions vexed her, and when Dat finished his short prayer, Katie lit a second lamp, headed for her room, and undressed for the night. Before pulling down the bedcovers, she resolved to pay Mary Stoltzfus a visit instead of Bishop John. First thing tomorrow after the milking, she'd talk things over with her dearest and best friend. Mary would know what was right.

That settled, Katie congratulated herself on this decision as she slipped between the cold cotton sheets and blew out the lantern.

Around midnight, muffled sounds were heard in the attic. At first, Katie thought she must be dreaming. But at five o'clock, when Dat's summons to get up and help with chores resounded through the hallway, she remembered the thumping noises overhead. Her heart leaped up at the prospect of investigating the attic—an unexpected opportunity to hold the beautiful satin fabric, the feel of it against her fingertips like forbidden candy. Perhaps one more delicious taste would satisfy her cravings.

Just once more, she thought while brushing her long, thick hair by lantern light. From sheer habit, she twisted the hair near her temples into a tight row on both sides, then drew the mass of it back into a smooth bun.

Dress modestly, with decency and propriety, not with braided hair or gold or pearls or expensive clothes. . . .

She set the white mesh kapp on top of her head, its ties dangling. Over thick woolen longjohns, she pulled on a solid brown choring dress and black apron.

Perhaps today she, Katie Lapp—soon to be the bishop's wife—might make a fresh start of things. Maybe today would be different. Maybe today she could be the right kind of woman in God's eyes. With all her heart, mind, and soul, she would try.

Katie heard the sound of Dat's voice downstairs; Mam's, too, as she leaned into the stairwell, listening. She was comforted by the thought that her mother was up, hopefully feeling well and preparing to cook a hearty breakfast.

If she did not delay, she might have time to visit the attic before morning prayer. She rushed back to her bedroom, reached for the oil lamp, and tiptoed to the ladder leading to the attic.

She climbed the rungs as quickly as she dared and, reaching the top, pushed the heavy attic door open. Then, scrambling up into the rectangular-shaped opening, she paused for breath before stepping over to the old trunk.

Silently, Katie set the lantern on the floor and opened the lid. With heart pounding and ears straining to hear her name in case Dat called, she searched the top layers of clothing in the trunk, exploring the area where she'd first discovered the satin baby dress. Finding no sign of the garment, she dug a bit deeper, careful not to muss things.

When she located Mam's wedding dress, she found that the spot next to it was vacant—obviously so. It was as though someone had deliberately removed the treasured item.

More determined than ever, Katie continued her search, pulling out lightweight blankets, solid white crocheted bedspreads and tablecloths, and faded cotton quilts, passed down from great-great-grandmothers.

There were the faceless cloth dolls Rebecca had made for her as a toddler, too, but not the satin baby dress. It simply was not there. The fancy infant gown was gone.

But where? And who had moved it?

She felt a deep sadness weighting her spirit. *Maybe it's as it should be*, she thought, reeling under the impact of the emotions warring within.

Attempting to shrug away her dark thoughts, Katie set to work reassembling the linens and things in the trunk before leaving the attic and joining the family in the living room. Her brothers and Dat—and Mam—were already on their knees, waiting for her.

"Thank you, O God, for all your help to us," Samuel prayed as soon as Katie's knees touched the hard floor. "Forgive us our sins and help us today with the land . . . *your* land. Amen."

Less than a two-minute ritual both at morning and at night, the prayers were an important pattern underlying the intricate stitchery of their family life.

When she stood up, Katie rejoiced at the light in her mamma's eyes; and her cheeks were no longer chalky white. But the splashes of rose in Mam's face reminded Katie of the frustrating attic search. Almost instantly, her happiness dissipated into thin air—like blowing out a match. She'd been deceitful by returning to the attic, hoping to indulge in one more moment of sinful pleasure. She had broken God's laws—the Ordnung, too.

"Mornin', Mamma." The greeting squeaked out. Katie kissed Rebecca on the cheek, and the two women headed for the kitchen. "I'm glad to see your color's back."

Rebecca smiled and nodded. "A good night's sleep was all I needed." She set a kettle to boil on the polished woodstove. She'd been up long before anyone else—an encouraging sign. And with her next remark, Katie was sure her mother was her old self again.

"You're mighty late coming down." She gave Katie a shrewd, sidelong look. "Are you feelin' all right?"

No doubt Mam was referring to the scene last night at supper. But Katie knew there was no use in bringing up the issue of the guitar and the tunes she loved to sing, nor her upcoming confession. And she dared not mention her wedding, which was only one week from tomorrow. Not after the fainting spell Mam had had last night.

Mary Stoltzfus was the one who would get an earful. Hashing things out with her would be much easier. Simpler, too. On both Mam and herself.

"Jah, I'm feeling fine." Katie took a deep breath. "I was up poking around in the attic this morning," she began. "That's why I was late for prayer."

She noticed her mother's eyebrows lifting in surprise. "Well, you better hurry now." She held out a plateful of jellied toast. "Dat's going to be wonderin' what's keeping you."

Katie carried the plate to the table and set it down. In the utility room, she sat on a stool and put on her work boots, then pulled an old choring coat from a peg. "Remember that little baby dress I was telling you about yesterday?" she called to her mother, barely able to restrain her eagerness to know more without divulging her sin. "I couldn't seem to find it just now."

"Baby dress?"

"Jah." Katie peered through the doorway to the kitchen, but Rebecca had turned to face the sink. "Don't you remember?"

"Things are a bit of a blur" came the tentative reply.

It was a good enough answer—enough to satisfy Katie that her mother hadn't been the one stumbling around in the attic last night.

"I'm sorry about coming down late," she blurted. "I won't be tardy again, Mamma."

Katie rushed outside with her piece of toast, feeling better for having confessed. Still, the thought of the satin dress haunted her. Where had it gone? And who would've taken it?

Rebecca waited for the sound of the door closing before going to the window to look out. Several sets of boot prints dented the hard snow covering the red sandstone steps. The steps led in a diagonal line through the side yard to the barnyard, where hay wagons and open market wagons ran to and from the barn during harvest season.

She watched as Katie hurried toward the barn door, coat-tails flapping in the cold. It seemed that here lately the girl was confessing every time she turned around. Last evening—about her music and not marrying the bishop because of it—and then again this morning, about being late to morning prayers. And once the deacon or the preacher was summoned, she'd be confessing again.

Rebecca sighed, not knowing what to make of it. She wondered if it was more than wedding jitters. A body could see that Katie wasn't herself. She'd even gone and changed her pony's name from Tobias to Satin Boy.

Rebecca thought about speaking with the bishop privately, but dismissed the idea and returned to the stove to begin frying up the cornmeal mush and some potatoes.

She looketh well to the ways of her household, and eateth not the bread of idleness. The words of a proverb ran through her head. No time to be idle around here.

Come breakfast time, there'd be eggs, liverwurst, and cooked cereal, too; bread, butter, and pineapple jelly, along with homemade apple butter—Katie's favorite.

Several times, before Katie and the men returned, Rebecca wandered to the kitchen door and stared out. Something was luring Katie to the attic. Hadn't she said she'd gone again this morning? Why?

Was it the baby dress? And if so, what interested her about it?

Rebecca pondered a bit, reassuring herself that the dress was safely hidden away, far from the attic trunk, never to be found again.

The family secret was safe.

She drew in a long breath and savored the tranquil scene through the window. The sun was still asleep over the eastern slope, where a Norway maple hung its stark branches over the stuccoed stone springhouse below. A weathered wooden bench near its wide trunk stood as a reminder of cheerful, sunny days dripping like golden honey.

Golden days. The thought brought a stab of sadness. *The best days.* Days spent doting on her beautiful infant daughter. She'd given Katie two full years of total acceptance and adoration, as was their way. Then in the blink of an eye, it seemed, her baby was a toddler being molded and fashioned into an obedient Amish child.

It seemed no more than a whisper of time before a well-mannered, yet rambunctious, dimple-faced girl with braids wound around her head was skipping down the lane to the one-room schoolhouse. Then, before Rebecca could turn around, Katie was riding off to Singings with her brothers and returning late at night with one eligible young man or another—the "running-around years," they called them.

It was along about then that Daniel Fisher walked into her life—right up the back steps and into their kitchen. And if he hadn't gone sailing in Atlantic City the weekend he turned nineteen, Katie would be sewing the wedding dress she'd be wearing for *him.*

But eighteen months after Daniel's drowning, Katie had made her vow to God and the church—her baptismal oath—the promise to follow the orally transmitted rules that must be kept unto death.

Katie, her dear, headstrong girl. Surely she wouldn't be letting her foolish notion about music come between herself and a chance to marry. Another year and she'd be completely passed over. The *alt Maedel* stigma was nearly impossible to avoid among the People. Not going through with marriage to Bishop John would be downright foolish—if not irreverent. A transgression of the worst kind.

Rebecca stiffened her shoulders and purposefully turned from the door window. She would see to it that Katie kept her mind on the task at hand—preparing for her wedding. The satin baby dress must be buried—along with the memory of Daniel Fisher.

When the time was right, Rebecca would double-check the new hiding place under the cedar chest. Maybe the dress wasn't as safely hidden as she'd first thought. Even Samuel had spoken to her about it early this morning.

Tormented with fear, she resolved anew to conceal the secret. It would follow her and Samuel to their graves. Most certainly, it *must*.

CHAPTER FOUR

When Katie arrived at the Stoltzfus farm, Mary was busy stewing chickens with her mother. Ten other women sat around the large kitchen table, chatting and sipping coffee. A quilting frolic! That's what it was, Katie decided. No doubt they'd be working on her wedding quilt.

Why else wouldn't I be invited? she thought. It was highly unusual for the bride not to attend her own quilting bee. But Katie suspected that since she was to become the bishop's wife, the People had planned something extra special out of respect for his position. Something in the nature of a surprise, which was more typical of the way Mennonites did things than their cousins, the Amish.

The quilting frames were set up in the large, sparsely furnished front room, where the women, ranging in age from eighteen to eighty, would sit on straight-backed chairs, sewing thousands of intricate stitches and chatting about vegetable gardens and flower gardens, new babies, and upcoming work frolics. Rebecca would tell her familiar tales, and some of the women might throw in the latest gossip. They would have contests over who could make the shortest stitches as they laughed and sang hymns and babbled endlessly. Later, there would be oodles of food, perhaps some of Abe and Rachel Stoltzfus's delicious pineapple ice cream—the crowning moment of such an event, especially for Katie, who often fought her craving for sweets.

"Something wrong?" Mary whispered, watching with a keen eye as Katie warmed herself near the black-metal stove. "You look all droopy."

Katie shrugged, glancing over her shoulder at her friend. "I'm all right." She wasn't in the mood for mentioning the strange commotion in the attic that had produced fitful rest. "I can't stay." The others would be wanting to get on with the quilting bee. "I best be going."

"But you just got here." There was a question in Mary's voice.

Her words went unheeded, though, and Katie turned to say good-bye to the group of women—women as fondly familiar to her as her own family. There was Rachel Stoltzfus, Mary's mother, and Ruth Stoltzfus, Mary's elderly grandmother on her father's side, as well as Katie's own great-aunt, Ella Mae Zook, also known as the Wise Woman, sitting beside her spunky daughter Mattie Beiler (married to the bishop's older brother), and Becky and Mary Zook, Ella Mae's daughters-in-law. Katie also spotted her first cousins—Nancy, Susie, and Rachel Zook; Naomi, Mary, and Esther Beiler—and more expected to arrive.

Each one greeted Katie warmly, eager to comment on her pending marriage. But none referred to the large piece of cloth and padding stretched over the frame, waiting for precut squares to be stitched into a colorful quilt. Or the fact that Rebecca, the mother of the bride, had not yet arrived.

Katie tried to be gracious, but at the first opportunity, she hurried outside and began to pick her way across the ice toward the family buggy.

She wasn't surprised when Mary Stoltzfus burst out of the back door, following close on her heels. "Katie, wait!"

But she kept going, watching her step as she crossed the side yard.

Mary was panting by the time she'd caught up, plump cheeks flushed from the cold and exertion. "You seem upset about something."

Katie stopped short and turned to face her friend. "We have to talk . . . and very soon."

"I'll come over after bit. Jah?"

Katie shook her head. "No. Not *my* house. We'll have to meet somewhere else—someplace private."

Mary slanted her a speculative glance. "Would've thought you'd be home sewing your wedding dress."

Katie forced a brief smile. "It's nearly done."

"Thought you'd have it *all* done by now."

"Jah, I know." Without explanation, Katie headed for the horse and buggy parked in the drive just west of the house.

Mary ran after her. "Maybe we could talk now"—she glanced apprehensively toward the house—"if ya hurry."

"There's no hurrying it. We'll chat later."

"Katie, something's awful wrong. I just know it."

At Mary's wide-eyed look of compassion, Katie felt the tears welling up, blurring her vision. "It's nothin', really." Her voice grew husky.

Mary reached for her with mittened hands, and Katie gave in to the heaviness inside. She buried her face in her friend's soft shoulder. "*Everything's* wrong," she cried. "Oh, Mary . . . everything."

Grabbing Katie's hand, she led her around behind the horse where they could not be seen from the house. "I knew it. Don't you see? Friends are for sharin'. The Lord puts people together for a reason, like how He put us—Mary 'n Katie—together."

At the sound of the familiar childhood connection, Katie's eyes grew even more cloudy.

"*Himmel*, it's not . . ." Mary paused, her expression grave. "This talk . . . it's not about the marriage, is it?"

Katie hesitated. But what she had to say was not for community ears. If there was even a slight chance that someone might overhear. . . . "Not now," she insisted.

"So, it *is* about your marryin' the bishop, ain't?" Mary prodded ever so gently.

Seeing the angelic, round face so concerned was a comfort. But Katie's heart sank as she looked into the all-knowing blue eyes. That look. It probed deep into her soul, reinforcing the sense that Mary always seemed to know what was good and right. "We'll talk tonight" was all Katie could say. "I'll ride over after supper."

Reluctantly, she climbed into the carriage and urged the aging horse toward Hickory Lane. She made the right-hand turn at the end of the Stoltzfus's dirt drive, now covered with deep, icy ridges from buggy wheels slicing into the encrusted snow.

Molasses pulled the buggy up the hill while a melody played in her head. For a time, she tried to put aside her doubts and ponderings, to allow the peaceful countryside to soothe her.

The smell of woodsmoke hung in the air as crows *caw-cawed* back and forth overhead. A bird sang out a low, throaty series of notes and flew away. Somewhere near the edge of the lightly forested area, on the opposite side of the deserted road, a lone deer—though she could neither see nor hear it—was probably watching her, heeding a primitive warning that it was not safe to cross this remote stretch of road buried deep in the Amish community. So isolated was the area that not even the smallest mark on the Lancaster map betrayed the existence of Hickory Hollow—home to two hundred and fifty-three souls.

One farm after another rolled into view—like a patchwork quilt of dusty browns and grays—as Katie trotted the horse over the two-mile stretch of the main road. On the way, she fought the notion that someone knew her as well as Mary seemed to. If Mary hadn't been the sweetest, kindest friend ever, Katie would have rejected outright the idea that a person could get inside your heart and know things almost before you did.

But back there just now, Mary had sized up the situation and guessed it was the wedding that was bothering her. Five years ago, she'd predicted that Katie would never love a man as much as she loved Daniel Fisher. She'd even had the nerve to say, when they were little girls, that Katie was her mother's favorite child. Yes, like it or not, Mary Stoltzfus was hardly ever wrong.

Quivering with cold, Katie tucked the lap robe tighter around her. Was it possible for someone to know you that well? Shouldn't a woman have her own sanctuary, that secret place in her heart and mind where no one else entered?

She slapped the reins and hurried Molasses along. *Maybe this time Mary is wrong*, she thought. *Maybe she's wrong about being right so awful much.*

At home, Rebecca was running late. The quilting bee would be starting soon, but first things first. She had something important to do before she could leave the house. It was a convenient time, too, since Katie hadn't returned with the family buggy. And Samuel and the boys had gone to purchase walnuts and hickory nuts for the wedding.

Hurriedly, she opened the door leading downstairs to the cold cellar. Here, with the help of women from her church district, she'd put up and stored eight hundred quarts of produce. She, in turn, had assisted her neighbors with their canning, as well. Piles of potatoes, onions, turnips, and sweet potatoes were stored separately, more than enough until the next harvest. There were rows and rows of canning jars filled with pickled beets, chow-chow, tomato relish, bean salads, and Rebecca's luscious jams and jellies.

But it was not food for her table that brought Rebecca to the cold cellar. In fact, food was the last thing on her mind as she crept down the narrow steps. In her hand, she held a baby gown wrapped in tissue.

She had felt uneasy about its former hiding place—the underside of the blanket chest. Last night after Samuel had fallen asleep, she'd gone to the attic, found the dress, and taped the lovely thing—still nestled in its wrapping—to the bottom of the cedar chest. So worried was she about someone, anyone, discovering it, that when Katie unexpectedly left with the buggy after breakfast, Rebecca decided to take advantage of the empty house. She would find a better, more secure location for the dress this time.

Sadly, the thought of destroying the garment had tempted her, but upon approaching the woodstove, another thought kept her from tossing the tiny gown into the fire. A frightening flash of reason—and absurdity.

What if someday this is all you have left?

She tried to shake off the preposterous notion, but in its place came a lump in her throat, nearly choking her. Stunned, she dropped the dress. As she leaned over to retrieve it, a tightness gripped her chest, and she felt as though her heart might break.

Carefully, she removed the garment from its wrapping and began to pray silently, pressing the soft satin fabric to her face.

O Lord God, heavenly Father, keep this dress safe from eyes that would hinder and disrupt your manifold great grace and goodness over our lives through Jesus Christ. Amen.

The words were a mixture of Amish High German and down-home emotion. Rebecca never spoke her prayers the way she "thought" them. The Lord deserved respect and reverence, after all. Oh, she'd heard of other folk who felt that it was all right to approach the throne of grace the way you would chat with a good friend. But such ideas seemed nothing short of heresy to her way of thinking!

Deep in the dim cellar-pantry, beyond the cabinets of canned goods and crocks of pudding, Rebecca spied the beautiful corner cupboard and its matching sideboard. She found a kerosene lamp, lit it, and quickened her pace toward the lovely pieces handcrafted by Samuel five years before, about the time Katie and Daniel were seeing so much of each other. The solid pine furniture had been banished to the dark cellar—not a necessary gift for this marriage, although there had been some talk that the bishop wanted to auction off his deceased wife's furniture to make room for Katie's things. That idea had been discarded, however, when nine-year-old Nancy—sentimental about her mother's belongings—had pleaded to keep the furniture for her own bride's dowry someday. So Katie's corner cupboard would remain in storage for now.

Perhaps Eli's bride would enjoy it. Or Benjamin's. Both boys were secretly courting girls, Rebecca was almost certain. A double wedding might be in the air come November of next year.

This year, however, was Katie's. She would be moving into John's house, where she'd have the use of his furniture—everything a married couple would ever need. A typical bride's dowry such as a sideboard for the kitchen or a corner cupboard for the parlor would not be called for. Not even a drop-leaf table.

But there *would* be a dowry gift, and Rebecca had planned something very special. In addition to a Bridal Heart quilt and some crocheted doilies and linens, she would give her daughter eighteen hundred dollars.

Though she'd said nothing to Samuel, she was sure he'd agree. In many ways, the money, which had accumulated interest over the past twenty-two years, was a befitting gift, and Rebecca found herself recalling the peculiar circumstances surrounding it. . . .

The morning sky had threatened rain the day she and Samuel climbed into the backseat of Peter and Lydia Miller's big, fancy car for the drive to downtown Lancaster. The trip seemed surprisingly fast—only twenty minutes—compared to the typical buggy ride of two hours or so, depending upon traffic.

Rebecca was grateful for the transportation at a time like this. Her contractions were much too close together, and she feared she might be going into premature labor. After two consecutive miscarriages and in her eighth month of pregnancy, she was weak with worry. She'd not felt life for at least a day now.

Married at eighteen, she was still quite young. Too young—at twenty-four—to be facing yet another loss. On some days, before this most recent pregnancy, she had found herself nearly frantic with longing and grief. Nearly two years had passed since Benjamin, her youngest, had come so easily that Mattie Beiler, the too-talkative midwife, was scarcely ready to catch him. But now there were problems. Serious ones.

Cousin Lydia had promised to pray for a safe delivery as her husband, Peter, stopped the car at the curb and let them out in front of the emergency entrance. But much to Lydia's dismay, Rebecca had insisted on going it alone. Not even Rebecca's closest kinfolk knew of her fears or the fact that the baby had stopped kicking. She needed only one person with her on this day. Samuel.

A tall, young orderly met them at the door with a wheelchair. Samuel answered the admittance clerk's questions while Rebecca sat very still, praying for life-giving movement in her womb instead of this dull and silent heaviness.

Forcing back tears, she thought of her little ones at home— happy little Benjamin, out of diapers now and a toddler of two;

Eli, a busy, confident youngster even at three. Her eldest, Elam, a fine, strong five-year-old, was already helping Samuel with the milking and plowing.

Oh, but she desired more children—a little girl . . . maybe two or three of them. Samuel, after all, had gotten his sons first off—three in a row—and Rebecca loved them dearly. Still, something was missing. A daughter to learn the old ways at her Mam's hearth, to bear many grandsons and granddaughters for her and Samuel one day.

The baby had come quickly. Stillborn.

Rebecca would not stay overnight in the hospital after her delivery. Her body was physically strong, but her emotions were scarred. How could she face the People—her loved ones and close friends—with empty arms?

Be fruitful and multiply, the Good Book said. Barrenness was a near curse, and among the Plain community, infertility, an unspoken blight.

The doctor's words had been guarded, yet they cut to the quick. "Be very thankful for the children you already have, Mrs. Lapp."

The children you already have. . . . Meaning that their boys would be hers and Samuel's only offspring.

The nurses were kind, sympathetic even. Some, she noticed, darted inquisitive gazes away from her kapp, trying not to stare. Their curiosity she could bear. But not their pity. Enough pity came from within herself, enough for all of them.

Samuel had been ever so gentle, standing by her side after the worst was over, staying strong for her as she lay there under the white sheet, brokenhearted.

Yet "providentially speaking"—as Samuel would later come to say—the anguish of those dismal hours had turned into a day of rejoicing. Everything had seemed to fit, right down to the encounter with the teenage girl and her mother.

Everything.

The timing itself had seemed somehow ordered—remarkably so. A divine appointment, she'd always thought. Who would've expected such an extraordinary thing to happen—within hours after losing their own flesh-and-blood daughter? But it had, and no one—*no one*—had ever known the difference.

The money—five hundred dollars cash—had come as a surprise later. But it had been there all the time, wrapped in the deep folds of the baby blanket. Rebecca had discovered it in the embossed, cream-colored envelope with the words "Please use the enclosed money for my baby's new life" written in a lovely, flowery hand and signed, "Laura Mayfield."

Wondering if they had gotten themselves caught up in some sort of trickery, Samuel hadn't wanted to keep the money at first. But the sum was soon forgotten, deposited in the bank to collect interest, awaiting an emergency or other needful thing. The tiny new baby—their precious Katie—immediately became the center of their lives. It was she, not the money, who'd soon won them over. As far as Rebecca was concerned, Katie was as much a part of her body as Elam, Eli, and Benjamin. She'd wet-nursed the infant until toddlerhood, coddled and loved her through sickness and health . . . just as she had her own sons. Katie was the same as her own flesh and blood. Just the same. Yet somehow—maybe because of the way the child had come to them—even more special.

The memories brought tears, and Rebecca turned, lifted the lantern, and beheld a pine baby cradle, perched high atop the corner cupboard. Eager to see it again, she placed the little dress on the bottom shelf, stepped on one of the old water buckets nearby, and reached for the cradle. When she'd recovered it, she noticed, quite unexpectedly, a milk white vase inside.

Rebecca smiled, remembering the flowers. Lydia Miller had

come for a quick visit that June day after baby Katie's arrival in Hickory Hollow. She'd arrived bearing a gift of colorful blossoms from her own garden. Rebecca had been surprised, and if the truth be known, a bit startled to see the vibrant blooms plucked off their stems. She and her friends never picked garden flowers; it was believed that they were to be seen and admired right where God put them. Because of this, there was no use for a flower vase in the Lapp home.

Days later, when the cut flowers were dry and dead, Rebecca had stored the vase here in the cellar. And years later, she had placed it in Katie's infant cradle.

The tall vase, quite narrow and deep, would make an exceedingly safe hiding place. Carefully, Rebecca rolled up the baby dress and pushed it down into the empty vase, wondering what Cousin Lydia would think if she knew how her gift was being put to use.

Rebecca never once thought how she would go about getting the dress out again, or even if there would come a time when she would need—or want—to do so. It was enough that the deed was done.

CHAPTER FIVE

Katie made her way slowly up Hickory Lane. The repetitious *clip-clop-clip* of the horse's hooves soothed her spirits and eased her mind somewhat. Out here on the open road, with only Molasses to hear her, she allowed herself the pleasure of humming. The tune was an old one. Familiar and cherished, it was the last song she and Dan had created together. Unlike the others, this melody had words. But Katie couldn't bring herself to sing them. Daniel—her love, her life—was gone. Drowned in the Atlantic Ocean, leaving her behind.

Too caught up in each other for trivial details, they'd not given the song a title back then. Their final sun-drenched days had been spent laughing and singing the hours away—as if time would stretch on forever.

On one such fine day, they had perched themselves on an enormous boulder, smack in the middle of Weaver's Creek, miles from Hickory Lane. There, with springtime shining all around them, the song had come easily, born of their love and their laughter, and the lazy, warm day.

Katie found herself humming much too loudly now, partly in defiance of the years. Years that had robbed her of Dan—someone to share her musical longings. Lonely years, in which she'd tried—and failed—to squash her stubborn need to sing, to give her heart a voice, accompanied by the joyful chords of Dan's guitar.

And now Dat was insisting she confess—before one of the deacons and Preacher Yoder—the sin that had kept her beloved's memory alive.

The idea seemed preposterous. To think of revealing the lovely thing that had connected her with Dan. Why, it would amount to betrayal, pure and simple.

She stopped humming, considering her options. If she refused to confess privately, then a *sitting* confession would be required. She must wait until after the next preaching service and remain seated in the midst of the members-only meeting. There, just before the shared meal, she would have to declare—in front of them all—that she had sinned.

Perhaps, she mused as Molasses picked up his pace nearing home, in order to come clean before God and the church, she should admit that she'd sinned repeatedly through the years—even after her father had caught her strumming the guitar in the haymow as a teenager and forbidden her to play. Still, she wasn't certain she'd tell the part about the repeated transgressions. It was bad enough—her humming forbidden songs on the way home from a quilting bee held in her honor, where the women were surely making hers and the bishop's wedding quilt.

Katie sighed, her breath hanging in the frosty air. Either way, she would be expected to say that she was turning her back on her sin, and mean it with all her heart. But she would keep Dan out of it. No need to place blame on someone whose body lay cold in a watery grave. Of that she was certain.

The confessing, private or otherwise, would be hers and hers alone. She would have to ask the deacon or Preacher Yoder to forgive her. Either that or go before the entire church membership.

Because if she didn't confess on her own, surely Dat would go to Bishop John himself and report her disobedience.

On the day of her baptism years before, Katie had agreed to this process of correction by the church. A time-honored ritual, it was the way things were done. Repentance must be a public affair. If she delayed the confession, then in order to be reclaimed, the bishop would come to her with another witness—possibly Preacher or one of the deacons. Matthew's gospel made the procedure very clear: " 'Take with thee one or two more, that in the mouth of two or three witnesses every word may be established.' "

Thinking of John being told, her face grew warm with embarrassment. She didn't want her future husband, bishop or not, caught in the middle. A decision would have to be reached on her own. She must give up her musical inclination and abandon her guitar, now hidden deep in the hayloft. She must give it all up, forsake the love-link between herself and Dan. Forever.

The dull clumping sound of the horse's hooves on the snow-packed road lulled Katie into a feeling of serenity despite the turmoil within. She could trust the old ways. Repenting would make things right. Somehow—though it galled her to think of it—she would have to do it. For her future standing with the People; for Bishop John's sake and his dear children, if for no other reason.

She leaned back against the hard leather buggy seat and sighed. If she'd known what to say to God, she would've said it then— spoken it right out into the icy air the way her mother's Mennonite cousins often did at family get-togethers. Though the social times were few and far between, Peter and Lydia Miller were the friendliest, nicest people anywhere. And they seemed comfortable talking to the Lord, during the table blessing or anytime. On the way home from such a gathering, Dat was always quick to point out to Katie and the boys how glib the Millers' approach to the Almighty seemed to be. Mam agreed.

Another gray buggy was approaching in the left lane, heading in the opposite direction, and she saw that it was Mattie Beiler's oldest granddaughter. Sarah was probably on her way to the quilting. They exchanged a wave and a smile.

Katie rode in silence for a while, then away in the distance, she heard her name. "Katie! Katie Lapp . . . is that you?"

Little Jacob Beiler had been playing with a rope and wagon by the side of the road, pretending to be the horse, it appeared. His deep-set, innocent blue eyes, framed by wheat-colored bangs peeking out from under his black hat, looked up expectantly as he ran and stood in the middle of the road, waving her down.

Here comes my new mamma! Jacob thought with delight. *Can't hardly wait 'til she comes to stay all the time. Hope she cooks good.*

Katie Lapp always sat up tall and straight in the carriage, holding the reins almost the way his own *Daed* did, her bright eyes shining. But she was different from all the other Plain women, no getting around it. Maybe it was her hair. It was sorta red-like. . . .

Jacob thought about it for a moment. Katie's parents had no such hair. And her brothers were blond headed—*like me.*

She was real pretty, too, and full of fun. And she hummed songs. He knew she did, because he'd heard her humming as she came up the lane—something he'd never heard his own mamma do. But then, he'd been just a baby when she died. Still, he was sure his Mam had never, ever done any singing except at preaching service. None of the other women he knew hummed or sang tunes. Katie was the first. He couldn't wait for her to be his real, come-to-live-with-him mamma. . . .

Katie slowed Molasses to a full stop. "Well, hullo there, Jacob. Are you needing a ride home?"

The four-year-old hopped into the carriage, hoisting his long rope and little wagon onto the floor. "Jah. Pa'll wonder what's become of me." He clapped his muffled hands together snug inside his gray woolen mittens and hugged himself against his heavy sack coat.

Katie wondered if his mother had made the mittens before she died. Or if they were hand-me-downs. With four older siblings, the latter was probably the case.

She covered his legs with her heavy lap robe, picked up the reins and gave them a plucky snap. "It's mighty cold for someone your size to be out playing, ain't?"

"Nah. Daed says I'm tougher'n most boys my age." His eyes sparkled as he spoke.

"I think he's probably right." She glanced down at the bundle of wiggles seated next to her.

"Daed's 'sposed to be right." A touch of healthy pride rang in his voice. "God makes bishops that-a-way, ya know."

Katie smiled. She wondered how it would be to hear John's youngest child chatter every day over little-boy things. Gladly, she'd listen to his babbling. Gladly . . . except . . .

Giving her love to Jacob and his brothers and sisters would mean giving up something besides her music. Last week, when she and John had gone into Lancaster to apply for their marriage license, she had scarcely been able to restrain herself from gawking at the colorful clothes the "English" women were wearing. Could she give up her seemingly endless desire to wonder, to dream, to imagine "what if"?

What if one day she dared to wear a pink or yellow dress; let her hair hang down her back in curls or pulled into beautiful braids? How would it feel? Would it change who she was inside?

Several months ago she'd discussed the topic discreetly with Mary, and her friend had said that it wasn't only the wearing of plain clothes that made them Amish, it was who they were. "It's what we believe," she'd stated with conviction. "We've been taught to 'make every effort to keep the unity of the Spirit through the bond of peace.' You know without me telling you what that means."

Katie knew. Her best friend was, of course, referring to the Scripture in Ephesians that taught uniformity of dress, transportation, and dwellings.

"What about the Englishers—what about *them*?" Katie had persisted.

Mary had become exasperated with her. "They don't know beans, that's what. They—those worldly moderns—keep on changing and changing their clothes and themselves 'til they don't know which end's up. They don't know who they are or whatnot all!"

Katie had listened, wincing inwardly at Mary's stern reminder. "Besides, it's much too late now to be questioning. You already took the vow for life." She'd paused for breath, pinning Katie with an unrelenting gaze. "Better never to take the vow . . . than to take it and break it."

Disobedience to the Ordnung brought dire consequences, Katie was well aware. The Ban and *Meinding* were a frightful, fearful part of the way things were—*das Alt Gebrauch*, the Old Way.

Without warning, Jacob jumped up in the buggy. "Oh, look, there's Daed!" He pointed toward a large, two-story white clapboard house.

Katie jerked her thoughts from their ramblings. How much of Jacob's boyish jabber had she missed? In her preoccupation, she'd nearly ridden right past the Beiler house!

Her guilt made her almost shy as she returned John's exuberant greeting from the high porch that spanned the entire front of the house. "Gut morning to ya, Katie!"

Katie reined Molasses in to the barnyard, where he halted on the frozen ridges made by the bishop's buggy wheels. As was the Old Order custom, John earned an income for his family from the land and the smithy, while serving God and community as a bishop. From the tracks, she could see that he'd already made several deliveries to customers this morning.

Katie let the reins rest loosely on her lap as she took in the snowy landscape extending far out and away from the road—John's long-ago inheritance from his father, now deceased.

It was a peaceful, sweeping spread of land, with three stately mulberry trees gracing the front yard. She could almost imagine the purple impatiens hugging the base of the trees on warm days, and the lush flower beds, well tended in the spring and summer by bright-eyed Nancy, the bishop's eldest daughter. Hanging from one of the low-lying branches, left over from the children's play, was a thick, long rope with an icy double knot tied in its tail.

Jacob turned to speak to Katie, short puffs of breath gusting in the cold air with each word. "Did I hear ya singin' back there just now . . . on the road?"

His innocent question took her by surprise. "Singing?"

"Jah, coming up the lane . . . I thought I heard a song."

Katie's pulse quickened. In a few long strides, John would be at her side. She certainly didn't want to be discussing her songs with Jacob when the bishop came to greet her.

"Oh, probably just a little humming is all you heard." Maybe the youngster wouldn't press her about it.

But he wasn't about to give up. "One of the hymns from the *Ausbund*?" Jacob asked. "I like singin' in church, too. I like 'The Hymn of Praise.' "

Katie smiled nervously. Here was a boy who loved music almost as much as she did. She only hoped that he hadn't noticed how different her song was from the ones in the sixteenth-century hymnbook.

With eyes shining up at her, Jacob pleaded, "Will ya come for supper tonight? We can sing some hymns then, maybe."

"Well . . ." She hesitated, uncertain how to answer, since his father had not yet declared himself.

"Oh, please, Katie? I'll even help ya cook."

John stepped up, tousled the tumbled curls, and drew the boy close just as the older children appeared at the window, waving and smiling, looking like a row of stairsteps.

"Then we'll invite not only Katie but her whole family, too." John's obvious delight was touching. Even in his heavy black work coat and felt hat—his full beard indicating his widowed status—the bishop made a right impressive sight. "And speaking of invitations, all my relatives and friends have been notified about the wedding. I finished up just this morning," he added with an air of satisfaction.

"Mamma and I are all through, too," Katie said, relieved that the first awkward moments had passed. "All except her Mennonite cousins, the Millers. We'll probably send them a postcard."

"Well, if you need to borrow any of our dishes for the wedding feast, just let me know." He reached into the buggy and touched her hand. "Will you come for supper, then?"

She fought back her fears and put a cheerful smile on her face. "Jah, we'll come. I'll tell Mamma when I get home."

"Gut, then. We'll be looking for all of you later." His blue-gray gaze held Katie's with an intensity and longing she'd not witnessed before, not in John Beiler's eyes. And he leaned close and kissed her cheek.

Despite the wintry temperature, her face grew warm and she looked down, staring at the reins in her lap. The desire in his eyes made her uncomfortable . . . aware of her own innocence and her femininity. She'd witnessed this look passing between other couples, long before she was old enough to comprehend its meaning. But there was no mistaking it now. Without further word, she inched Molasses down the slippery slope toward the main road.

"*Da Herr sei mit du*—the Lord be with you," John called after her.

"And with you," she replied, willing the sting out of her cheeks.

CHAPTER SIX

Rebecca was in the kitchen pulling on her boots when Katie arrived. "I'm awful late," she sputtered in a flurry to put on her shawl and black winter bonnet. "What's been keepin' you, anyway?"

"Oh, I rode down to Mary Stoltzfus's for a bit."

Rebecca's lips twitched with the beginning of a smile. "Mary's?"

Katie grinned. "Everyone's there waiting for you, Mamma. Ella Mae, some of the cousins . . . and probably lots more by now. Better hurry."

"Jah, I 'spect they're waiting, all right."

She bustled out with a wave and a gentle reminder to Katie to finish sewing her wedding dress.

It seemed odd not to be attending the quilting bee today. Quiltings were popular in winter, Katie knew. When the land was resting, the women of the church district often got together to do their needlework, waiting for the first spring thaw that would wake the good earth again.

Katie could almost hear the chatter and laughter as she thought about the frolic and the quilt they'd be finishing by sometime around dark tonight. Some of the women would probably mention how lonely poor Bishop John had been these past years since his first wife went to Glory, and how *wonderful-gut* it was that Katie had accepted his proposal. Most likely, they'd be passing on a bit of gossip, too, from time to time. And always there would be Mam's tales.

Katie wondered which story it might be today as she hurried to find her sewing basket. With the wedding only a few days away, she'd better listen to her mamma and finish up her wedding dress. She sank down into a rocker and was nearly halfway around the hem when she remembered Bishop John's invitation for supper. She'd forgotten to tell her mother.

And she'd forgotten something else. Mam would be happy to hear that she'd abandoned her doubts and decided to go ahead and marry John, music or no music. All around, it was the best thing. The *right* thing, as Mary would say.

Still, in spite of everything, Katie struggled with a restive feeling. She picked up her sewing and headed through the kitchen to the long, rectangular-shaped front room, where they gathered for Sunday preaching when it was their turn to host the meeting. Had she not been marrying a widower, her wedding night might have been spent here in this very house. As it was, her first night as John Beiler's wife would be spent at his place, a spacious farmhouse brimming with children. She would sleep next to him in the bed he had shared with his first wife.

Brushing tentative thoughts aside, Katie hurried to the doorway connecting the stone house with a smaller addition—the white clapboard house her ancestors had built many years ago. With both sets of grandparents now deceased, the *Dawdi Haus* remained vacant. But someday, when her father was too old to work the land, it would become her parents' home. Then Benjamin, the youngest son, would inherit the main house and forty-five acres of fertile farmland—passing the family homestead from one generation to the next.

Katie opened the door and surveyed the living room of the smaller house. Sparse furnishings had been left just as they were when her maternal grandparents lived here—matching hickory rockers with homemade padding on the seats, a drop-leaf pine table near the window, and a tall pine corner cupboard. Colorful rag rugs covered the floor, but the walls were void of pictures except for a lone, outdated scenic calendar hanging in the kitchen.

Katie closed the door behind her and entered the Dawdi Haus, wandering through the unheated rooms, wishing *Dawdi* David and *Mammi* Essie were alive to witness her marriage. She imagined them sharing in the joy and the preparation of the community ritual, knowing they would have delighted in becoming instant step-great-grandparents to five young children.

Katie sat down in Mammi's rocker, the unhemmed wedding dress still in her hands. She leaned back against the wooden slats and shivered. It was much too cold to sit here and sew, yet she remained seated, recalling a childhood memory involving her mamma's mother, Essie King—twin sister to Ella Mae Zook, the Wise Woman.

Mammi Essie had caught young Katie humming a tune, just as Jacob Beiler had earlier today. One of those fast, made-up tunes—way back when Katie was but a schoolgirl, around first or second grade. She couldn't remember which grade exactly, but it really didn't matter. The memory that stuck in Katie's mind was what Mammi Essie had said when she looked up from snapping peas.

"Lord have mercy—you're like no little girl I ever knowed! Like no other."

At the time, it seemed like a reproach—the way the words slipped off her wrinkled lips and stung the childish heart.

Condemning words, they were, and Katie had blushed, feeling ashamed.

Yet, as she thought back to the incident in their backyard, where honeysuckle perfume hung in the air and bees buzzed messages back and forth, it seemed that Mammi Essie was making more than a verbal rebuke. Had her grandmother sensed a streak of stubborn individualism? Such a thing was strongly discouraged; Katie knew that. By the time you were three, the molding of an obedient Amish child was supposed to be evident. That is, if the parents had done a thorough job of teaching the ways of *Gelassenheit*, total submission to the community and its church leaders.

Katie had overheard her grandmother talking with some of the other womenfolk at a quilting frolic not long after. "Rebecca gives the girl a little too much leeway, if you ask me. But then little Katie's the only girl child—and the last 'un at that, it appears."

Leaning down, Katie placed her sewing basket on the floor beside the rocker. Silently, she crossed the room to inspect a deep purple and magenta afghan on the back of the davenport. She lifted the crocheted afghan and held it, feeling the rough texture in her hands.

"Mammi Essie knew I was different," Katie said aloud. "And she knew it had nothing to do with Mam's doting on me—nothing like that. Mammi knew there was something inside me . . . something longing for a way to let the music out."

There were no tears as Katie refolded Essie's afghan. Her Mammi had died suspecting the truth—that the music had been a divine gift within Katie. God, the Creator of all things, had created her to make music. It wasn't Katie's doing at all.

Still, no other living person truly understood. Not even Mary Stoltzfus. Only one had fully understood and had loved her anyway, and he was dead. Maybe it was because Daniel Fisher had shared the same secret struggle, the same eagerness to express the music within. While everyone around them seemed to be losing themselves—blending together like the hidden stitches of a quilt—Katie and Daniel had been trying to *find* themselves.

Looking back, Katie wondered why she hadn't been stronger in her stand, hadn't at least tried to follow the church rules. But, no, she'd gone right along with Dan's suggestion that they write out their songs. He'd shown her how to use the treble clef to sketch in the melody lines, notating the guitar chords with letter symbols.

Why hadn't she spoken up? Had she been too weak in spirit at seventeen to remind him of what the church required of them? Too much in love with the boy with blueberry eyes?

Trembling with cold, she heard a faint sound of voices through the wall. The men were back inside, no doubt warming themselves by the stove. They'd been out all morning—removing loose stones from the fields—and would most likely welcome some black coffee before taking the cab wagon down the road to a farm sale.

Katie hoped her father had not already summoned the preacher for a private confession. Reluctantly, she picked up her wedding dress and the basket with her needle, thread, and scissors, and opened the door leading from Mammi Essie's former home. Then she trudged into the front room, toward the toasty kitchen awaiting her on the other side of the stone house.

"Ach, what a beautiful quilt this'll be," Rebecca said, hurrying to find her place at the large frame in the Stoltzfus house. She pulled out the only vacant chair remaining and sat down with a sigh. She waited a moment to catch her breath, then picked up the needle.

"A warm quilt'll come in mighty handy on such cold nights, jah?" Ella Mae asked in a near whisper.

Rebecca glanced over at her petite aunt. Lately, the old woman's bouts with laryngitis seemed to linger longer and longer. But at her age, it was a wonder she continued to carry on as she did—attending quiltings and rug braidings, tending her herb garden, having the women in for pie occasionally, and even assisting her middle-aged daughter, Mattie Beiler, with her midwifery duties. Not all the young wives went to outspoken Mattie to have her "catch" their babies, but a good majority did.

"Ain't it lovely . . . our Katie getting married to Bishop Beiler?" Mary Stoltzfus remarked, speaking as only a best friend could. She tied off an intricate row of stitches and snipped the thread free.

"It's such a long time for the bishop to be without a wife— too long—raising all them little ones by himself," Mary's mother commented.

Rebecca agreed, thinking it would soon be time for her to entertain the quilters with one of her best stories. She'd told them all—the same tales over and over—so often that the women knew them by heart. But still they called for more. Did they believe the stories . . . that they were absolutely true?

She glanced again at dear Ella Mae, the Wise Woman. Through the years, the slight woman had been found to be trustworthy with shared confidences, as well as wise in counsel. Rebecca noticed that her wispy white hair nearly matched the kapp perched on her head till a body couldn't tell where one left off and the other began. The woman looked downright angelic— the way the light streamed in from the window. And today, for some reason, she looked more like Rebecca's own mother, Essie King, than she'd remembered. Being her mother's twin, Ella Mae had every right to look like Essie, of course, but Rebecca had forgotten how closely they resembled each other until now.

Maybe it was the way the brightness shone through the curtain-less windows, highlighting her aunt's pleasant, dimpled face and high forehead. Maybe it was the way Ella Mae sat with back erect, defying her eighty years.

Rebecca had always been interested in searching out the physical characteristics in families—especially the similarities between mothers and daughters, sisters and brothers. She hadn't meant to stare, but evidently she was staring now, because Ella Mae's wide hazel-gold eyes met hers.

"Something on your mind?" The hoarse voice penetrated Rebecca's thoughts.

"Oh, nothing . . . nothing a'tall. You just look . . . well, so lovely." Rebecca's words surprised even herself. She wasn't given to complimenting folk; it was not the way of the People.

Ella Mae was silent. To acknowledge such a remark would be to imitate the ways of the English.

"In fact, you're looking near like an angel today," Rebecca blurted out, blushing furiously.

Ten other heads jerked up at the mention of a heavenly messenger. Ella Mae chuckled demurely but said nothing.

If they could have read Rebecca's mind, they would know that she yearned for a resemblance between herself and her auburn-haired daughter—the same as others in this room. These family traits were like the very threads the women stitched into the fabric of Katie's quilt—joining, attaching . . . linking them one to another.

"The Samuel Lapp family is expanding by six more come next week," Mary Stoltzfus said, changing the subject.

"A gut thing, jah?" There was a twinge of doubt in Ella Mae's whispery voice, as though she suspected something amiss.

"Ach, we all know how ferhoodled Katie gets before time to do something awful important," Mattie Beiler cut in. "But my brother-in-law, the bishop, is a patient, kind man—no question about it. He'll be gut for her."

Hearing Bishop John referred to as a patient man was not surprising to Rebecca. As long as she'd known him, she had felt at ease around him. He ran his farm well—working long hours every day—as well as handling much of the blacksmithing in and around Hickory Hollow. And he managed his children soundly, with help from young John—nicknamed "Hickory John" to distinguish him from his father—and Nancy, the oldest daughter, always admonishing the youngsters in the fear of the Lord.

But what had Rachel just said about Katie—that she got herself ferhoodled sometimes? "My daughter does no such a thing," Rebecca spoke up.

"But she does, and you know it," Mattie retorted.

Rebecca's eyes shot blazing darts across the quilt frame. "I'd be obliged if you'd not speak about my Katie that way."

A familiar look of disgust, accompanied by a snort, was Mattie's answer. The rift between the two women remained strong. Twenty-two years strong.

Rebecca was certain she knew what her cousin was thinking. Mattie figured she'd been deliberately snubbed on the day of Katie's birth. Instead of calling for the local midwife, Rebecca had gone to Lancaster General to have her premature baby. She'd let an *English* doctor catch her baby.

"Well, Katie and I'll be sisters-in-law very soon," Mattie managed to say. "I couldn't be saying nothing but gut things about her."

But in Rebecca's heart, she knew better. Here sat the very woman who'd made a big fuss over the plans for Daniel Fisher's graveside service, them having no body to bury and all. Even with Katie crying and pleading, Mattie and her husband, David, had gone to the Fishers and persuaded them to contact the bishop.

"Burying an empty coffin just ain't never done," David Beiler had insisted.

So Katie had visited the Fishers herself, begging them at least to have a simple burial service for their son—a quiet gathering of some kind, perhaps a prayer and a spoken hymn. And a wooden grave marker.

Sooner or later, Rebecca knew she'd have to forgive her cousin for the added grief Mattie had caused Katie. But not now. She pursed her lips and kept her eyes on her work—sewing her tiny running stitches into the wedding quilt.

It was a good thing Mary Stoltzfus spoke up about that time, asking Rebecca for a story . . . and the Telling began.

The women were soon responding with their usual lighthearted laughter. Everyone but Mattie.

And sensing hostility brewing, Rebecca was cautious today, avoiding any mention of her boys' childhood escapades . . . or of Katie's homecoming. It wouldn't be wise. Not wise at all. Not with Mattie Beiler acting up the way she was.

———————

Katie was grateful. Neither the deacon nor Preacher Yoder were waiting in the kitchen for her when she arrived from the Dawdi Haus.

Quickly, she made hot coffee and warmed up a fat, juicy jelly roll each for Dat and her brothers. But the minute he and the boys left for the farm sale, Katie headed for the barn. With her heart hammering and long skirt flying, she made her way through the barn and up the ladder to the hayloft.

The day was not as sharply cold as it had been for the past few weeks. Not a single cloud in sight and a powerful-good sun shining through the rafters. The perfect time to pull the guitar out of hiding. She found it under the old hay, back in the west corner near one of the hay bins.

Lovingly, she brushed the fine gray dust off the case with her wool shawl. She opened the case, lifted out the instrument, and cradled it under her right arm. Without hesitation, she found the frets and began to tune. Might be the last time for a long time—or maybe forever.

She sang several of Dan's songs first, then her own. She saved for last the love song they'd written together, knowing that it wouldn't matter really how many times she sinned by singing them between now and the confession she must give. Feeling the old rebellion rise up, she willfully disobeyed and played it again. And again.

While she played, she remembered. . . .

The sun glinted off the back of Daniel's sleek horse as the steed, groomed to perfection, pulled the brand-new open buggy down the road toward Weaver's Creek. His arm brushed against Katie's, sending tingling sensations up her spine. When he took the curve too fast, she leaned hard against him, making him chuckle. Then he put his left arm around her, holding the reins with his right hand and keeping his eyes on the road ahead.

"No matter what happens," he said, "remember I love you, Katie Lapp."

Her heart thrilled to his words, and she listened carefully to the echoes in her mind. She'd never felt so cherished, so safe.

They rode along in silence a bit farther. Then, quite unexpectedly, he reined in his horse and, in broad daylight, turned to look her in the face. She saw the longing in his shining blueberry eyes, the quiver in his lip.

"You love me, too, don't you?" he asked gently, holding her hands in both of his.

Katie glanced around. "Maybe we shouldn't be—"

"I want you with me, Katie, always," he whispered in her ear, and the worries about being seen like this skittered fast away.

She snuggled against his chest and whispered back, "I've loved you since I was a little girl. Didn't you know?" She felt soft laughter ripple through him as she relaxed in his arms.

"You're *still* a girl."

She pulled away and looked him square in the face. "I'm old enough to go to Singing, and don't you forget!"

He leaped out of the buggy and ran around to stand on the left side, offering first his hand, then disbanding with chivalry and opening his arms wide to her. Not thinking—nor caring—what would happen if they were seen doing such a thing, Katie hopped down, letting him catch her and hold her.

He didn't let her go until he'd cupped her face in his hands and tilted it to meet his gaze. "You're the most beautiful creature on this wide earth, and I want us to get married tomorrow."

Katie sighed, understanding. "I'll grow up quick," she promised. "You'll see."

His face inched closer, and wistfully he gazed at her lips. "Oh, Katie, whatever happens . . ."

She didn't hear the rest. Dan's words were lost as he drew her close. His lips touched hers, lightly at first, then pressing ever so sweetly.

It seemed to her that he was never going to stop kissing her, and she wondered if she shouldn't be the one to do the stopping, because now her head was spinning and she'd never felt so wobbly in her knees before.

"Oh my," she finally said, pulling back and smiling up at him.

When Dan reached for her again, she purposely turned and looked at the old covered bridge up ahead. Some people called them "kissing bridges," but that wasn't why she wanted to go there.

She needed some air—a bit of distance between herself and Dan. "Maybe a walk would do us good," she suggested.

"Jah, let's walk." He tied the horse to an old tree stump and held out his hand to her. "Did I offend you just now?" he asked as they made their way down the old dirt lane.

"No . . . no," she said softly.

At the old bridge, they turned away from the road and headed down the banks of Weaver's Creek. "Hold on now," he said. "I won't let you fall."

"I know you won't." She smiled, eager to trust this boy with the disturbing good looks, who stood out in the Amish community for his bright spirit.

"I've never been lip-kissed before," Katie admitted as they stepped barefoot across the creek, one stone at a time, finally reaching the huge boulder in the middle of the rushing water.

"Maybe it's time I caught you up . . . on kissing, that is." Daniel grinned.

"You been kissing for a while?" She had to know, even though she wondered if it was right to be asking.

"Not really, not like . . . back there."

"A peck then?"

"The smallest peck . . . and on the cheek."

Again, she listened to his words, studying his face. Mary Stoltzfus had always said that if you watched a fella's face when he talked, you could see if he was telling the truth.

So what did he mean—"a peck on the cheek"? Who, but his mother or sisters, would he kiss that way?

"You have to tell me who you kissed," Katie said, surprised at her own bold curiosity.

"I have to?" His eyes twinkled. "Well, ain't *you* the bossy one!"

She didn't mind the name-calling. Not with Daniel doing it.

He could call her most anything he pleased, if he only told her the truth about whoever it was he'd pecked on the cheek.

She sat there with her long green dress draped over her knees, hugging her legs as she balanced herself on the boulder next to him. "I'm waiting. . . ."

To that, he burst out laughing. "It was a little baby. I was two years old and she . . . well, *you* were just this big." He measured the space with his hands.

"Me? You kissed *me* when I was a baby?"

"Jah, when Mamma went to visit ya for the first time. Your Mam's Mennonite cousin came, too. She brought flowers in a vase, from her garden."

Katie threw back her head, a ripple of laughter startling a bird on a branch overhanging the creek. "People don't remember things like that so long ago. How could *you*?"

"Maybe it's because Mamma talked about it so much. It was a big day—your coming into the world, Katie. Your Mam was happy beyond words, finally getting her first daughter." He paused, then took up again. "Might be I just *think* I remember that day— hearing about it so many times and all." He tossed a stick into the creek, and they watched it float downstream and disappear under the bridge.

Dan slipped his arm around her waist, and the two of them sat quietly, lost in their own world. "Just tiny . . . brand-new, you were," he whispered. "So pretty—even back then."

She turned to look at him, resplendent in the glow of the sun's reflection, slanting off the creek.

"Your Mam had just come home from the hospital, and there you were—all pink and pretty." A chuckle broke through. "Guess I just couldn't help myself."

"The hospital?" Katie was puzzled. "Did you say the hospital?"

"Jah."

"But I thought everyone around here had the midwife—Mamma's first cousin, Mattie."

Dan shrugged. "Sometimes when there's a problem, even the Amish use the English doctors."

"Oh." Katie pondered the thought. She'd never heard that explanation. She would be speaking to her mother about it later. But for now, it seemed Dan had other things on his mind, starting with the song he wanted to write. He pulled a sheet of staff paper out of his pocket.

"What's that?"

He pointed out the lines and spaces, and within twenty minutes or so, they'd written their love song. It seemed that even the birds joined in on the chorus, and the gurgling brook carried the melody all the way to the bridge . . . and beyond.

Katie couldn't recall now how many times they had sung the song that afternoon. But each time, Dan would gaze deep into her eyes and pledge his love—it was that kind of song.

She now remembered one thing, though, although the notion hadn't once crossed her mind that enchanted afternoon five years ago. She remembered his words. His strangely prophetic words. *No matter what happens . . .*

He'd said it at least twice that joyous day, the day he'd declared his love. What did it mean?

There'd been no apprehension in his face, no hint that he sensed what was coming. Yet, thinking back, Katie wondered. Had he known somehow that he would die . . . exactly one week later?

Some folks seemed to be able to predict such things with a kind of inner knowing. Ella Mae had told her so. She was chock-full of wisdom, that woman. Everyone knew it. Hickory Hollow was populated with Plain folk who'd gone to confide in Ella Mae Zook at one time or another.

After Dan's death, Katie, too, had gone to her great-aunt—not to share secrets, but out of desperation. At the time, she'd been surprised to hear such a thing. Yet looking back, it was comforting to know that just possibly her darling Daniel had not been completely startled by his own untimely death.

Her fingers having grown numb from the strumming and the cold, Katie placed the guitar back in its case. Slowly, she closed the lid. She'd never play again.

She would marry John Beiler come next Thursday. Hard as it would be, she must.

CHAPTER SEVEN

Supper at John Beiler's house was served promptly at five-thirty. Katie knew that to be so. The bishop kept to a strict schedule, and his household hummed with the precision of a well-oiled machine.

The table was set for eleven people. Nancy and her younger sister, Susie, age six, carried the serving bowls to the table and set them in front of their father's plate.

When Katie offered to help, Jacob hopped off the bench and stopped her. "This is our doin's tonight," he said. And by that, she knew that the children—without the usual assistance from two helpful aunts—had fried up the chicken dinner, complete with homemade bread and jam, macaroni, green beans, corn, chow-chow, applesauce, and banana nut bread.

"Find anything useful up at Noah's sale today?" John asked Samuel after the silent prayer.

"Oh, not much, really. Nothing we needed."

"We saw some nice-looking hickory rockers, matchin' ones," Hickory John spoke up. "But we figured we wouldn't be needing 'em anytime soon." He cast Katie a sidelong glance through long lashes framing clear blue eyes.

Wondering if he were thinking of future Beiler babies, she felt her cheeks grow warm. His mamma's rockers would have to do when that time came, she thought, half wishing she were bringing her own furnishings—along with her hope chest linens—to this house. Then she felt guilty for her ingratitude. Wasn't it enough that someone wanted to marry her?

Surely that was what Mam was thinking this very minute over there at the opposite end of the supper table—that Katie shouldn't be fussing about not bringing her own dowry to this marriage. That she shouldn't be fussing about anything at all. She sighed and took another bite of the delicious banana bread.

After the meal, Jacob startled her by asking, "Now will ya sing for us?"

For a breathless moment, Katie felt as if her heart would stop.

Nancy grinned, egging her on. "Jacob says you have a real nice singin' voice."

The others were waiting for her answer, while Dat glared. "Maybe we could all sing something together," she managed. "I could lead out on 'Sweet Hour of Prayer.' "

Dat frowned and shook his head. "Too fast."

She wasn't surprised to hear that opinion coming from her father. Samuel Lapp preferred the slow tunes in the *Ausbund*. But Katie hadn't expected to be setting the pitch and singing the first syllable of each line of those old, old hymns tonight the way the *Vorsinger*—song leader—did for the congregation at Sunday preaching.

The atmosphere was taut with tension. Katie prayed silently with unorthodox fervor, *Please, Lord, let Jacob keep still about what he heard today. Don't let Dat mention my sinning over the music. . . .* Above all, she was hoping that the others wouldn't notice her heart hammering wildly beneath the green serge of her dress.

Bishop John came to her defense. "Oh, I don't think Katie has to lead out in singing just now." The slight reprimand in his tone sent Jacob's small shoulders drooping, but the boy said nothing.

All five children, including mischievous Levi, age eight, sat straight and still as fence posts on the bench across from Katie—looking a little disappointed.

Katie thought the matter was at an end when Jacob seemed to take on a burst of fresh enthusiasm. "But, Daed," he persisted, "couldn't she just sing the tune I heard her hummin' today on the road?"

John's eyes widened, but before he could respond, Samuel intervened. "No, Jacob, she won't be singin' tonight—and that's that."

Katie felt Dat's hard gaze on her.

When John shooed his children away from the table as though they were a flock of chickens, Katie welcomed the opportunity to escape and left the table to help with the dishes. She was worried, though. What if Dat brought up the subject of her music with the bishop, her willful sinning?

So terrified was she that she did her best to eavesdrop on their conversation, much to the dismay of Jacob and Susie, who were trying to engage her in lively dialogue as she stood in front of the sink, elbow deep in foamy suds.

"I can hardly wait for you to come be our Mam," the little boy was saying.

"Me too." Susie's blue eyes were wide and bright.

Nancy stood near the sink, ready to dry the first cup. "*All* of us can hardly wait," she added in her soft voice.

Katie gave a wry smile. "Well, you'll have to be patient with me, jah? I've never been a mamma before."

Nancy giggled. "We'll be patient, all right. Just havin' you here all the time will be wonderful-gut."

"And we can even teach ya—'bout being a mamma, I mean," little Jacob prattled on.

The poor little things must be lonely, Katie decided. *They seem so eager for their father to remarry.* Well, no doubt they needed a mother. Someone to share their chatter after the school day. Someone to teach the girls how to can and preserve the bountiful harvests yielded by the land. Someone to be a role model, passing on the traditions of the People.

Nancy had six or seven more years before she'd come into her "running-around" years—*Rumspringa*—when Amish teenagers were allowed to see what life was like on the outside. During her Rumspringa, she'd also be meeting Plain boys at Singing every other Sunday night and ultimately having to decide between the world and the church.

Jacob, on the other hand, had many more years at home to be loved and nurtured and shaped. When Katie looked into those innocent blue eyes and heard his husky little-boy voice, she felt a strong tug. Already there was a soft spot in her heart for this child . . . for all the Beiler children.

Levi—a rascally glint in his eye—handed the dishes to Nancy without a word. He stared at Katie as she emptied the dishwater and dried off the counter. What thoughts were swirling around in his head? Levi had sat too still, too quiet throughout the entire meal, never once speaking. Now, it seemed as though there was something stirring inside him. Something he was itching to say.

Katie decided to make it easy for him. "You're a right tall boy, nearly as tall as your big brother," she said with a smile.

The smile was not returned.

While she was fumbling for another topic of conversation, Nancy stepped in to ease the strain. "Levi never says much," she volunteered.

"I say what I need to say."

There was a chorus of chuckles from the other children at their brother's abrupt announcement. Then Jacob began pulling on Katie's apron, tugging her over to the rocking chair near the woodstove. "Will ya play me a game?"

Nancy's eyes lit up. "Jah! Checkers it will be!"

The others—Hickory John, Susie, and Jacob—sat cross-legged on the linoleum floor with the identical checkered pattern as Rebecca Lapp's kitchen. Most of the kitchens around Hickory Hollow looked alike—same black woodstove in the center, same gold-flecked countertops, same checkered linoleum. A gas lamp hung over the long table, and a tall corner cupboard stored books and odds and ends. On the far wall, near the steps leading to the cold cellar, was a picture calendar with farmland scenes. But no other ornaments decorated the walls.

Levi went to sit near the bishop, who was still talking with Katie's parents and brothers at the table. Twice Katie caught the boy glancing over at her playing with the other children. Should she invite him to join them?

Uncertain as to the approach she should take, Katie went on with the game. For a moment, she wished for Mary Stoltzfus. Mary would know just what to do to win over a boy like Levi Beiler.

"Crown my king!" Jacob ordered as his black playing piece made it through the maze of Katie's red ones.

"Already?" she said, suddenly aware that the child had been paying closer attention than she.

An hour later, when the time came for the Lapps' departure, each of the children gave Katie a hug. All but Levi, who stood aloof beside the bishop.

"I'll see you again soon," Katie called to Levi, deliberately singling him out.

The boy's cold-eyed stare met hers. There was something unsettling in his face. What was wrong?

On the ride home, Katie cringed when Samuel brought up the music and the fact that little Jacob had heard her humming. "Were you singin' those songs of yours right out in the open for all the world to hear?" he demanded.

"Jah, Dat . . . I was." Katie's voice, from her buggy seat behind her parents, was subdued.

"That's no example to set for a young boy and his brothers and sisters, now is it?"

She had no answer. So this was how Levi Beiler must have felt tonight. As if he was cornered, with no way out.

She could hear Dat mumbling something to Mam, then his angry words burst out. "There's just not many left around these parts who live the way the Lord God intended from the beginning."

An uncomfortable silence followed, and Katie could feel the pull of the powerful undertow. She had precious little time to apologize.

When she did not reply, Samuel spoke again. "I have no choice, daughter. I'll be speakin' to Bishop John first thing tomorrow."

"But Dat, I—"

"Save your arguments. It's too late," he said with finality. In that dreadful monotone her father assumed for solemn occasions, he began to recite the Scripture about the bitter and sweet water. Eli and Benjamin sat soberly on either side of her, listening.

To say she was sorry would be a lie. Katie wished she could ask for forgiveness and mean it sincerely, but how could she? The songs she'd hummed and played today had marked the end of her singleness. She had celebrated her memories of Daniel Fisher. There on the road and later in the barn, she had reveled in the last bright days spent with her love. And when the song was done and the guitar put away, she had decided to turn her back on the music, once and for all. Yet, in all of it, she knew she had defied Dat, had knowingly and willfully partaken of one last forbidden expression.

"It would be displeasing to the Lord if I said nothin' to Preacher Yoder or Bishop John." Her father's righteous indignation seeped into the damp darkness. So heavy and oppressive was it that Katie felt it close in around her, suffocating her.

Rebecca was weeping now in the front seat as the horse pulled the carriage down Hickory Lane toward the sandstone farmhouse. Katie didn't have to see Dat's face to know what he must be feeling. Still, even as stern and devout as her father was, surely he was also torn between doing God's bidding and altering his only daughter's future.

John Beiler read his children an evening prayer from the standard prayer book, *Christenpflicht*, before heading upstairs to his bedroom. It had been a long day, but an even longer night stretched ahead of him.

How fetching Katie is, he thought, settling down under the covers and quilts. *So kind and cheerful. . . . No wonder my children already love her.*

As for himself, he'd admired Katie Lapp from the day he'd become aware she'd grown into a young woman. From the day she'd knelt before him there in Preacher Yoder's barn in front of all the People. As the presiding elder, it had been his duty to administer the rites as the tin cup spilled baptismal water over her head and down her face. But he'd not been prepared for the silky feel of her auburn hair beneath his fingers.

Waiting for Katie to reach marrying age had not been easy for a man whose children needed a mother and whose own bed had been long empty. More than three years he had waited. And soon, very soon, she would belong to him.

He yawned and stretched, then let his tired body relax, eager for their first night of intimacy, when he would gather his new bride into his arms here in this very bed—hold her tenderly and demonstrate his love for her. Of course, a woman's beauty was not the main consideration when taking a mate, but when a woman was as pretty as Katie Lapp, the spark was stronger. Still, it was far more important that Katie create connections with the People as a married woman. Together, they would start their wedded life, taking on the added responsibilities of a bishop and his wife.

He yawned again and was dozing off to sleep when he heard the floor creak. In the inky darkness, he felt a presence. Which one of his children was out of bed?

"Daed," whispered his second son, "are you awake still?"

John sat up. "Come on in, Levi."

Levi, carrying an oil lamp, approached the bed.

John saw the look of hesitancy on the boy's face. "What is it? Can't you sleep?"

"I have to tell ya something, Daed," Levi said softly. "I can't put it out of my mind."

"Put what out of your mind?"

"Today after school, someone . . . a stranger . . . stopped by the house."

"Go on."

"A lady came up to the front porch—an Englisher. I went to the door . . . that's when I saw her face." His sleepy eyes were wide now with the telling. "She was askin' for directions 'cause she'd gotten lost or something."

"Well, I hope you helped her out."

Levi nodded. "I tried to tell her how to find her way back to the main road. She seemed ferhoodled some, said she'd looked and looked but couldn't find Hickory Hollow on the map, nohow."

John chuckled. "Hickory Hollow was never meant for outsiders. What was she doin' out here, anyway?"

Levi sobered. "Said she was tryin' to find someone's friend . . . a woman in her early twenties. Didn't know the exact name."

John was as puzzled as his son. "Mighty strange . . . an English woman away out here. And looking for the Hollow on her map, you say?" He squinted at the boy, who was breathing hard. "What's got you so worried?"

Levi shrugged. "Just curious, I guess."

"Why's that?"

" 'Cause she had hair like I ain't never seen before . . . 'cept for Katie's."

John suppressed a chuckle. Wouldn't do to be thought mocking his shy son. "Lots of folks have red hair."

"Not around here."

The boy was dead serious, and because Levi rarely spoke, John knew this information was more than a little troublesome. "Why don't you head on back to bed. We'll talk more tomorrow, jah?"

"Jah . . . good night, Daed."

"Good night, son."

When the boy was gone, John reached for the quilt and drew it up under his bushy beard. He reflected on Levi's words. 'Twas a curious thing. Why would an Englisher say she was searching for a Plain friend, yet be way off course? Seemed to be some kind of contradiction.

The more he thought on it, the more John realized that the woman might've been telling the truth. Maybe the stranger had simply lost her way on the winding paths off the main road. But even as he tossed about, trying to find a comfortable spot in his bed, John pondered the matter. He did not rest easy that night.

In another Beiler home, Ella Mae sat quietly as Mattie's husband read from the German Bible. A familiar passage from Exodus, chapter twenty—the first of the Ten Commandments: " 'Thou shalt have no other gods before me,' " David Beiler read. " 'Thou shalt not make unto thee any graven image, or any likeness of anything that is in heaven above, or that is in the earth beneath, or that is in the water under the earth: Thou shalt not bow down thyself to them, nor serve them; for I the Lord thy God am a jealous God, visiting the iniquity of the fathers upon the children unto the third and fourth generation of them that hate me; And shewing mercy unto thousands of them that love me, and keep my commandments.' "

Ella Mae folded her arthritic hands for the German prayer, but long afterward, her thoughts were on Rebecca Lapp and the peculiar way she'd acted at the quilting. Rebecca had gawked at her, calling her "lovely" and "near like an angel," for goodness sake. What foolishness! And she'd kept staring with those clouded eyes. Worry-filled eyes.

Something about it didn't add up, not the way Ella Mae knew her niece inside out—almost as well as a woman knew her own child. After all, a twin sister's offspring had to be linked more closely to yourself, or so she'd always thought. And if that wasn't true, then why did Rebecca Lapp resemble Ella Mae herself almost as much as Mattie did?

The old woman sighed. What had gotten into Rebecca today, anyway? Her mind wandered. And why was it that Rebecca's daughter, young Katie, had not inherited a single one of their closely linked twin genes? At least, not so's a body could tell it. Where was the broomstick hair and the hazel eyes—their family mark? Or the high forehead and the deep dimples?

Ella Mae had never been one to worry her head over silly goings-on. She was the sensible one people brought their worries to—not the other way around. Still, she thought it mighty peculiar how Katie's reddish hair had shown up out of nowhere. Not even as far back as great-great-Grandmammi Yoder had there been a speck of red hair. Ella Mae knew that for a fact. Even though there were no photographs to prove it, the People of Hickory Hollow passed on the stories of their kin, knew what they'd looked like—right down to the last eyelash.

Not only that, she'd secretly traced the family line back several generations on Samuel's side—to the man who'd built one of the best-looking sandstone homes in all of Lancaster County. Samuel Lapp's ancestor, Joseph Lapp.

Later, after the family had gone to bed, Ella Mae closed the door between Mattie and David's big farmhouse and her smaller attached Dawdi Haus. She sat in her tiny front room, rocking and thinking about the events of the day, then snuffed out the only lantern in the room.

How long she sat there in the darkness, she did not know. But around the time the moon started its climb into the sky, through the wide branches of the old elm tree on the east side of her house—about then—she heard the distinct sound of a car motor out front. Turning, she peered out the curtainless window. The pane was a bit frosty, but clear enough to see a long black car creeping down Hickory Lane. The closer it came, the better she could make out its front bumper and chrome-trimmed doors.

Seconds later, the fancy car—a lim-ou-sine, she recollected—came to a gentle stop across the road from the house. The lone yard light cast an eerie glow over the streamlined chassis.

Ella Mae abandoned her rocking chair to stand in front of the living room windows, staring out at the unusual sight. Then, quite surprisingly, the window glided down on the passenger's side. A woman's face stared out into the semidarkness. Had it not been for the full moon, Ella Mae might have missed seeing the white fur hat slip back away from the woman's face, revealing a billowy cloud of hair. Such a splendid burnt red it was that instantly she thought of her grand-niece Katie.

"My, oh my," she whispered into the darkness. "Who is *this*?"

She inched closer to the window, knowing she could not be seen from the road. As she watched, a light came on inside the car. A man, dressed all in black and wearing an odd, beaked hat, unfolded a large paper. The woman and her driver bent over to study what must be some kind of map, best Ella Mae could make out.

"Strange," she said to herself. "Imagine bein' lost on a wintry night like this." If she hadn't been feeling her age tonight—what with the cold weather and all—she might've put on her warmest shawl and snow boots and tromped outside to help. Not wanting to risk a fall on the ice, though, she waited and watched from inside.

Soon, the English car rolled down the lane, and Ella Mae turned away from the window and headed for bed.

There were two large flashlights in Benjamin Lapp's open buggy. Katie found them quickly and took one along with her. She stopped by Satin Boy's stall just long enough to whisper to him, "I won't be gone long," then quietly hitched up Molasses to the family carriage. Dat and Mam surely were asleep by now—Eli and Benjamin, too.

The wind was stiff and cold as she rode to Mary's house.

Once there, she shone her brother's powerful flashlight up at

Mary's bedroom window, grinning to herself. Her friend would probably think a young man was outside, wanting to propose marriage. That's how it was done in Hickory Hollow. The boy waited till he was sure—or hoped, at least—that the girl's parents were soundly sleeping. Then he'd park his open courting buggy out by the road, run to the house on tiptoe, and shine the light up to his sweetheart's bedroom window until she opened it to tell him she'd meet him downstairs.

When the window opened, Mary peeked out. "I gave up on you ever coming over and went to bed," she began apologetically, "but come on up. The door's unlocked."

"Did you think this was your night?" Katie teased as Mary closed her bedroom door behind them.

Mary was wearing a long white nightgown, her unbound hair hanging down past her waist. "When I saw your flashlight, I sat right up and said to myself, 'O God bless me, he's come!' " Mary confessed with a light laugh. "But someday soon it'll be so."

Katie knew she was thinking of either Preacher Yoder's middle son, Jake, or one of Mary's own second cousins, Chicken Joe, who helped his father run a chicken farm. "Are you sure your parents are sleeping?" Katie asked, removing her coat and heavy black bonnet and perching on the edge of Mary's bed.

"Jah . . . listen. You can hear Dat snoring!"

Katie leaned her ear to the wall. Abe Stoltzfus was sawing more logs than one, and with that kind of racket going on, Mary's mother couldn't possibly hear what Katie was about to say. "When I was here this morning—before the quilting—you thought I wasn't going through with marrying John Beiler, remember?" she began. "Well, since then, things have gotten worse."

Mary frowned, leaning forward. "Worse?"

"Oh, I'll marry Bishop John all right, but Dat's making things mighty hard for me."

"What do you mean?"

"Somebody heard me singing today." Katie took a deep breath and dropped her gaze to her apron. "Little Jacob heard me . . . and told."

Mary gasped. "I thought you put your guitar away years ago!"

"It wasn't the guitar he heard. I was humming on the road home from your house this morning—and it wasn't a tune from the *Ausbund.* Dat says he's going to take the matter straight to the bishop."

"Over Preacher's head?" Mary asked, aghast.

Katie nodded, feeling the shame of it.

"So, then, are you guilty of sinning?"

"Guilty as ever," Katie replied. "But it's over and done with, the music is. And that's the truth."

"Then hurry and tell your Dat!" Mary was adamant. "Don't let him go to Bishop John—whatever it takes, ya have to confess!"

Katie stared at Mary in disbelief. "You're saying this only because you don't think anybody else'll have me if the bishop lets me go, ain't so?"

Mary shook her head. "You know that's not true. You're a good and kind woman, Katie, everybody knows that. And any man with eyes in his head can see you're just as pretty on the outside."

It was the first time Katie had ever heard her friend speak this way. She mulled it over before replying. "What good are looks when stubbornness gets in the way?" she muttered. "I just plain run the fellas off."

Mary was silent for a moment. "But there was someone who didn't run off. *He* knew about your humming and singing, didn't he? That's why he gave you the guitar."

She was right, of course, but Katie was determined not to

let on about Dan. Not even to Mary. "Dan's long dead. Leave him be."

Mary scooted over and put her hand on Katie's. "You still love Daniel Fisher, don't you? You're still clinging to him hard . . . but he's gone."

"Not his memory. *That* ain't gone!"

"No," Mary whispered. "Still, have you thought what you'll do when you're married to a man you don't love?"

Katie jerked her head around. "John's a gut man," she insisted. "He'll be a right fine husband, and I'll come to love him . . . in time."

"Maybe you will . . . and maybe you won't."

The two friends sat in silence, as still as their fathers' fields in winter. Katie wished the conversation hadn't taken this turn. Why was Mary asking these questions?

"I'm living the Plain life best as I can—" Katie stopped herself before adding "without Dan."

"You're angry, though." Again, Mary seemed able to read her heart. "You don't really like being Amish, but you're stuck."

"I never said such a thing!" Forgetting the lateness of the hour, Katie raised her voice, then clamped her hand over her mouth. Surely Rachel Stoltzfus would come running now, wondering what on earth was so important as to be discussing it in the middle of the night. Katie waited, listening. . . .

When no sounds of footsteps were heard in the hallway, she relaxed. "To be honest, it's no fun wearing these long, heavy dresses and dull colors," she admitted. "But that's nothing new—you always knew that about me."

"Jah, but you should be clean past that by now, Katie. You should be moving on to higher ground. How can you be a good Mam to the bishop's children if you can't control yourself—can't submit to the rules of the church?"

Mary had a point, but Katie didn't want to hear it. "Well, then, so you're saying I shouldn't marry the bishop—that it's not fitting or right?" The words tumbled out, echoing her own doubts.

"You're a baptized member of the church, Katie. That makes you eligible for a church wedding to any man—bishop, preacher, deacon, whoever."

Katie pressed harder, needing a straight answer from her best friend. "You'd say that—knowing what you know about me? Am I respected enough among the People, do you think?"

" 'The Lord God exalts those who humble themselves,' " she quoted. "It's not your doing, Katie. Things are ordered by Providence—ordained by God."

So that was that. Mary honestly thought Katie had been chosen by God to be the bishop's wife. Katie stood up and tied on her black bonnet, then pulled her shawl around her shoulders.

"Just remember," Mary said, looking solemn, "you can tell me anything. Isn't that what best friends are for?"

"Yes . . . and I'm real glad for that." Katie walked toward the bedroom door and turned to regard Mary with a helpless shrug. "So will you pray that I'll quit being so hardheaded? That I won't always be tempted so?"

"Temptation is not the sin. Yielding to it is." Mary jumped up to give her a hug. "Remember, 'Blessed are the peacemakers.' "

Katie smiled, agreeing with her friend. "I'll make peace with Dat first thing tomorrow. I'll catch him before milking and confess—make things right between us. I'll tell him I'm sorry about the music, and that I'll never sing or hum anything but the *Ausbund* for the rest of my born days."

"Des gut," Mary nodded briskly. "And after chores, Mamma

and I and a bunch of the cousins will come over and help scrub down your walls and paint, too—for the wedding."

Katie left the Stoltzfus house with Mary's wise words ringing in her ears: *He that humbleth himself shall be exalted.* She was deep in thought all the way up Hickory Lane—so deep that she scarcely noticed the long black limousine that slowed, then passed on the opposite side of the road.

CHAPTER EIGHT

Eager to speak with her father, Katie rushed to the barn the next morning. Eli and Benjamin were prepping the herd for the morning milking, but Dat was nowhere to be seen.

"He's out runnin' an errand," Eli replied nonchalantly when she asked.

"This early?"

"He left about four-thirty," Benjamin volunteered. "I heard him out hitchin' up Daisy before we ever got up."

Katie went about her chores without saying more. She fed the chickens and pitched hay to the draft horses and her pony, Satin Boy, then to Zeke and Molasses—the older driving horses—and last, to the mules, wondering if her father was, even now, reporting her wayward behavior to Bishop John.

I should have talked with Dat last night—even if I'd had to wake him! she thought. Groaning inwardly, Katie headed for the milk house.

Ben was leaning over to get some fresh, raw milk from the Sputnick, a small stainless-steel mobile contraption used instead of milk cans to take milk from the cow to the large refrigerated bulk tank, its power supply coming from a unique twelve-volt motor attached to a battery. Ben had always liked the taste of raw milk. "Has a fresh, green taste about it," he'd often said, gulping down a dipperful.

Katie filled three large bowls for the barn cats, wishing she had the nerve to take the market wagon or sleigh and ride over to the bishop's place. As embarrassing as it seemed, there still might be time to prove her sorrow and repentance. The whole disturbing episode could then be dropped, and life could go on as planned. Wouldn't be the first time an errant soul had found forgiveness in the privacy of someone's barn.

"When did Dat say he was coming back?" she asked timidly, not wanting Ben to guess how worried she really was.

"He didn't say."

"So then you really don't know where he went?"

Ben stood up and narrowed his gaze. "If it's what you're thinking, jah, I do believe he went to talk to Bishop John. Dat sticks by his word, ya know."

Katie stiffened. Her brother was telling the truth. Not once had she known their father to back down on something he said he would do.

"If only I hadn't been so stubborn," she muttered to herself.

"Jah, awful stubborn ya were, Katie . . . *terrible* stubborn."

Deliberately, she turned away and clumped outside through the dirty snow toward the house.

Down the main road, familiar road signs dotted the snowy landscape, directing visitors and tourists to the Hickory Hollow General Store. Levi, seeing that he was one of the first customers of the day, pulled on the reins, urging Dumplin', his tan pony, into the wide parking lot. Only seven or eight enclosed gray buggies were here ahead of him. But his sleigh was the only one of the kind in sight. He tied Dumplin' to the hitching post and hurried inside.

The faint smell of peppermint greeted his nose, and he spied the jar of green-and-white striped candy sticks near the cash register.

"Mornin' to ya, Levi," called Preacher Yoder, the silver-haired man who owned and operated the small Amish store. "Let me know if you need help finding anything, ya hear?"

Levi waved and nodded silently, his usual greeting. Grown folks used up way too many words, he'd always thought.

He wandered over to the glass display case where spools of white, black, and several colors of thread were stored under the old wood-paneled counter top. He stood there a moment surveying the sewing supplies, then pulled out a tightly folded list his older sister had written down.

"Don't forget to bring back everything—and I mean *every-thing*—on this list," Nancy had admonished him before sending her brother out into the cold. "And whatever you do, please don't dawdle . . . or we'll be late for school."

Nancy doesn't wanna be late, he thought. *But I wouldn't mind it one bit.* He chuckled under his breath.

Truth be told, he liked school well enough; he made good marks in penmanship and arithmetic. But today he had more important things on his mind—like that Englisher with red hair—the one who'd come to the front door yesterday, asking for directions. He secretly hoped the stranger-lady might still be riding around lost on some back road in her long black car with those shiny bumpers. That way, maybe somebody else in Hickory Hollow would lay eyes on her and that fancy car of hers. Then Daed would have to believe his story.

Levi unfolded the piece of paper, placed it on the counter, and smoothed out the wrinkles as best he could. Without speaking, he made a mental note of each of the desired items—two spools of black thread, four of white, a silver thimble, and five yards of white Swiss organdy. Nancy was making new head coverings for herself and Susie. Brand-new capes and aprons, too.

All's because we're gettin' a new Mam, he thought to himself. He was mighty glad the Lord God hadn't made *him* a girl. Such fussy things as aprons and capes! And always that clean white color till a girl turned thirteen. Give him an old pair of "broadfall" trousers—broke in good—and he was happy.

When Preacher Yoder came over to help, Levi simply handed him the list and pointed. He wasn't one to speak much to people outside his own family. And Katie Lapp would be no different, he decided while the preacher filled his order.

"Shall I bill it to your Pop?" Preacher asked with a smile.

Levi nodded and accepted the sack of sewing supplies, careful to hold it out a ways—not too close. Now if that bag had held a fistful of peppermint sticks like the ones over on the counter, he'd have grabbed it right up next to him. Just so's he could snitch one or two of the delicious mints out of the sack on his way down the narrow grocery aisle.

He breathed in the soft, minty smell one last time before reaching for the knob on the jingle-jangle door.

From the corner of the store, someone with a raspy voice spoke to him. "Well, hullo there, little Levi."

He turned to see who was calling him "little." Because he was no such thing!

"Come on over here," Ella Mae Zook said, motioning to him as she sat at a square wooden table, having a cup of hot chocolate. "I could use some company." She smiled and her deep dimples danced for him.

Levi realized with a jolt that not only was the Wise Woman right here in the general store, but Mattie Beiler, his aunt, was with her—over at the sewing counter, picking out dress material. His mamma, before she died, had told him all about his aunt Mattie and how she'd helped bring him into the world. It hadn't been an easy birth, but he'd finally come, all blue and barely breathing. Mattie had saved his life eight years ago, and to Levi, who believed himself to be near half grown, that was a good long time past.

Ella Mae pulled out a chair for him, and he slid onto it. He couldn't honestly remember ever being this close to the woman whose daughter had saved his life. People said things about Ella Mae, called her "wise" and other such grand things. But now, looking up into her wrinkled face, Levi couldn't see anything too awful special about her. Except maybe for the way her kinda goldish eyes—like the barn cat's—seemed to look straight through somebody—deep into your heart somehow.

To his surprise, she ordered and paid for another cup of cocoa without even asking if he wanted any, then settled back to enjoy her warm drink. "Guess you ain't all that little now that I see ya up close," she said, squinting her eyes a bit.

Levi only smiled.

"Ah . . ." She put her hand on her heart. "That smile of yours reminds me of your dear mamma. And ya know something else?"

Levi shook his head.

"I think you got more than just her smile." The old woman took a sip of cocoa, not explaining herself, which made Levi a bit jumpy, wondering what on earth she was talking about.

Well, he had to know. "What do I got that's like my mamma?" He leaned forward, his elbows on the old table, his ears wide open.

Ella Mae straightened up, and her wrinkly face broke into a broad smile. "Curiosity . . . *that's* what. You're interested in people— think long and hard about 'em, now don'tcha?"

Levi blinked. Did she know, could she tell, that he'd been

thinking about someone? Could she tell that he'd been thinking long and hard, so hard that his head felt stiff from the notions a-stirring around in his brain—about that stranger-lady with hair as red as Katie's?

"I . . . I guess so," he stammered. "Jah, I'm curious sometimes."

She nodded slowly, then picked up her cup and saucer, letting the steam rise to fog her spectacles. She was silent for such a long time that Levi began to think Ella Mae had forgotten all about him. He sat back in his chair and stared at the glass jar of unclaimed peppermints on the counter across the wooden floor. His mouth watered just thinking about them.

"It's mighty gut to be interested," Ella Mae spoke up out of the blue. "It shows you're thinkin' . . . just don't go and think too hard. Save your brain for schoolwork."

He thought she might tell him to drink his cocoa right down and run along. But when she didn't, he figured it was the same as asking him to tell her what was on his mind—that curious question he'd been pondering on. "Where do you think . . . I mean, uh, where do family looks come from—like hair and eyes, ya know?"

Ella Mae slid her cup and saucer away and studied him thoughtfully before she spoke. "Parents have physical traits that get passed down to their children—just like your blond hair came from your mamma and the point of your chin from your Daed."

He sat up straighter. "And I'm tall like him, jah?"

"That you are."

Levi glanced around because what he was about to say was for Ella Mae's ears only. "Can ya keep a secret?" he whispered.

"Do you trust me, Levi Beiler?" she replied, looking him square in the face.

Studying her for a moment, Levi remembered all the things he'd heard about the little old lady sitting across the table. Hickory

John and Nancy had both looked her up several times after their mamma died. And Levi wasn't exactly sure, but he thought even his own Daed, the bishop, had come to see the Wise Woman secretly—when his heart was near breaking in two.

Once, Nancy had said right out loud at supper that Ella Mae Zook seemed to listen like she believed every last word you told her. Never handed out a bunch of *shoulds* and *shouldn'ts* neither. Just let a body settle for himself what he ought to do.

So, Levi decided, if they—and most everyone else he knew in Hickory Hollow—had told Ella Mae their secrets at one time or another, why shouldn't he tell her just one of his own?

He drank his cocoa half down, then set the cup on the saucer with a clink. "I was just wonderin'," he said softly. "Who do ya think Katie Lapp gets her red hair from?"

Ella Mae didn't seem the least bit bothered by the question. "Oh, probably from a relative somewheres down the line."

Levi scratched his head, puzzled. "Wait now, *you're* related to Katie and she doesn't look nothin' like *you.*"

Ella Mae smiled. "Every now and again, God gives us a wonderful-gut surprise."

"Like red hair?" He sighed, thinking about the stranger-lady. "Like shiny black cars stretched out longer'n three fence posts?"

Ella Mae jerked her head back a bit, her eyes wide with surprise. "Where on earth didja ever see a car that long?"

Levi felt his mouth go dry. Did he dare mention the English stranger and the flashy automobile parked and waiting on the road? "I . . . uh, I saw it yesterday after school . . . right in front of our house."

The whole secret was out now. What would the Wise Woman say? Levi stared at her, trying to read what was behind those know-everything eyes. Would she believe him—the way Nancy said she always did? Or would she brush him off like Daed had last night?

Her words came slowly at first. "About that car . . . was a man in a black uniform driving it?"

"Jah."

"And was there a woman all decked out in a white fur coat?"

Levi accidentally let go of his sack. Spools of thread flew all over the place, and he went running, chasing them across the floor. He stuffed Nancy's sewing supplies back into the sack and sat down at the table again, blinking his eyes to beat the band. "A white fur coat, ya said?" He leaned so close he could smell Ella Mae's chocolaty breath. "Then you musta seen the Englishers, too."

She nodded.

"Ya did? You seen 'em?"

Ella Mae frowned and opened her mouth to say something else. But Levi interrupted before she could get a word out.

"Didja get a good look at 'em?"

"I saw 'em. Both of 'em."

Levi kept his voice low, but he was about to bust wide open! "Didn't that lady have the reddest hair you ever seen?" He didn't wait for Ella Mae's reply but asked another question. "Where'd *you* see 'em?"

"Out front, parked in front of our house—like they was lost for sure."

"So then, they was still lost after sundown?" The thought excited him. "Do you think they're still 'round here somewheres?"

Ella Mae's worry lines deepened. Then, in the very next minute, a funny little smile played across her lips.

Levi couldn't help but grin. She'd seen right through him. "I just wanna have another look at that long black machine," he admitted before she could point it out, "that's all."

"Levi Beiler," she scolded softly. "I do believe ya best be runnin' along to school now."

He scooted his chair back. The Wise Woman of Hickory Hollow had witnessed the exact same thing he had yesterday. She'd just told him so. Now Daed would *have* to believe him—for sure and for certain.

"Ach, I left my basket on the counter," Mattie told her mother outside the General Store as they were leaving close to thirty minutes later, and she handed her the reins.

"Now you hurry back, ya hear?" Ella Mae called from her warm nest of woolen lap robes in the front seat of the buggy.

Moments later, a shiny limousine pulled into the parking lot and came to a stop in front of Preacher Yoder's store.

Ella Mae gave the English couple a quick, astonished look; so as not to stare, she looked away. But it wasn't any time a'tall before she heard the sound of feet crunching in the snow and someone approaching the buggy.

"Please, excuse me."

Ella Mae looked up into the face of the woman she'd seen last night—the one with the burnt red hair.

"I am very sorry to intrude," the woman said, "but I've been trying to locate someone. Perhaps you can help?"

Ella Mae sniffed. She knew that scent. Lavender—sweet and delicate. "Who would you be looking for?" she asked, taking note of the woman's fur coat and leather gloves.

"I wonder . . . would you happen to know of an Amish woman named Rebecca living in this area?" the soft voice came again.

Ella Mae stifled a chuckle. "At least ten or more."

The woman sighed. "I'm sorry I can't give you the last name." Her shoulders sagged, and it was then that Ella Mae noticed something much heavier than disappointment weighing her down. The woman seemed downright desperate.

Tugging at her fur coat, the red-haired woman shivered. "Would there be a young woman in your community—about twenty-two years old—whose mother's name is Rebecca?"

Without much thought, Ella Mae calculated several daughters of her friends in the church district. "Sorry, but I can't be much help to ya if I don't know the last name."

"This Rebecca . . . I believe she would be in her mid- to late-forties. And her husband was somewhat older."

"Could be any number of folk, really," Ella Mae replied, wondering why the Englisher referred to the couple in the past tense.

The lady straightened a bit and continued to stand there, now leaning on the carriage. She took a deep breath before speaking again. "You've been very kind. I do thank you." She smiled a tiny, weak smile that faded like dew in the morning sun. Still her deep brown eyes twinkled with hope, matching the diamond choker at her throat. But it was the determined set of her jaw that caught Ella Mae off guard, and for the blink of an eyelash, the spiffed-up woman reminded her of someone.

Before she turned to leave, the lady reached deep into the pocket of her coat and pulled out a sealed envelope. "This may seem a bit presumptuous, but it would mean so very much—more than you could know—if you, or someone else could pass this letter on to some of the Rebeccas in your community—the ones with a twenty-two-year-old daughter. Oh yes, I forgot to tell you . . . the daughter's birthday is June fifth."

June fifth? There was only *one* woman who fit *that* description.

All of a sudden, the Wise Woman knew which Rebecca the fancy lady wanted, and why her face had seemed so startlingly familiar. As sure as she was Ella Mae Zook, she knew.

The lady handed her the sealed envelope. "With all my heart, I am forever grateful." And she was gone.

Mattie returned in time to see the tail end of the black limo pulling out of the parking area. "Some mighty fancy Englishers around today, jah?"

Ella Mae did not speak.

Mattie touched her arm. "Are you all right, Mamma?"

She nodded, then—"Are you going over to help Katie and Rebecca Lapp spruce up the house this mornin'?"

"Thought I would. How 'bout you? The company'll do ya good, Mamma."

"I'm all wore out, child," Ella Mae said, her thin voice sounding rough and hoarse again. "I best be gettin' off my feet and sit a spell."

Mattie trotted the horse up the lane toward their gray, wood-frame farmhouse. "I'll help you into the house, then, if you're sure you're not coming."

Ella Mae stepped down out of the buggy, holding on to her daughter to steady her footing. With her free hand buried in the folds of her long woolen shawl, she clutched the envelope. The envelope with a fine linen finish and the name *Laura Mayfield-Bennett* centered on the back.

Mary Stoltzfus and her mother, Rachel, made their way down the narrow road toward the Lapps' house, a large basket of sticky buns fresh from the oven nestled between them on the buggy seat. Even by carriage, time passed quickly this morning—their conversation punctuated with speculation about the Englishers who'd been seen by both Levi Beiler and Ella Mae Zook only an hour earlier.

Before they knew it, they were turning into the Lapps'

tree-lined lane and pulled up in the side yard, coming to a stop beside a row of identical, boxlike gray buggies. Mary helped her mother down, and they walked across the packed snow toward the farmhouse, waving at Eli Lapp, who'd come over from the chicken house to unhitch their horse and lead him to the barn for hay and water.

A four-sided birdhouse, accommodating as many as twenty purple martins in springtime, cast its tall shadow over the snowy walkway as the two women hurried up the back steps to the kitchen door.

At their first knock, Katie opened the door. "*Wilkom*, Rachel. *Wie geht's*, Mary." She hugged them both and helped Rachel off with her wrap.

"It's nice to see ya all smiles again," Mary whispered in Katie's ear.

"The smile's for hope, nothing more," Katie said under her breath.

Mary followed Katie into the bustling kitchen where cousins and friends had come to help the bride-to-be do a thorough house-cleaning—a community effort. Everything must be thoroughly spotless for the wedding service next week.

So it was much later before she was able to have a moment alone with Katie. It was then Katie confided that her father had gone off on an early-morning errand. "And so far, he hasn't come back."

There was no mistaking the look of concern on her friend's face. "Do you think he's over at the bishop's, then?"

"Ben thinks so."

"Oh, Katie, I'm sorry. It scrambles things up so."

"Jah." Katie's smile was forced, no doubt about it. "Now I'll have to be confessing to my future husband." Suddenly her mood shifted. "Come on to the kitchen. Maybe something sweet will take our minds off my problem."

She headed for the kitchen with Mary in tow. Together, they sampled the gooey pastries.

"Here, try one of mine." Mary reached down and tore a generous portion of sticky bun free from the rest.

Katie took a bite, finished it off, and licked her fingers. "*Du konst voll*—you do very well, Mary. You'll make a gut wife someday."

Then, glancing around for possible eavesdroppers, Katie dropped her voice to a whisper. "Will it be Chicken Joe or Jake Yoder?" she teased.

Mary felt her cheeks heat. "Don't worry. You'll be the first to know, most likely."

" 'Most likely?' " Katie slanted her an appraising look. "No, no . . . you have to *promise* me."

"We'll never be far apart, you and me . . . we're best friends, remember? Why on earth wouldn't you be one of the first to know?"

The look in those bright blue eyes told Katie that Mary would keep her word, as always. Mary could be trusted. It was one of the many reasons she had latched on to the jolly girl with the face of an angel. And a heart of pure gold.

"Then that's that." Noticing some of the women already at work, Katie jumped to her feet. "Can't let the others do all the chores for my wedding day."

The women had set about cleaning the house, beginning with the upstairs bedrooms and working their way down to the main level of the house—washing down walls and scrubbing windows till they sparkled. Every inch of the house would be needed for Katie's special day, so some touch-up painting was done in several rooms.

Before the noon meal was served, the men began to arrive, including Dat. It was the first time Katie had seen him all morning, and she was apprehensive. Since the men were served first, she helped with their light lunch—cold cuts, pickles, red beets, and a variety of cheeses—careful to avoid her father's end of the table. Instead, Mary served him and the others seated nearby.

Afterward, while the women sat down to their own meal, the husbands set about enclosing the large front porch to allow for more room for the many guests who would be coming for the wedding.

Bishop John stopped by shortly, bringing with him additional plywood and sheets of plastic, temporarily sealing off the porch. Katie felt his gaze on her, but pretended not to notice and managed to get lost in the crowd of women cleaning up the lunch dishes. Time enough to deal with him later.

"When will you be confessing?" Mary asked when she and Katie were alone once more upstairs.

Knees weak, Katie sank down on the edge of her double bed. "Not 'til everyone's gone," she said, then frowned. "But maybe John should know ahead of time, so he'll stay around after the other men leave."

"If you want, I'll tell your father, and he can tell Bishop John you need to speak to him," Mary offered, heaving a big sigh. "After that, things'll be right back on track where they ought to be, honest. You'll be forgiven and feeling gut again, jah?"

Katie nodded, unsure of herself. The confessing was to be her first ever.

Mary's smile was reassuring. "It'll all be over before you know it."

"Jah," Katie said, thinking the confessing was really only the beginning. *It'll be over, all right,* she agreed silently, then allowed her mind to wander. *If only Dan had lived. . . .*

With the thought of Dan Fisher came the realization that she'd gone for nearly twenty-four hours without humming or singing their love tunes. Not a single one.

CHAPTER NINE

Katie waited in the kitchen until the last few women had left the house before strolling into the front room as nonchalantly as she could manage.

"Come," Bishop John said, extending his hand to her as he stood to his feet. The blue in his dove gray eyes seemed to brighten as she made her way across the room.

"Dat told you about my songs?" she said in a near whisper, taking a chair across from him.

John nodded, and they sat facing each other. "It is a redemptive thing you're about to do, Katie. Unless a person backs up from takin' that first step away from the fold, the second and third steps will most likely follow. Those first steps can lead a person far, far away from the church. . . ." He paused, gazing at her tenderly. "Come, sister, find your peace where you lost it."

He continued on, now into his preaching mode, although it seemed to Katie that he was going about his admonition in a gentle way, in keeping with the Scriptures. "We must crucify our flesh, resist the things of the world. Do you agree to turn your back on songs not found in the *Ausbund*?"

"Jah," Katie responded, doing her best not to cry, not to think of Dan's love songs.

"And the guitar . . . will you destroy that instrument of evil?"

Katie caught her breath. Dat had told John Beiler everything! The request caught her off guard. What could she say? If she argued with the bishop, asking for an alternative to his demand, she raised the possibility of being banned—excommunicated from the church—for to talk back or argue with a church leader was definite grounds.

John had been chosen by lot, by divine decree. He'd prayed the baptismal prayer over her only a few years before. How dare she dispute with God's elect?

She lowered her head, staring at her folded hands. Her voice shook as she spoke. "I will destroy the instrument of evil."

John stood and turned his palms toward her. Hesitantly, she placed her small hands in his large callused ones and rose to stand before him. "This day, a sister has been restored to the faith," he declared.

Mary Stoltzfus was right, as usual. The confessing part was over quickly, made less painful by the obvious anticipation in John's eyes and the kind expression on his ruddy face. In fact, if Katie hadn't known better, she might have thought her soon-to-be husband had glossed over the issue of her singing, somewhat playing down the offense. Except for the startling request to destroy the guitar.

Little Jacob's words rang in her memory. *Daed's 'sposed to be right . . . God makes bishops that-a-way.*

Katie would have to follow through on her promise. A person just didn't go around making a vow to the bishop without meaning it. She didn't know how she would bring herself to it, but the Lord knew, and He would give her the strength when the time came.

She was greatly relieved, however, when their conversation— John's and hers—turned from sinning to the wedding. Still, she was wondering if John might mention her father's state of mind when he'd reported her transgression earlier that morning. But nothing was said.

With the confessing behind them, they headed for the kitchen, where Rebecca had set out apple pie and slices of cheese on the table.

"Have you decided who you want for *Newesitzers?*" John asked, referring to Katie's wedding attendants, who, as was customary, were not to be dating couples, but single young people.

Katie nodded. "I asked my brother Benjamin and my friend Mary Stoltzfus. Mary's already done sewing her dress and cape."

John smiled and reached for her hand as they sat down on the long bench at the table. "I asked my youngest brother, Noah, and . . ." He paused, casting a thoughtful glance at Katie. "Ach, I would've chosen my oldest daughter, but Nancy is still a bit young, I suppose."

Katie agreed. Surely he wouldn't have seriously considered asking a child to be an attendant. And in the next breath he was telling her that he'd chosen Sarah Beiler, Mattie's oldest granddaughter, John's grand-niece.

"How do you feel about Preacher Yoder being one of the ministers?" she wanted to know.

"Gut." John grinned at her, showing his gums like an exuberant young boy. "And I thought I'd ask Preacher Zook from over in SummerHill. He and I go way back to early days in Lancaster."

Katie wondered if Preacher Zook might be a relative of John's deceased wife. But she was silent, practicing the submissive role she had learned from Rebecca through the years.

It was settled. Two of their favorite preachers in the Lancaster area would preach the sermons right before the wedding ceremony. Other decisions had to be made as well, including the *Forgehers*—ushers—and the others who would assist at the all-day affair. Waiters, potato cooks, and "roast" cooks had to be chosen, and *Hostlers*—the boys who took care of the horses. Men to set up the tables and take down the benches were next on Bishop John's list, followed by a number of women who would launder and iron tablecloths for the enormous dinner crowd of around two hundred guests. The helpers were to be married couples, and occasionally a man would help out in the kitchen on the day of a relative's wedding—the one and only time such a thing would occur. Katie smiled, thinking of her older brothers Elam or Eli trying to cook up anything in their mother's kitchen.

Katie was grateful to John for allowing a large wedding with a feast to follow. Typically, out of respect for the loss of a widower's first wife, a second wedding was far less elaborate. But John, being the bishop, had waived the usual practice, much to the amazement of the People.

Before he left, John kissed her on the lips for the first time. She was glad no one was around to witness the kiss, for it was such a private thing and somewhat awkward, as well. Katie knew it might take some getting used to—this lip-kissing with the bishop.

Katie went upstairs to her room and contemplated the day. Things had turned out the way Mary had predicted, for which Katie was profoundly grateful. She felt more determined now to take on the task of daily crucifying her flesh—putting her wicked ways behind her. Confession *was* good for the soul, she decided.

Long after John's visit, but before the afternoon milking, Rebecca met up with Samuel in the barn. "I think we oughta go ahead and give Katie the money . . . that money from her birth mother, I mean," she blurted out when no one else was around, "as a dowry gift."

Samuel nodded. "A wonderful-gut idea for Katie and the bishop."

"I'll go and get it out of the bank on Monday, then." And

without further discussion, Rebecca hurried out of the barn, glad that Samuel had agreed. Every wedding detail was settled now. Things had fallen into place nicely. Everything. Right down to Katie's confessing to the bishop about her music.

The wedding would be her only daughter's crowning day. Rebecca had never felt so good about anything in her life. Not since the day she'd gone to the Lancaster hospital and returned home with little Katherine Mayfield.

Rebecca was so elated that when a horse and buggy stopped in the side yard, bringing Ella Mae Zook, she bounded over to greet her like a young colt. "Wilkom!" she called, then helped the older woman out of the carriage and into the house.

"Have a cup of coffee with me," Rebecca said, pulling up the rocking chair close to the cookstove.

"Ach, I can't stay long," the Wise Woman muttered as she sat down. A look of concern deepened the frown lines in her forehead. "Are we alone?"

"Jah. Samuel is out in the barn. So's the boys and Katie."

Ella Mae sighed deeply and began to speak. "A young English woman stopped by Preacher's store this mornin'—and started askin' questions." She glanced down at her lap. "She gave me this envelope. I believe it's for you, Rebecca."

"For me?"

"Jah, and I feel it may be best if you was to read it in private."

A paralyzing dread numbed her limbs and brought an involuntary gasp from Rebecca. "Wh-what do you mean?"

"I think . . . I have reason to believe it's only for your eyes," the Wise Woman advised. She handed over the envelope.

Rebecca trembled when she read the name penned in the flowing script—*Laura Mayfield-Bennett*—grateful that Ella Mae was kind enough not to ask questions.

"I best be going," the old woman said. "Mattie's expectin' me for supper."

Rebecca followed Ella Mae out to the carriage and helped her back inside. "Da Herr sei mit du—the Lord be with you," she said, her voice breaking.

"And with you, child." Ella Mae's tone—raspy as it was—had never sounded so sweet, so full of compassion, and Rebecca's eyes welled with tears.

Before picking up the reins, Ella Mae turned to Rebecca and spoke once more. "*Wann du mich mohl brauchst, dan komm ich*— When you need me, I will come."

Rebecca glanced down at the fine white linen envelope. "I know ya will," she whispered, shivering against the cold . . . against the unknown. "I know."

Katie finished up her chores in the barn, trying to shake off the nagging thoughts. Her gaze wandered to the hayloft high overhead, where Dan's guitar lay hidden safely in its case. Forcing her eyes away, she headed toward the milk house, noticing her mamma waving to someone in a departing buggy. *Wonder who that could be?*

John's words tumbled over and over in her mind: "It is a redemptive thing," he'd said about her confession. And it was, of course. Her act of confession assured her a good standing in the church. So she must obey the rules. Her future depended upon it.

Yet why did she feel stifled? Trapped? Her heart imprisoned along with the forbidden songs?

Hours before, she'd come clean, but her heart felt wicked still. Not at all the way she thought she would feel after baring her soul. What was keeping her from the straight and narrow? What more could she do?

Dan Fisher had spoken of this very thing once during a buggy ride home from a Singing a few days before his drowning. Katie had listened in confusion as he rattled on and on about something he'd found in Galatians, where the apostle Paul spoke about not building your faith on church rules, but on Christ. Dan had even read aloud the verses from chapter 5, and she remembered being surprised that he was carrying a paraphrased version of the New Testament around in his pocket. An odd thing for a baptized Amishman!

"The Ordnung can't save us, Katie," he'd said with a serious look in his eyes. "Our forefathers weren't educated in the Scriptures . . . they didn't study the Bible so they could teach it to the People. They made rules for the Old Order to follow. Man-made rules."

Katie had heard about the four elderly bishops back in 1809, who'd issued a ruling about excommunicating members who failed to obey the Ordnung. But she was in love, and whatever Dan chose to believe about their Swiss ancestors was fine with her; she wasn't going to argue with him. Besides, he'd probably gotten himself invited to a Mennonite Bible study or prayer meeting somewhere. The Mennonites were known for seeking out the truths of God's Word, and many of them ended up becoming missionaries.

At the time, Katie figured Dan had encountered some Bible-thumpers, that was all. But she hoped he'd be careful about his affiliation with outsiders. Especially Mennonites. He could get himself shunned for such things as that!

Katie cringed. Die Meinding, the shunning, was a frightful thing. The word itself stirred powerful emotions among the People. Feelings of rejection, abandonment . . . fear.

She could remember her Mammi Essie telling about a man who had been shunned for using tractor power. None of the People could so much as speak to him or eat with him, lest they be shunned, too.

"It's like a death in the family," Essie had told her. And Katie, only a youngster at the time, had been sorry for the outcast man and his family.

But it wasn't until she met his little daughter, Annie Mae, during a spelling bee at their one-room school, that Katie understood
the depth of sadness involved. No one knew what to say to Annie
Mae. They either said nothing at all or were extra nice, as if that
could somehow make up for her father's pain.

Even though the children were pretty much sheltered from
church affairs, they could all see that after the shunning, Annie
Mae was no longer the same. It was as if she'd been stripped bare,
robbed of something precious. Katie had even been fearful that,
unless Annie Mae's father submitted to a kneeling confession and
pleaded for forgiveness, his little girl might suffer for the rest of
her life.

Along with all the other children in the Hickory Hollow church
district, Katie had been taught never to deviate in the slightest from
the Ordnung. Once you began to stray, you were on your way out
the church door.

Well, nobody'll ever hafta worry about me, young Katie had
thought after witnessing the plight of Annie Mae's father. Never
would she willfully disobey and disgrace her family and her
church. Never would she step so far from the fold as to be
shunned. . . .

———————————

Moments after Ella Mae Zook lifted the reins and drove her
carriage toward the western horizon, now deepening to smoke gray,
Rebecca stumbled into the house, her heart thumping hard against
her rib cage. This letter in her hand, this stationery . . .

She clutched it to her, casting furtive glances about the
kitchen to be sure she was alone. Alone, as Ella Mae had kindly
suggested.

The room, strangely cold, fell silent. Rebecca reached for a
butcher knife and sliced through the envelope, making a long,

clean opening at the top. Fingers trembling, she reached inside to find a business-size letter folded in thirds. Slowly, she opened the page and read:

Dear Rebecca (the adoptive mother of my child),

I am sorry to say that neither my mother nor I took the time to learn your last name that day in the Lancaster hospital twenty-two years ago. Unfortunately, things were spinning out of my control that June fifth morning.

Perhaps I seemed too young to be presenting you with my newborn daughter. And yes, I was young. Irresponsible, as well, to have conceived the tiny life. The guilt is long since gone, but the grief for my lost child remains, forever imprinted on my heart.

It is with great apprehension that I contact you in this way. My prayer is that you may understand my motive, for I must be honest with you, Rebecca. The baby girl I gave to you has been living in my heart all these years. Yes, I must speak the truth and say that I am sorry I ever gave her away. Now more than ever, because, you see, I am dying.

A number of specialists have suggested that I "get my house in order" as I have only a few months to live. With this recent news, you will understand why I am desperately longing to see Katherine—if only once more—before I die.

Of course, it is very possible that you and your husband did not choose to keep the name I gave my baby, and perhaps, wisely so. However, I respectfully request your help in making a way for our initial meeting—my daughter's and mine. Since I am praying that you will respond favorably to my plea, I am enclosing my address.

Thank you, Rebecca, for all you have done for Katherine, for the years of love you and your husband have given her. Please be assured that I have no plans to interfere in her life or yours in any mean-spirited way. My search for my child is purely a love search.

May the Lord bless you always,
Laura Mayfield-Bennett

Halfway through the first paragraph, Rebecca had to sit down. "Oh my, no . . . no," she muttered to herself. "This can't be. It just can't."

She reread the letter several times, tears welling up when she came to the part about Laura's sadness over losing her baby. The loss of a child—any child—whether to adoption or to death was a searing, life-altering experience, she knew. She *knew*.

Yet everything in her resisted the notion of arranging for the meeting of this—this *woman* with her precious Katie! She—Rebecca Lapp, not Laura Mayfield-Bennett—was Katie's mother!

Still, hadn't the young woman said she was dying? Dying! What age would she be? Late thirties? Maybe even younger. Rebecca had no idea, for there had never been any information exchanged between the two families. The adoption had never been finalized. The infant girl had needed a home; she and Samuel had just lost their tiny newborn. Heartsick and barren, Rebecca had accepted the baby as a gift from the hands of the heavenly Father.

God, in His great Providence, had put her and Samuel in the path of the pitifully sad teenager with auburn hair. And that teenager—Laura—had kissed her baby girl good-bye and placed her in Rebecca's open arms. Who was to question the rightness, the legitimacy of such an act?

But in her heart, Rebecca knew that the identity of the infant she'd named Katie—and raised on a Pennsylvania farm in a sandstone house passed down from one generation of Lapps to the next—had never truly existed. Not really. Such a flimsy arrangement would never hold up in a modern court of law. No, if truth be told, Katherine Mayfield, the daughter of a fancy woman . . . Katherine, with English blood coursing through her veins . . . Katherine, with a bent for forbidden melodies and guitars—*she* was the girl who had lived here and grown up Amish all these years.

"And now her real mother wants her back," Rebecca moaned,

rocking back and forth. "She'll probably come right back to Hickory Hollow . . . and take Katie away from me."

She felt her heart skip a beat and the startling sensation caught her by surprise, taking her breath. With a great sigh, she stood up, crumpling the letter in her hand. "I won't be writing back, Laura Mayfield-Bennett. I won't!"

Without regard for Samuel's interest in the matter, or asking his advice—without thinking any of that—Rebecca got to her feet, walked directly to the old woodstove, and fed the letter—envelope and all—into its blazing belly.

As if from a great distance, she heard the back door swing open and Katie come rushing inside. She did not look up, but stared at the fire as it licked up the remains of the secret past.

"Mamma?"

She recognized Katie's voice and wondered how long she herself had been standing there, gazing into the red and orange flames.

"Mam, are ya all right?" Katie touched Rebecca's arm and she straightened, calling up all the strength left in her.

Slowly, she turned to face her daughter. "Where's Dat?"

"He's on his way in. He and the boys are coming for supper soon."

Rebecca went about fixing leftovers and forced a smile—a frozen mockery of a thing. Katie must not suspect that anything was wrong. She must never know that another woman, a complete stranger, had given birth to her. Or that this woman was even now dying of a terminal disease. Or that the letter—the one that might have opened the door to fancy dresses and mirrors and music—was shriveling in the heat of an Amish cookstove, only inches away.

CHAPTER TEN

The third Sunday in November was an off Sunday. Every other Lord's Day, the Amish community had a day of rest. The time was to be spent quietly at home or, as was more often the case, visiting friends and relatives.

Katie and her family had planned a peaceful day together, tending only the necessary chores and, in general, enjoying one another's company—the last such Sunday before her wedding day.

After lunch, Mary Stoltzfus stopped by with the finished wedding quilt, eyes shining as she greeted each member of the Lapp family. Eli seemed to pay more attention than usual when Mary walked through the kitchen and into the front room. This did not come as a surprise to Katie, for her dearest friend was glowing today.

Mary's mother, Rachel, had often warned, "Perty is as perty does." If the old adage was true, then Mary was the model, for she was as pretty inside as out.

Eli followed them into the front room and sat down on a straight-backed cane chair across from them, looking up occasionally from his crossword puzzle as they made over the quilt. Then Benjamin came in and suggested to his brother that they "take to visitin'." But from the twinkle in Ben's eyes, Katie suspected that they were on their way to see their girlfriends.

"So long," Mamma called from her wooden rocker across from Dat, who was snoring softly in his matching chair. The boys waved but continued on through the kitchen to the utility room, making plans in low tones and laughing softly.

"Will your *Beau* be comin' over after a bit?" Mary asked.

"Jah." Katie couldn't hide a blush. "John will be coming to take me with him to pay a visit to his preacher friend over in Summer-Hill. There's been some trouble with a few boys at the Singings."

"Really? What kind of trouble?"

"Oh, just boyish rowdiness, I guess. Some of them have been bringing fiddles and guitars—such like that."

At the mention of guitars, Mary frowned slightly, and Katie wondered if she was going to ask if she'd gotten rid of hers yet. To fill the awkward silence, she spoke up quickly. "I heard they even had a portable CD player over there one night. Can you imagine that?"

"CD player? What's that?"

"Oh, it's some sort of machine that plays music on tiny little records."

"Well, if that don't beat all."

"I tell you, Mary, things are changing mighty fast around here. I remember when we weren't even allowed harmonicas at Singing."

Mary nodded. "You're right, and they still don't use them much here in the Hollow. Not since John Beiler was ordained bishop a few years back. He's stricter than some, you know." She reached for Katie's hand. "But I'm glad we have a firm, *standhaft* bishop, really. And, just think, come Thursday, you're going to be his bride."

Katie smiled, gripping Mary's hand tightly. "And everything's all ready for the wedding." She looked around at the freshly painted walls and scrubbed floor. "Dat and the other men did a right fine job of closing off the porch, don't you think?"

She led Mary to the front door, where they looked out, inspecting the long porch area through the heavy, double-paned glass.

"Oh, Katie, I almost wish I was you," Mary whispered, her face close enough for her breath to cloud the windowpane.

"Really? Why?" Puzzled, Katie turned to regard her friend. "Did *you* want to marry the bishop?"

Mary's hands shot up to cover her flaming face. "Ach, no—I meant nothing of the kind!"

"What then? How could you be wishing you were *me*?"

Mary glanced at Dat, who was still napping, and dropped her voice to a hushed tone. "I just meant I wish I was getting married soon."

"Oh, Mary . . ." Katie reached for her friend and hugged her hard. "You'll have your day, you'll see. One of the fine fellas around here—one of them will be shining his flashlight at your window someday real soon now." She sincerely hoped she was speaking the truth—that it would happen just as she had predicted. "Come on now. There's apple strudel left from lunch!"

In the kitchen, Katie served hearty slices and filled two cups with her Mam's good coffee.

"Mm-m, des gut," Mary said after her first bite. "Is it your mamma's recipe?"

"Jah."

"Then I best be getting it."

"I've tasted your pastries, Mary Stoltzfus. You need no help there!"

They finished off their dessert, still chattering on about the wedding plans. "I couldn't be happier about you being my side sitter," Katie said, referring to her attendant for the preaching service, held during the first two hours of the wedding.

"Well, who else would you have picked?" Mary's eyes sparkled.

"Nobody. You're my one and only choice. I never had sisters to choose from, you know."

Mary brushed the crumbs toward the center of the table. "I'm glad . . . in a way. If you had, then maybe I wouldn't be getting to have a place of honor at your wedding. And maybe . . . we'd never have been such close, dear friends."

There was a moment of silence while they pondered the changes Katie's marriage would bring. "Oh, Mary, how will it be, me going off and getting married and leaving you behind, all single? Wouldn't it have been wonderful-gut if we could've had a double wedding?"

Then, thinking out loud, she added, "Maybe I should wait a bit longer, put the bishop off . . . 'til Chicken Joe asks you to marry him . . . or Preacher's boy."

Mary's mouth dropped wide. "Don't you go saying such things! God's ways are best, Katie. Besides, poor Bishop John's been waitin' an awful long time for you as it is."

"A long time?" Katie was surprised to hear it. "How do you know?"

Mary frowned, and it appeared that maybe her friend feared she'd spoken out of turn. But Katie pushed for an answer. "Just what are you saying?"

Mary cocked her head and narrowed her gaze. "I know it's true. The bishop's had his eyes on you for a gut long time. I've seen the way he watches you. Ach, I wouldn't be surprised if he's been in love with you since before your baptism."

Katie groaned. "But Dan and I were in love back then, so how could it be that the bishop—"

"Oh, I'm not saying Bishop John was *jealous* of Dan," Mary quickly interrupted, eyes wide. "I didn't mean that at all."

Thinking back, Katie realized what Mary must be referring to. "Oh, *that*. John was just being extra kind and helpful after Dan drowned, that's all."

"Well . . . maybe so. John Beiler's a kind, God-fearing man, of course." Mary sighed. "It must be awful gut to have someone like that eager to be marrying you."

Katie cleared off the table, then came back over to sit across from Mary. "Before, when you were talking about John watching me . . . well, you didn't mean he had that serious, uh . . . that intense look in his eyes, did you?"

"Katie Lapp! I never meant to be putting such a notion in your head!" came the fiery retort. "John Beiler's an ordained bishop, for goodness' sake!"

Katie nodded, thinking, wondering. John Beiler was also a human being. She had seen clear evidence of longing in his eyes, but it wasn't something she felt she should share—even with her closest friend.

"Please, whatever you do, don't go telling anyone what I said just now, you hear?" Mary sounded almost desperate.

Katie nodded in agreement, but her mind went swirling off, thinking back to the way John had glossed over her confession. Was it because of his fondness for her? Because he didn't want to be harsh with his future wife?

"Whatcha thinking now?" Mary asked, straightening her apron as she stood and went to the cookstove to warm her hands.

"Nothing much." Katie remained seated, watching Mary, wishing things could stay the way they were between them.

"Well, that's gut, because I don't want you thinking at all 'til after the wedding. Then, in a couple of days, I'll come visit you over at the bishop's house and hear all about the names you've picked out for your first baby come spring." Her broad grin revealed slightly crooked front teeth.

"Why, you . . ." Katie hustled over to her, jostling and poking at Mary's ribs. If it hadn't been the Lord's Day, she would have been tempted to hale her friend outside for a snowball fight. As it was,

Katie's prayer kapp was knocked askew, and Rebecca had to shush them from the front room.

"We're still just like two kid goats, ain't?" Katie whispered, trying to squelch another giggle. "And here you are—talking about the little ones you think I'll be having soon."

Mary shrugged. "Maybe one of your children will have red hair. Wouldn't that be right nice?"

"My hair's not red!"

"Well, what do you call it, then?"

"It's auburn," Katie insisted. "But you're right about one thing. It's about time for someone else in the Hollow to have colorful hair, don't you think?"

Mary was thoughtful, unexpectedly so. "You know, I guess I never thought about it, but you're the only one around here with auburn hair."

Fearful of continuing on that conversational course, Katie rose and motioned Mary upstairs to the bedroom, where she dropped to her knees, opened her cedar chest, and showed her friend the many handmade linens and doilies she'd collected.

"Does it feel strange moving into a house that's already set up with furniture and whatnot?" Mary asked as they were refolding the dainty things.

"Oh, I can't say it feels strange, really. The bishop and I talked about it. We think it's best this way . . . for the children, that is. . . ." Her voice trailed away, and she sat back on her heels, staring off into space.

"But it bothers you, doesn't it?"

There she went again. Mary seemed to know instinctively what the real truth was. "Oh, it's bothered me a little off and on, I suppose, but I'll get used to it," Katie replied, closing the lid of the chest and getting to her feet. "I'm sure I will."

What she didn't say was that marrying *any* man other than her first love would bother her somewhat, at least for a time. Perhaps a good *long* time.

Elam, Katie's eldest brother, and his petite, but expectant, young wife of one year arrived a few minutes after Mary left the house. Both Elam and Annie hugged Katie and Rebecca as they came in.

"We have our dishes all ready to load up for the wedding feast," Annie said, smiling as she removed her winter bonnet, revealing dark chestnut brown hair under her white kapp. "Elam will bring them over tomorrow sometime . . . whenever it suits."

Katie was pleased to be borrowing Annie's good dishes. Her sister-in-law was probably the sweetest girl Elam could have chosen to marry, even though he had to be the orneriest brother God ever made. Of their union, a new little Lapp was soon to arrive—in mid-January. Eager for her first niece or nephew, Katie wondered if the baby would look anything like Annie's younger brother—her beloved Dan.

The first time Katie had mentioned the possibility, her sister-in-law had nodded sadly, saying she truly hoped so. "Dan had the dearest face in all the world, I do believe."

Katie had agreed wholeheartedly. She would have loved to pursue the matter with Annie, but because her wedding date had recently been published and was widely known among the People, no more public talk of Dan Fisher was appropriate.

"I think Mam's gonna ask you to be servers at my wedding," she whispered as Annie settled into the rocker near the woodstove.

Since his favorite chair was in use, Dat went to sit at the head of the table. He rested his arms on the green-and-white checkered tablecloth, looking as though he might be expecting a piece of *schnitz* pie, perhaps.

"Of course, Dat and Mam should do the asking," Katie spoke

up, glancing at Rebecca across the kitchen as she pulled dessert dishes from the cupboard.

"Ach . . . ask away," Elam said, giving Mam a peck on the cheek. "We can always say no, now can't we?"

"Well?" Rebecca eyed her son. "Would you and Annie consider being servers for the wedding?"

Katie noticed Annie purposely glance at her tall, handsome husband, waiting submissively for Elam's reply. He would make the decision for the two of them.

"Jah, we'll serve," Elam replied cheerfully, without a trace of teasing on his ruddy face. "It'll be an honor, you know that." He grinned at Rebecca. "Who else will you be asking, Mam?"

"Oh, Aunt Nancy and Uncle Noah, and Dat's youngest brother and his wife. Close relatives, mostly."

"What about David and Mattie Beiler?" Elam taunted her. "Wouldn't you like to have them help, too?"

Before their mother could answer, Katie spoke up. "Mattie will probably be doing other things, but Abe and Rachel Stoltzfus will be helping out in the kitchen."

"Ah!" Elam threw up his big hands. "So . . . the best friend's parents are pushing Mattie out, jah?"

"Elam Lapp," Mam reprimanded softly, "hold your tongue."

Katie stifled a smirk. The scene was a little comical; interesting, too. She continued to observe the joshing between her brother and Mam, keenly aware of their striking resemblance—clearly visible, even to strangers. No one would ever doubt who had given birth to the robust twenty-seven-year-old man. She envied the bond between each of her brothers and her parents—especially the obvious physical link between the firstborn of the Lapp family and Rebecca herself. Even with a year's growth of whiskers, Elam's facial features matched hers closely—the high forehead, the dimples, the straw-colored hair. No doubt about it, he was her boy.

Elam had always seemed comfortable cutting up in front of Mam. Today was no exception. In spite of his sometimes obnoxious friskiness—Elam had a tendency to carry things a bit too far at times, Katie thought—he exuded a warmth of spirit, a connecting tie even now, as a married man living twenty minutes away from the old stone house. A married man come home for a Sunday afternoon visit, true, but one who loved his homeplace still. Katie sensed it, perhaps more strongly today than ever before.

"So . . . it's final, then—we won't be including Mattie?" Elam persisted, teasing his Mam.

"Jah, final" was Rebecca's firm answer.

"Are you sure, now? Don't you want mad Mattie over here taking charge of your kitchen, Mam?"

Dat let out a grunt of displeasure. After all, it was the Lord's Day.

Elam poked his finger into Katie's rib, carrying the frivolity one step further. She backed away, shaking her head. Mam would have to deal with her eldest son's never-ending shenanigans.

And deal with him, she did. Rebecca served up schnitz pie, a hefty slice of stink cheese, and black coffee to keep Elam's hands and mouth busy.

More relatives—Noah and Nancy Yoder, Rebecca's sister and husband, and six of Katie's first cousins—showed up in time to enjoy the dried apple dessert. And if it hadn't been a Sunday, the women would have made quick work of the walnuts and hickory nuts still waiting to be cracked for the wedding. Instead, Rebecca invited all of them back on Tuesday morning for a work frolic.

"Will you be telling your stories again?" one of the cousins asked.

"Oh, most likely." Rebecca grinned, and Katie realized that her mother had taken the question as a compliment.

Mam was beaming today—her extended family gathered around her like chicks around a hen. Warmth and goodwill seemed to permeate the house, and by the time Bishop John arrived on the scene, Katie was genuinely glad to see him.

John took the cup that was offered him and swigged down a few sips of Rebecca's delicious black coffee. Greetings were exchanged around the kitchen, with many relatives mentioning the upcoming wedding on Thursday.

When the good-byes were said, Katie bundled up in her warmest shawl and headed out to the buggy with John, wondering what it would be like to bring her new husband home for a Sunday afternoon visit.

CHAPTER ELEVEN

The air was icy and sweet on Monday morning as Katie hung out the wash. She thought how much more pleasant it would be doing the same chore with Nancy Beiler, the bishop's eldest daughter, at her side. It was difficult to believe that three days from now, she would be saying her wedding vows. The hours seemed to be speeding by like wild horses, much too fast.

"Be sure and lock up the house when we go," Rebecca told Katie before leaving with Samuel to tend to some business at the bank.

Katie puzzled over her mother's strange request. Here in Hickory Hollow, folks had never felt the need to do such a thing. Nevertheless, she went around and locked the front and back doors, waiting until her parents were out of sight and Eli and Benjamin were off to a cattle sale before going to the hayloft. It was time to make good her confession promise to the bishop.

The smell of hay filled the drafty haymow, and although she was momentarily tempted to play the instrument of evil when she found it, Katie kept the guitar case securely closed and tucked it under her arm. Surefooted, she made her way down the long wooden ladder to the lower level, where the cows came in for milking and the horses and Satin Boy were stabled and fed. Her pony whinnied playfully, but she didn't take the time to go over and caress his beautiful long neck.

Nor did she allow her thoughts to wander from her original purpose. Resolutely, she headed for the house. Once inside, she opened the round grate on the top of the woodstove, almost succumbing to the reckless impulse to burn the guitar and get it over with—once and for all. But when she lay the case out on the table and unsnapped both sides, she hesitated. If she opened the lid and so much as *looked* at Dan's old guitar, her promise to the bishop might wither and turn to ash—much like the kindling consumed by these flames.

But what could she do to rid herself of this wickedness without forever reliving the heart-wrenching memory of the final, destructive act, carried out by her own hands?

There was always the cemetery. . . .

The notion startled her at first, but it was an option. A simple wooden grave marker designated the empty spot in the earth, making note of the fact that Daniel Fisher had drowned on his nineteenth birthday. Why not bury the guitar there?

But it was faulty reasoning, and she knew it. The ground was much too frozen now.

Katie snapped the guitar case securely shut and carried it downstairs to the cold cellar, uncertain of her next move. Had Bishop John meant for her to do away with the guitar completely? She tried to remember his exact words at her confessing. But the more she tried, the more difficult it was to believe that such a kindhearted man would have insisted on destroying a lovely, well-crafted instrument. Surely, it would be no problem to merely put it out of sight somewhere. The idea was appealing.

She knew she was grasping at straws, though, rationalizing away the bishop's actual words as she crept past the rows of canned goods in her mother's tall storage cupboards. Undaunted, she hurried through the narrow passageway to the darkest part of the cellar, where Dat had stored her former dowry furniture. Because it was dark, she backtracked, locating the flashlight Rebecca always stored in the bottom right-hand cupboard in front of several old tablecloths used for summer picnics.

She pressed the button, and the area ahead sprang to life. Katie aimed the beam toward the corner cupboard in the depths of the cellar and wondered what it would be like to flick a switch and bathe a room in light. The reckless thought was momentary, for her gaze fastened on the lovely piece her father had made for her. She forced down the lump that tried to form in her throat and clung to the guitar, staring at the dowry furniture that might have been hers. And all the wondrous, innocent love it represented.

With guitar in hand, she decided the tip-top of the corner cupboard was a good choice for the hiding place. She propped up the flashlight on the floor, shining it toward the cupboard, and pulled over an old water bucket to stand on, steadying herself as she hoisted the guitar case high overhead. When it was close enough to the edge of the cupboard top to slide it back and out of sight, she bumped into something.

"What's up there?" she said aloud, determined to accomplish the deed before anyone caught her in another act of disobedience. Carefully, she hefted the guitar case down and retrieved the flashlight, shining it high to reveal a wooden baby cradle. She thought it amusing that her mother had stored the baby bed in the exact spot—the same dark, out-of-the-way place—that she had planned to conceal her forbidden guitar.

Katie stood on the bucket again and reached for the cradle. When she did, something rolled out and fell to the floor, smashing into pieces around her.

"*Himmel!*" Annoyed, she got down and turned to investigate. There, in a beam of artificial light, lay an infant's dress covered with shards of white milk glass. Had the dress been stuffed into the vase somehow?

Startled by the thought, Katie leaned down and picked up the garment and gently shook away the splinters of glass from its satiny folds. Then she held the flashlight closer, completely amazed. This baby dress was strikingly similar to the one she had found in the attic.

Driven by an urgency to know the truth, to be absolutely sure, she checked the back facing. The name stitched there was "Katherine Mayfield."

It appeared that someone had purposely hidden the dress. But why? She fought back unanswered questions.

Quickly, she made her way through the dim cellar to the steep steps, climbed them, and snatched up a broom and dustpan from the utility room. She felt herself becoming frantic, her pulse racing as she surveyed the side yard for any signs of her brothers, who sometimes returned home to get something they'd forgotten. When she saw that no one was coming, she flew back down the steps to sweep up and discard the broken fragments of glass.

Moments later, she rushed over to the Dawdi Haus next door and deposited the guitar in a crawl space. The instrument would be safe there, far from the eyes of Bishop John. And Dat.

Back in the main house, she sat down in the front room unashamed. The deed was done—a deceitful act—yet she felt absolutely no remorse. Why should she . . . when someone in her family was being dishonest with her? Still, did another's sin justify her own? She dismissed the annoying thought.

The fact remained—Katherine Mayfield's infant gown had been moved on purpose. Sadly, Katie suspected her mother. She was so certain of her supposition that, if necessary, she was prepared to confront Rebecca with the evidence.

Rather than indulge herself in a mountain of misery, Katie

set to work cleaning the oil lamps in the house, all of them. She struggled with her emotions, asking herself how her Mam could have possibly lied to her.

She thought about last Wednesday morning, when she had inquired about the baby dress after a second look in the attic had turned up no clues. What had Mam said? Something about everything being "a bit of a blur"? Was it that she truly could not remember? Or was she simply avoiding the issue entirely?

Katie had dismissed her mother's response as proof of her innocence. But now? Now everything seemed to be pointing to trickery. Why?

To keep her mind occupied, Katie set about making two green tomato pies and a pot of vegetable soup for lunch. But she found herself rushing to the kitchen door and peering out every time she heard a horse and buggy on the road. She continued to busy herself, hoping her parents might return in time to share the noon meal with her.

When they hadn't arrived by eleven-thirty, she went to the front room and sat in her mother's hickory rocker, twiddling her thumbs and staring at the lovely baby garment in her lap. The minutes seemed to creep by, taunting her. She examined the workmanship, the seams, the stitching—and came to the conclusion that the gown had not been purchased in a store but rather was homemade, with the aid of an electric sewing machine.

When Mam and Dat failed to appear, Katie went outside to check the clothes on the line. They were still a bit damp, so she left them hanging in the pale sunlight and went back inside.

Still restless, she carried the little dress with her each time she darted to the kitchen to look at the day clock—ten times in fifteen minutes—pacing back and forth between the two rooms. What was keeping them?

Things just didn't add up. But no matter how long it took or what measures she had to resort to, Katie planned to move heaven and earth to discover the truth. Beginning the minute her parents arrived home.

The lobby of the bank was crowded; the line seemed longer than usual for a Monday morning, Rebecca thought. But she waited patiently with the other patrons, most of them Englishers, although there were a few Mennonites and other Plain folk. None, however, that she recognized.

When she finally reached the head of the line and the next available teller's number appeared in red dotted numerals on the counter screen, Rebecca hurried to booth five and set her wicker basket down in front of her. Hastily, she filled out the withdrawal form, while the woman in the open booth waited.

"I want to close out this account." Rebecca pushed the bank slip in the direction of polished red fingernails. "And I'd like the balance made out to Katie Lapp—in a money order, if ya don't mind."

The owner of the red nails nodded and promptly left to carry out the transaction.

Later, when Rebecca met up with Samuel at the designated street corner, she walked beside him in silence, ignoring the stares of the people whizzing by in their fast cars. The notion that one of those people might be Katie's natural mother was horrifying. Instinctively, Rebecca moved closer to Samuel's side, wondering if that woman—that Laura Mayfield-Bennett—was out there somewhere right now—observing her, watching her every move, in the hope that Rebecca would lead her to the child she had loved for so long but had never known. . . .

Once she was safely bundled into the carriage, sitting to Samuel's left, Rebecca felt protected. Their familiar rig, pulled by old Molasses, stood as a shield against the modern English world.

"Did you get the dowry money for Katie, then?" Samuel asked, glancing at Rebecca.

"Jah, I have it."

"Wouldn't it be right nice to give it to her tonight at supper? That way Eli and Benjamin can be in on the celebrating."

Rebecca rallied somewhat at the prospect of a festive evening, sitting a bit straighter as they headed through the traffic toward the Old Philadelphia Pike. "Jah, a gut idea. Won't Katie be surprised, though?"

Samuel's face broke into a wide grin, and Rebecca knew she must tell him about the letter right away. But she would break the news as gently as possible. "It's a smart thing for Katie to be marrying the bishop this week."

"He's been waitin' for her long enough now."

"No, no, I didn't mean for the bishop's sake," Rebecca corrected. "I meant because . . . well, because something's come up."

"What do you mean?"

She took a breath for courage. "Our dear Katie . . . ach, how can I put this?" She sighed, then began again. "Our daughter's mother, her birth mother, is looking for her."

Samuel jerked his head around so fast his hat nearly flew off. Rebecca could see his struggle for composure as he pushed it down on his head and resumed his questioning. "This can't be. What're you saying to me?"

Dear Lord God, Rebecca prayed silently, *help me to speak the complete truth*. She eyed her husband tentatively, then began to explain. "Ella Mae brought over a letter last Friday, before supper. It was signed, 'Laura Mayfield-Bennett.' "

Samuel seemed thoroughly confused, and his brows beetled with an ominous frown. "Why on earth didn't you tell me before?"

Rebecca did her best to fill in the details, and by the time they made the turn onto Hickory Lane, Samuel had the whole story as best she could recall it.

"So you're saying that the young girl who gave Katie up is all growed up now and . . . she's dyin'?"

The pain in Samuel's voice ripped at Rebecca's heart, but she suspected that he was equally concerned about not having been told sooner. She could see now that burning the letter had been a grave mistake, and that it had created a thorny distance between herself and her husband.

She sucked in some fresh air and held the raw cold inside her lungs for a moment, then let it out slowly. "I never gave it a second thought, honest I didn't. I should've known how you'd be feelin', though. I'm sorry, Samuel, so awful sorry."

He nodded. "I see why you said what you did about gettin' Katie married off. If she'd waited any longer, who knows what might have happened next?"

"Jah, who knows?" Rebecca was sick with worry that the stranger might just show up on their doorstep. Perhaps today, while she and Samuel were gone . . . too far away to protect their daughter.

Rebecca shivered and tried in vain to shake off the nagging fear.

Katie forced herself to sit calmly in the front room when the carriage turned into the lane and Dat stopped to let Mam out. It was almost impossible to remain seated as though nothing were wrong. But *everything* was wrong, and when the back door opened and she heard the clunk of her mother's boots against the utility room floor, it was all she could do to keep from flying through the house.

"Katie?"

"I'm here, Mamma . . . coming." She gripped the baby dress and stood, steeling herself, and made her way toward the kitchen.

Rebecca rushed to greet her with a great smile on her face,

arms outstretched. "Oh, Katie, wait'll Dat comes in. We have such a wonderful surprise for you."

Katie held the little dress behind her back. "Can I have a word with you first?"

Her mother's smile faded a little, and she touched Katie's face, letting her hand linger there. "Child, what is it?"

"Mamma, I'm *not* a child. I'm a grown woman—about to be married."

But her Mam seemed too preoccupied to hear and turned as Dat came huffing into the house. "Samuel, come," she called to him.

He tossed his heavy sack coat and hat onto a hook and hurried into the room.

"Let's give Katie her dowry now." Katie had never heard her mother's voice so full of eagerness, or seen her eyes more heavenly hazel than at this moment.

"I thought we agreed to wait 'til supper, so the boys can be in on it." His words, directed at her mother, were almost a reprimand.

"At supper, then."

What was this tension between them? But Katie didn't ponder long. Whatever her parents had agreed on presenting to her at supper was not half as important as the questions burning in her heart. So, without any warning, she flung the satin baby dress down on the kitchen table in front of them.

Her mother saw it first and gasped, backing away. But Dat reached for the tiny dress almost reverently, touching the hem as if recalling a fond memory.

"Dat?" Katie whispered. "Have you ever seen this before?"

Rebecca had now positioned herself in such a way that she was standing guard over the dress. She spun around, eyes glazed. "It's best you don't know!"

Katie grabbed the dress and clasped it to her. "What's there to know? It's an English baby dress, that's all—ain't?"

"Don't go asking about something that's nobody's business."

From the firm set of Mam's jaw, Katie sensed there was more—much more. "It seems . . . well, I think someone keeps hiding this dress. First in the attic . . . and now—"

"That's enough foolish talk."

"Foolish?" Katie studied Mam's face, knowing full well she was treading on thin ice. "Maybe you're hiding something from me, is that it?"

Dat glowered and moved in front of his wife protectively. "Your Mam deserves respect, daughter. Never, ever speak to her in such a way."

Seeing the quiver in her mother's lower lip, Katie left off the questioning, even though it was obvious that they knew far more than they were willing to tell. "Forgive me, Dat . . . Mam." She turned and left the room, her head in a whirl.

By now her stomach was churning, too, and she decided against eating lunch, despite the mouth-watering aroma wafting from the vegetable soup, now ready to be served.

Katie knew she couldn't remain silent forever, though. She would wait, possibly until evening. By then she might be able to approach her parents more discreetly. At least she'd try.

Still, the thought that her mother had been somehow deceitful was the most troublesome of all. Katie felt the old rebellion rise up in her. If her gentle, honest Mam—the soul of integrity—could be guilty of such a thing, then, "I ought to be able to have my own opinion sometimes," she spouted off to no one but herself and curled up on her cold, hard bed, remembering something she'd heard years ago.

Somewhere in Ohio, a group of New Order Amish had separated from the Old Order in the late sixties. There, the women not only wore brightly colored dresses, but weren't above having ideas of their own. In fact, at this moment, as Katie simmered and stewed, the idea seemed downright appealing. And if her memory served her correctly, little Annie Mae's father had moved his whole family out to Ohio several months after his shunning probation. The New Order had welcomed them with open arms. At least, that's how word had it here.

She dozed off, dreaming of life in such a place. . . .

A welcome change in temperature—a foretaste of Indian Summer—lured Katie out of doors when she awoke. For old times' sake, more than anything else, she went out to the barn and hitched Satin Boy to the pony cart.

Without a word of explanation, she left the premises.

Most of the snow had already melted, clearing the way for two buggy-sized paths on either side of Hickory Lane. Numerous sets of buggy wheels had left their imprint—folks on their way to the cattle auction, most likely—which had served to turn the ice to slush. She rode on, enjoying the balmy weather, until she came to the turnoff to Mattie Beiler's house. And suddenly Katie knew what she must do.

There was not a sign of life at Mattie's place when Katie arrived, and she walked around back to the Dawdi Haus where Ella Mae lived. She tapped on the door, knowing it was unlocked, but waited for the Wise Woman to invite her in.

The sun shone steadily, warming her, and for a moment Katie amused herself with the thought that she might not have to bother with a shawl on her wedding day.

"Ach, come in, come in," Ella Mae said as she opened the door, panting a bit. "I was just cleanin' out from under my bed." She paused to give Katie her full attention. "It's so nice to see you again." And with that, she turned to the cookstove and set a teakettle on to boil.

Katie knew better than to decline Ella Mae's tea, for it was widely known that two sprigs of mint from the old woman's herb garden went into each visitor's cup. The brewing and the sipping went hand in hand with a visit to the Wise Woman.

"I always love it when the days get warmer along about now." Ella Mae stood near the stove, waiting for the water to boil. "Indian Summer makes for a right fine weddin' season."

"Jah, it does." Katie was eager to pull the satin baby dress from her basket right then and there, but the tea-brewing ritual mustn't be rushed.

"How's everybody at your house?" The quavery voice took on a little strength.

"Oh, the boys are down at the Kings' auction, and Mam and Dat just got home from tending to some business."

The old woman nodded. "Last-minute business for a daughter's weddin', most likely."

When the tea was ready, Ella Mae poured two cups, then settled down at the table across from Katie, sipping, then stirring in a second teaspoon of sugar.

In the momentary lull, Katie reached down into her basket and pulled out the baby dress. "Have you ever seen such a beautiful thing?" she asked, handing it across the table.

The old woman took the infant dress, fingering its sleeves and the long, graceful folds. "It's awful perty, ain't?"

"It's satin . . . English, wouldn't you think?"

Ella Mae nodded thoughtfully, then glanced up at Katie with a curious glimmer in her eyes.

"I'm mighty sure it's English." Katie showed her the name sewn into the facing. "*Mayfield* sure isn't Plain." She took a deep breath, then launched into her story, including the suspicion that someone had been hiding the dress from her.

When she finished, Katie sat silently, hoping Ella Mae would offer some word of wisdom, tell her what to do.

Ella Mae took a long sip of tea, then set her cup down with a clink. "Talk to your Mam about it."

"Even if it means confronting her?"

The old woman's gaze was as tender as her words. "Talk to your mamma, child. Speak kindly to her."

"Mam won't like being accused."

" 'In quietness and in confidence shall be your strength,' " she quoted. "You can't be sure how she'll take it 'til you try. Go to her . . . in love."

Katie didn't feel altogether charitable toward her mother just now, but she would consider taking Ella Mae's advice. "If you don't mind, I'll have some more tea."

The Wise Woman beamed and rose to get the kettle.

During the next hour, Katie found herself pouring out her heart. This time, unwilling to reveal too much, she spoke in riddles. "Several days ago I agreed to something that I just can't bring myself to do, after all," she began hesitantly.

"Katie, our dear Lord was the only perfect Person who ever walked this earth. And if you're sorry and repent, you'll be following His teaching," replied Ella Mae. "Perhaps in due time, your promise will be kept."

Reassured by Ella Mae's quiet perception, Katie opened up a bit more, feeling her way through the maze of revelation. "Just today, I figured out another way to do this thing—a different way—from what I promised. And I'm not feeling sorry for it yet."

Katie doubted that the Wise Woman understood much of her vague explanation. But even in spite of that, she felt better for having told someone. It seemed to lift some of the load of guilt.

" 'In quietness and in confidence shall be your strength,' " Ella Mae quoted once more, this time her voice fading to a whisper.

But Katie wondered how she would manage to remain quiet if her mother spoke sharply to her again. Confidence was one thing, but the quiet part was something else.

She squared her shoulders. It was settled. She would bring up the matter of the satin dress at supper tonight . . . in love.

My Dear Reader-Friend,

This novel will always be special to me, because it was inspired by the life and courage of my dear maternal grandmother. *The Shunning* is loosely based on her excommunication from an Old Order Mennonite church, and her eventual shunning.

Die Meinding—the shunning—is practiced in Plain communities to this day. And while it is intended to bring the wayward back into the spiritual fold, it continues to spawn heated debate and to divide families and churches as it has for more than three hundred years.

When the Hallmark Channel chose to bring *The Shunning* to life on film, I was delighted. To think my family's amazing story is now fleshed out on screen . . . Thanks to Director/Producer Michael Landon, Jr., Coproducer Brian Bird, and a remarkable cast, *The Shunning* is a compelling and inspiring film in every way. I hope you'll have the opportunity to see it!

Within these pages, you will rediscover the original story, as well as beautiful stills from the movie. As you watch the movie or read the book, my hope is that you will be captivated by the spirited Katie Lapp of Hickory Hollow, who embodies the profound courage and faith that carried my grandmother through her darkest hour.

Happy reading!

Beverly Lewis

Cast

Nancy Saunders
(Ella Mae Zook)

David Topp (Daniel Fisher) and Danielle Panabaker (Katie Lapp)

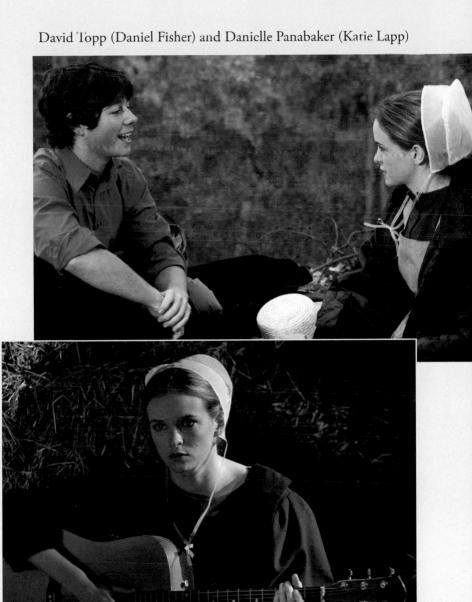

Danielle Panabaker (Katie Lapp)

Danielle Panabaker
(Katie Lapp)

Bill Oberst Jr. (Samuel Lapp) and Sandra Van Natta (Rebecca Lapp)

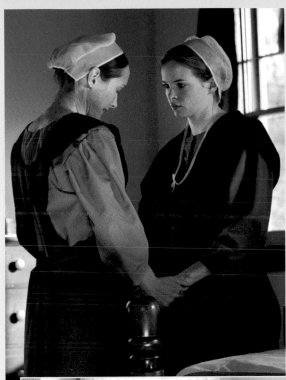

Danielle Panabaker
(Katie Lapp) and
Sandra Van Natta
(Rebecca Lapp)

Burgess Jenkins (John Beiler), Danielle Panabaker (Katie Lapp),
Jimmy Hager (Preacher Yoder)

Danielle Panabaker
(Katie Lapp) and
Bill Oberst Jr.
(Samuel Lapp)

Danielle Panabaker
(Katie Lapp)

Danielle Panabaker (Katie Lapp)

Danielle Panabaker (Katie Lapp)

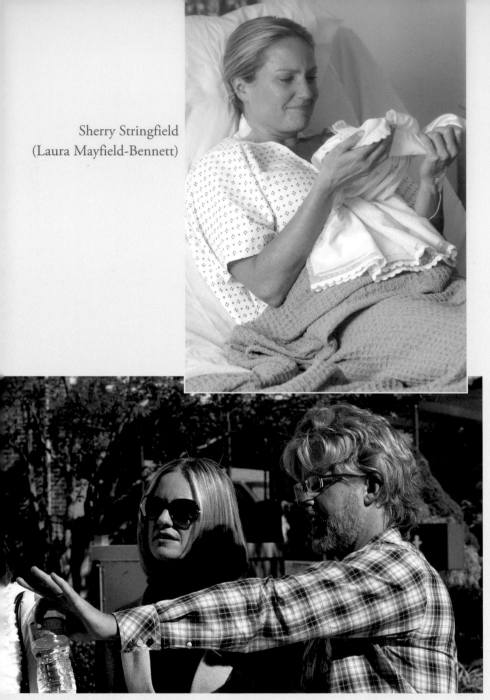

Sherry Stringfield
(Laura Mayfield-Bennett)

Sherry Stringfield (Laura Mayfield-Bennett) and
Michael Landon Jr. (Director)

CHAPTER TWELVE

Katie arrived home in time to help with the afternoon milking, feeling a bit weary and quite hungry now, having left in a huff and without her lunch.

Samuel and the boys did most of the heavy work—feeding the horses and hauling the milk to the milk house. It wouldn't be long before the three men would be doing all of the outdoor work. Katie would take her place in the world of married Plain women, attending work frolics—quiltings, cannings, and, once in a blue moon, a cornhusking, not to mention tending to the Beiler children and eventually her own babies.

Katie was thankful for her past experience with several English families outside Hickory Hollow—cleaning their houses and tending to their young children. The extra spending money had come in handy, and she'd enjoyed riding in a car occasionally. But all that had come to a halt a few months ago when Bishop John had asked her to become his wife.

"Will you be missing me when I get married?" she asked Satin Boy, stroking his glossy mane. The pony kept right on eating. "I'll come back and see you sometimes, I promise."

Eli hurried past her. "Don't be wastin' time talkin' to that pony. Best go on in and help Mam with supper. She's feelin' *grenklich.*"

Mam, ill again? It seemed to Katie that their mother was getting sick a lot these days. Strange, too, when she'd always been the picture of health—hearty and robust and working from sunup to sundown. In fact, now that she thought of it, before Katie found that baby dress, she didn't recollect Rebecca Lapp ever fainting—even once.

Concerned, she left Satin Boy to his supper and dashed toward the house. When she had hung up her work coat and winter bonnet, Katie found Mam standing near the woodstove, staring hard at it.

"Mamma? Are you all right?"

She started, then straightened quickly. "Oh my, yes. I was just off in a daze somewhere, that's all. The wedding . . . and all."

"Eli said you were ill."

"I think it's just a touch of the flu, maybe. Not to worry." Then she brought up the question Katie had been dreading all afternoon. "You wanted to talk to me about something?"

"About the fancy baby dress, that's what it was."

Rebecca seemed relieved and went to test the potatoes with a fork. "Oh. I thought somebody might've stopped by while we were gone. You did lock all the doors, didn't you?"

What was Mam talking about? "Was Mary Stoltzfus supposed to drop by?" Katie thought for a second, then realized her friend had said nothing at all about visiting today.

"No, no, not Mary. I wasn't speaking about anybody in particular, really."

The evasive reply piqued Katie's curiosity. "Who, then?"

A worrisome look clouded the hazel eyes. "A young woman, maybe? A stranger?"

Katie went to stand beside her mother. "Forgive me, Mamma,

but you're not making a bit of sense. Now start over. Tell me again."

Rebecca waved her hand in front of her face, a motion that usually signaled the end of a frustrating conversation. "Aw, just forget now, forget I ever said a word."

Katie leaned hard against her Mam and felt ample arms wrap around her. For a moment there, she almost gave in to the fear that her mother might be slipping—mentally, at least—and wondered if she should say something to Dat.

The supper table was set with Rebecca's finest dishes and silverware when Katie came into the kitchen later. In the corner, near the utility room, her parents were talking together quietly, their expressions sober. Katie made her presence known with a light cough, and they broke off their conversation abruptly. Then both of them stood looking at her—heads tilted to one side, eyes slightly narrowed—as though calculating how she might receive what they were about to say.

Alarmed, Katie glanced from one to the other. "Is something wrong? Is Mamma really very ill?"

"No, nothing's wrong, nothing at all," Rebecca tossed off a casual reply and turned to dish up the food.

Still not convinced, Katie washed her hands and helped set the serving platters on the table. Eli and Benjamin slid onto the long bench, and the family bowed their heads for silent prayer.

Afterward, Katie observed Dat cueing Mam with a nod, and Rebecca promptly pulled out an envelope from her pocket. "Katie, here is your dowry gift from your Dat and me."

"Dowry?" Katie was speechless. "But I don't need—"

"We want you to have it," her father interrupted, sporting a rare smile. "Someday you and the bishop . . . well, you may have need of it—to expand the house, or who knows what all."

Katie caught her breath when she saw the amount. "*Wie viel*—how much *is* this, for goodness' sake!"

"Ach, just enjoy it." Dat helped himself to the potatoes and gravy, dismissing her exclamation of disbelief.

Mam seemed content to sit and watch as Katie slipped the envelope into her side pocket. "This is quite a surprise, really," Katie added, suddenly mortified at the thought of the fuss she'd made earlier over the baby garment. Now she knew why her parents had been so secretive—getting off to themselves and talking that way. She was relieved that they'd apparently given no further thought to her outburst.

Eli and Benjamin seemed more interested in feeding their faces than inquiring about the dowry money. It was not until Benjamin had satisfied his hunger that he spoke up at all. "Which of my white shirts should I be wearin' on Thursday?"

"One of the new ones I sewed for you last week," Katie put in, glancing at her mother's drawn face. "And wear black stockings, too, and don't forget to shine your good shoes."

When the conversation turned to preparations for moving her belongings to the Beiler home tomorrow, Katie was happy to see that her mother seemed as keen and alert as ever. "I know you'll be wanting your own things over there . . . and with the bishop's first wife's furnishings taking up so much space . . ." Rebecca waved her hand. "Ach, I do believe that house is big enough for both. Maybe even the corner cupboard Dat made you—"

"Mamma!" Katie interrupted, horrified. "Why would you say such a thing? You know Dat made it for—" She broke off before she embarrassed herself again.

"Well, I don't see why you shouldn't take it on over to John's place, after all." Instantly Mam took on that glazed, cloudy expression again that settled in her eyes as she spoke.

Dat must have noticed it, too. "Let's just be thinkin' about it for now," he soothed.

"Jah, *think*," Eli teased. "Just think about Katie bein' mighty holy—holy enough to be the bishop's wife."

"Eli Lapp!" Dat scolded. "You will say no such thing!"

His sharp rebuke snapped Rebecca out of her daze. "Well now, who's hungry for dessert?" She sprang to her feet and began to move back and forth between the kitchen counter and the table, serving apple cobbler and ice cream.

Katie observed her, wondering when she should bring up the topic of the satin baby dress. If at all.

The moment came later, while Samuel was having his coffee. Black. Not a speck of cream or sugar.

"If it wouldn't be too much bother," Katie began hesitantly, "I want to ask about that baby dress . . . the one I found in the attic." To the best of her ability, she did as Ella Mae had advised, approaching the subject gently. In a spirit of humility.

"I thought I told ya to leave it be." Dat stirred his coffee with a vigor.

"No, no." Mam touched his forearm lightly, letting her hand rest there. "We really ought to discuss it, Samuel. The time has come."

Dat shrugged.

"I have to make you an apology," her mother pressed on, looking now at Katie. "It was wrong of me to do what I did." Her voice grew velvety soft—the tone she usually used when telling of the day Katie was born. "You see, *I* was the one hiding the dress."

Eli and Benjamin looked up in surprise, lips still smacking over the tasty cobbler. And Dat . . . his eyes widened, then squinted into slits. "Maybe it'd be best if we did our talking to Katie . . . alone."

There was no mistaking the meaning in her father's look. Eli gave a bit of a grunt and gulped down another glass of milk before the final silent grace, then left the kitchen for the barn, lantern in hand. Benjamin bundled up and headed for parts unknown, leaving Katie alone with her parents in the warm kitchen.

Katie was aware of a portentious feeling, as though something she had always known deep down was about to be revealed—like the missing piece of a life-sized puzzle, maybe, or an explanation she'd waited her whole lifetime to hear.

Rebecca began, softly at first. "We—Dat and I—have to tell ya something, Katie. Do try and bear with us 'til we're all through, jah?" Her eyes were soft and misty. She took in a deep breath.

Then, before she could launch into whatever it was she had to say, Dat stopped her. "Wait, now. I'll be the one tellin' it." He got to his feet and lumbered over to the woodstove, turning to face them.

Mam leaned her elbows on the table, seemingly relieved that, for tonight at least, her husband would be the storyteller.

"When we first laid eyes on ya, Katie . . . well, there was no doubt in our minds that you came to us, straight from the Lord God in heaven himself."

Rebecca nodded. "We always considered you the same as our own flesh and blood."

"Wait!" Katie threw up her hands. "What are you both saying? I don't understand a word of this!"

"Aw, Katie, my dear, dear girl," Mam said, her chin beginning to quiver. "It's time you knew. It's time you heard how it was that you came to be ours." Her tears welled up and spilled over, leaving a watery trail down her flushed cheeks.

"You mean . . . I'm not your own . . . daughter?" The thought was too large, too shattering to bear, yet her mind was racing frantically. Somewhere from the misty past, something Dan Fisher had said drifted back from that summery day. Something about kissing her on the cheek "the day you came home from the Lancaster hospital." Some problem Mam had had giving birth. But Katie had been so deliriously happy that day, so giddy with Dan's nearness that she'd paid scant attention to anything but their love.

"It comes as a shock to ya, no doubt." Through the veil of tears, Katie could see the concern on her father's face. He paused for a moment, breathing hard.

"Dat and I, we love ya so—honest we do." Mam picked up the conversation. "Seems now it's our turn to be beggin' your forgiveness. You see, we never told you the truth, Katie—not all of it."

"What . . . truth?" Katie's heart was pounding, ringing in her ears until she could only hear as if from a great distance.

"The truth about who you are . . . really." Rebecca broke down, her tears giving way to sobs.

But Katie couldn't comfort her, couldn't move. She was rooted to the spot while the room spun crazily, tilting this way and that, like a windmill in the spring. "What do you mean . . . you never told me the truth? If I'm not Katie Lapp . . . then who am I?"

Her father came to hover over Mamma as she looked up, her eyes swollen and red. Her voice came out in a whisper, trembling with emotion. "You're Katherine Mayfield, Katie, that's who you are."

Katherine Mayfield. The name sewn into the satin dress.

It was Dat who attempted to explain. "You're English by birth and Plain by adoption."

The words came as a blow. "I'm . . . what? *Adopted?*"

"In so many words," he said, resting his big, work-roughened hands on Mam's shoulders. "We never made it legal . . . didn't see the need, really. We loved ya from the start, and love was enough."

"But I'm not *yours* . . . not your own *real* daughter?"

"Now, now, nothing's changed at all," he was quick to say. "Nothing's diff'rent because of your knowin' it. You're ours and ours forever, and in our hearts you'll always be our little Katie."

"But you never told me . . . not in all these years. No one ever told me." Katie could hear herself whimpering. Suddenly she felt cold and crisscrossed her arms in front of herself as if to create a shield against the complete and utter shock of it all.

"Not a soul knows of this," Samuel said. "Though a few may suspect it, I do believe."

Rebecca blew her nose and spoke at last. "You don't carry the family's traits in looks, you know."

"My hair's *red*, that's all." Katie was shocked at the words from her own lips. She'd never before used that term to describe her hair. *Auburn*, of course. But never red. Red was for worldly English barns and highway stop signs—not for the single most beautiful feature God had ever given a woman. But she didn't stop to correct herself; her thoughts were flying way ahead. "So no one in Hickory Hollow knows I'm not Amish?"

"But you *are* Amish, Katie, through and through," her Mam said gently. "In every way, 'cept blood."

Katie propped her head in her hands as the truth began to dawn. *I'm adopted. . . . I'm someone else. Someone else . . .*

Slowly, she looked up at them. "Do my brothers know?"

Dat shook his head.

"Shouldn't they be told, then? Shouldn't everyone know the truth?"

Mam gasped. "What business is it of anybody's? Life can go on just as it always has."

"No," Katie replied. "Things can *not* go on as they always have. Everything's changed, don't you see? *Everything!*"

She ran out of the kitchen, tears dripping off her cheeks. Without a lantern to light the way, she stumbled up the stairs and fell across her bed, sobbing into the inky darkness. "Oh, dear Lord in heaven," she cried, "let this be some awful dream. Please . . . oh, please . . ."

It was only the second time in her life she had used such desperate, non-German words in addressing the Creator of the heavens and earth. She lay there weeping and trembling, remembering another dark and grievous time when her body had heaved with sorrow. And she could not be comforted.

Rebecca's rest was fitful. Three or four times in the night, she got up to look in on her grown children as they slept, her heart breaking anew as she stood at the door of Katie's room and heard the intermittent hiccups that come from crying yourself to sleep.

Finally, past midnight, she gave herself permission to stretch out on the bed beside Samuel. She made herself lie there, trying, but not succeeding, to shut out the voices of the day. Wondering if she and Samuel had done the right thing. Hoping against hope that all of them could go on with their lives and prepare for Katie's wedding.

Despite the brightness of the moon, a cloud of gloom descended over her as she stared, teary eyed, at the ceiling. She knew full well that the whole wretched truth—that an English woman was searching for her birth child—had been withheld. That neither Samuel nor she herself had mustered the courage to tell Katie the complete story.

At last, she slept. And as she slept, she dreamed—a dream both distorted and hopeful. In her desperation, she reached into the belly of the cookstove and retrieved the charred English letter, burning her fingertips. But instead of hiding it from Katie's eyes, she handed the letter over to her.

Katie shrank back in horror, determined to have nothing to do with something so fancy—not the fine stationery nor the woman who had penned it. Instead, Katie fell into Rebecca's arms, declaring her love and loyalty, forever and ever.

Rebecca awoke with a start, not knowing whether it was outright fear or love that propelled her out of her warm bed and down the hall to check on Katie, asleep in her childhood room. On her way down the cold hallway, Rebecca wondered why she had not been able to part with the satin baby dress all these years.

Now, as she cracked the door to Katie's moonlit bedroom, she saw that her daughter, too, had been drawn to the small garment. For there on the feather pillow, clasped tightly in her hand, was the infant dress she'd worn home from the hospital.

The dress—was it a symbol of the wicked outside world? Had Rebecca herself been too attached to it, to the glorious memory of their day of days? Was this dress the cause of all their present heartache?

What had Katie said before flying off to her room? That everything had changed? That learning she wasn't their "real" daughter meant things could not go on as before?

Katie stirred in her sleep and murmured a name. "Dan . . ."

Was it Dan Fisher she was still dreaming of? Poor Katie, her darling child . . . losing Dan . . . and now *this*? Poor, dear girl.

Rebecca blamed the dress, and she blamed herself. *If only I'd told Katie the truth from the very start*, she groaned inwardly. *If only I hadn't been so proud.*

Pride. One of the deadly sins the People prayed against daily, lest it bring about their downfall.

Rebecca backed away from the bed, inching her way out of

the room. She could only hope that her past sins would not scar her daughter for life, that Katie wouldn't let her impulsive nature drive her to some reckless decision. That she would put the shock of her true identity behind her and get on with her new life. A glorious new life with Hickory Hollow's finest widower, the bishop John Beiler.

CHAPTER THIRTEEN

"Katie doesn't think before she speaks . . . never has," Samuel grumbled to Rebecca at breakfast the next morning. "She leaps before she looks, ya know."

The milking and early-morning chores done, they sat at the table sipping hot coffee—just the two of them. Eli and Benjamin had excused themselves to go finish up some work in the fields, and Katie was still in bed.

"Where *is* that girl?" he went on, looking around with a frown on his face. "She ought to be up helpin' you."

"Aw, she's exhausted from crying," Rebecca told him, her heart in her throat. She wished he wouldn't go on being hard on the girl. It wasn't kindly of him, not when Katie was suffering so. "Our daughter's like a wheel with two spokes missing."

"Two?"

Rebecca didn't even attempt to explain. Matters of the heart made little sense to her husband, practical man that he was. Things such as losing your first sweetheart to the sea and then, on top of that, losing your own sense of who you were. Well, she couldn't fault him for not understanding. He was just like that.

"Our dear girl's lost right now, Samuel, swimming in an ocean of sorrow and—"

"You're not makin' sense yourself," he interrupted. "You can't be babyin' her along when she's got things to do to get this weddin' done up just right."

Among the People, weddings were a reflection on the father of the bride. Rebecca knew that her husband had high hopes that Katie's special day would come off without a hitch. Besides, no father had ever loved a daughter more, she thought, gazing fondly at his strong profile.

Rising briskly, Rebecca cleared the table. "I best run on up and see how she's doing. She's probably got herself a real bad headache."

"Jah, and I'll be havin' one, too, if we don't get her things moved over to the Beiler place 'fore sundown," he groused. "And don't you go lettin' her make you feel bad," Rebecca heard him say as she dried her hands on the kitchen towel. "Katie owes her life to us, ya know."

That's where you're wrong, Samuel Lapp, Rebecca thought. *Don't you know it was our Katie who gave me a reason to live twenty-two years ago?* It was Katie's coming that had filled Rebecca's empty heart, her empty arms.

She climbed the long, steep steps leading to the second floor, bracing herself for whatever hurtful words Katie might fling at her first thing. Her love was strong enough to endure it. Strong enough.

As it turned out, when Rebecca knocked on the sturdy bedroom door, Katie's voice was only a muffled, sleepy sound. "Come in, Mamma."

Putting a smile on her face, Rebecca tiptoed inside. At the foot of the bed, she looked down at the rumpled quilts and covers. "Were you able to rest at all?"

Katie yawned and stretched, then sat up and pushed up her

pillow behind her back. "I don't remember sleeping much . . . but I must've. I dreamed some."

"Bad dreams?"

"Jah, bad ones, all right."

Rebecca sighed. "Well, a good breakfast will do ya some good." She hated to remind Katie that a group of cousins would be arriving soon to help crack nuts and polish the silver. "Elam came over yesterday with Annie's dishes while you were out somewhere with Tobias and the pony cart."

"Satin Boy. His name is Satin Boy now, remember? I renamed him."

"Ah, I keep forgetting. A new name does take some getting used to, I must say."

Their eyes locked and held, and for one chilling moment, Rebecca felt her daughter's incredible pain. She could see in Katie's eyes the reality of what growing up Amish had done to the girl. How it had changed her entire life—stripped her of her true origins. What it meant to be the birth child of a wealthy, worldly family, never having been told of your real roots, yet knowing it in your bones as sure as you were alive.

"It must take a lifetime of gettin' used to," whispered Rebecca. "But you're Katie now . . . Katie Lapp, soon to be Katie Beiler, the bishop's gut wife."

Neither spoke for a moment. Then Katie patted the spot beside her, and Rebecca moved silently to sit on the edge of the bed. "I don't blame you, Mam," came the gentle words. "I just don't understand why it had to be such a secret."

Nodding, Rebecca reached for her hand. "I was ashamed, you see. There was a baby . . . one that died before it ever got a chance to live. And after it was born dead . . . well, the doctor said I was barren, said I'd never have any more children." She stared down at the floor and caught her breath. "I felt cursed . . . wanting more babies . . . and knowin' I'd never have 'em."

Katie listened without interrupting, letting Mam pour out her own pain.

"Then when we saw you—your Dat and I—it was like the Lord God himself was saying to me, 'Here's your heart's desire, Rebecca. Rise up and wash your face . . . put a smile on your lips. The daughter you've been longin' for is here.' And that's what we did—brought you right home to be our little girl."

"Just like that?" Katie asked, full of wonder, not pressing to know how or when or what had happened to bring all this to pass.

"Exactly like that."

"And the People? They never suspected I wasn't your real baby?"

"Not for a single minute."

"And you never once thought I looked like a 'Katherine'?"

"Not after we undressed you and put away the satin dress. Once we renamed you, I guess . . . well, you always looked like a little girl named Katie to Dat and me." She thought for a second, glancing at the ceiling with her head tilted to one side. "Jah, I can say here and now, you looked just like a Katie . . . right from the start."

Katie stared dreamily into space. "Who named me Katherine? Was it my first Mam?"

The words were a hammer blow to Rebecca's heart. Oh, not today. Not with the wedding so near. Not with Laura Mayfield-Bennett driving around Hickory Hollow, searching.

"Jah, your biological mother named you, I think."

"Did you meet her?"

"Only for a little bit." Rebecca's encounter with Laura and her mother in the hospital corridor had been brief. In fact, she seemed to recollect Laura's mother more clearly than she remembered Laura Mayfield herself.

"Did you see her long enough to know what she looked like?"

Rebecca was thoughtful. "You have her brown eyes and auburn hair."

"Anything else?"

She shook her head. "I don't remember much now."

"Well, it doesn't really matter, I guess," Katie said. "I know who my *real* mamma is." She slid over on the bed and hugged Rebecca, giving her a warm kiss.

While Katie dressed and had a late breakfast, Rebecca jotted down a list of things to be done before tomorrow. In between the writing, though, she wondered at Katie's response. She marveled that the girl hadn't ranted and raved, hadn't caused a fuss. Hadn't threatened to tell the People the truth. But she'd done none of that.

Rebecca should have felt relieved. Instead, she felt curiously unsettled.

Katie stood at the tall window in her bedroom, looking out. The best times of her life had been before she'd learned that she was the only adopted child in Samuel and Rebecca Lapp's household. Maybe the only adopted child in all of Hickory Hollow. The best times had been the carefree days of her childhood.

Blinding hot summer days . . .

She and Mary Stoltzfus—two little Plain girls—running bare-foot through the backyard, Mamma's white sheets flapping on the clothesline, past the barnyard to the old wagon road connecting Dat's farm with a wide wooded area and a large pond that lay sparkling in the sunlight.

Two little Plain girls, telling secrets as they worked the oars of the rickety old rowboat, on their way out to the island in the middle of the pond.

Two little Plain girls—birds swooping overhead, oars splashing, sending lazy ripples through the water—laughing and chattering away the sun-kissed summer hours. . . .

In those days Katie was simply . . . Katie. Not Katherine. Not someone sophisticated. Just Plain Katie, inside and out. At least, as Plain as she could be in spite of the constant inner tugging toward fancy things. Still, she did try to follow the rules—what was expected of the People, according to the Ordnung.

But things were changing. Had already changed—overnight, it seemed. And it appeared that they would keep on changing—just like the ripples on the pond, ever circling out and away into the distance. Far, far away.

She was not Katie inside or outside, neither one. The girl with autumn brown eyes and reddish hair had come to see herself as a different person. Someone she didn't know, didn't recognize. Someone with a mother who had given her an English name. A fancy, worldly name.

Katherine.

The name did not sit well. She fought the fog of numbness, attempting to sort out her feelings, to push resentment aside. The growing resentment she was feeling for her parents, the *adoptive* parents who had kept their secret locked up for more than twenty-two years.

For a moment, she allowed herself to wonder about her real parents, especially her birth mother. Who was she? *Where* was she? And why had she stayed away for so very long?

The first thing Katie wanted to do when she saw Mary coming through the back door was to take her aside to a secluded corner of the old farmhouse and tell her the secret. Instead, she greeted her calmly and ushered her into the kitchen, along with about ten of her cousins. Then she rounded up extra chairs for the nut crackers as

Mam put on a kettle of water to boil. There would be hot chocolate and marshmallows for everyone and slices of cheese, fresh bread, and melted butter. Apple butter, too, and pineapple preserves for those who preferred a tart topping on their warm bread.

Katie went through the motions, performing her duties like a sleepwalker, barely registering the chitchat and laughter swirling around her. She made it through—without a soul suspecting that anything was wrong—all the way to the end of the day, when Eli and Benjamin hauled her cedar chest off to the bishop's house along with several suitcases, the satin baby dress hidden inside one of them.

That evening, five men arrived to help Dat and the boys move furniture out to the barn for storage, to make room for the long wooden benches that would accommodate two hundred wedding guests indoors.

Early Wednesday morning, John Beiler and his son Hickory John arrived to help set up the benches when the two bench wagons arrived—one from the Hickory Hollow church district and one from a neighboring district. Several uncles and male cousins, as well as close neighbors, assisted in unloading the benches, unfolding the legs outdoors before taking them in the house and setting them up, following a traditional plan—the way it had always been done.

Since John Beiler, at his first wedding, had observed the customary ritual of chopping off the heads of thirty chickens needed for the wedding feast, he delegated the task to three of his brothers and other close relatives, out of respect for his deceased wife.

Rebecca, along with her two married sisters, Nancy Yoder and Naomi Zook, and their husbands, began to organize the workers, including those assigned to peeling potatoes, filling doughnuts, making cole slaw, roasting and shredding the chicken and adding the bread mixture, cleaning celery, baking pies and cakes, and frying potato chips.

Twenty-two cooks—eleven married couples—had been assigned their duties, as well as the four wedding attendants, including Katie's bridesmaid, Mary Stoltzfus, who arrived just after seven-thirty.

"You seem awful quiet again," Mary said as they escaped to Katie's bedroom for a reprieve.

Katie spread her wedding attire on the bed, leaving it out to be inspected one last time. She had starched her white apron and cape and ironed the wedding dress until there was not a wrinkle anywhere. From the sound of the hustle-bustle going on below, she knew there were only a few minutes left to tell her friend what she wanted to say. If anyone could understand, it would be Mary. "You might be surprised at what I'm going to say now," she confided.

Mary listened, her eyes darkening with concern.

"I'm thinking that I might not be able to love John as much as I should," Katie whispered. "Might not be enough to make a gut marriage, but I'll do my best. I'll do my very best." Having admitted this, she felt a weight lift from her heart.

Mary spoke tenderly. "I know ya will. And you might even surprise yourself and fall in love with the bishop. In fact, I'm sure of it. It'll happen, sooner or later."

"He's been awful kind, deciding to marry me." Katie touched the white cape, a symbol of purity. "I might've been passed over if he hadn't—"

"Now, listen," Mary interrupted. "That kind of talk won't get you anywhere. You got a lot to be thankful for, that's true, but when it all boils down, Katie, you are supposed to be marrying the bishop and don't ya ever forget it. He's a wonderful-gut man."

The way Mary said *wonderful-gut* made Katie wonder. Was her friend harboring some secret interest in the bishop? "Just what are you thinking, Mary?"

"Well, I guess you haven't been paying much attention," Mary said, dumbfounded. "Don't you think John's nice-looking?"

"Well, I guess I never thought of him that way, really." *Not after staring into Dan's face the way I used to,* Katie thought, *wondering how on earth the Lord God could make such a handsome fellow. . . .*

"Well, you oughta be taking another look," Mary advised, slanting Katie a curious look. "You're lookin' through tainted glasses . . . and I know why. It's because of Dan, ain't? He's clouded everything up for you. But you're *supposed* to marry the bishop now."

Supposed to? If she only knew the truth. *I'm not even* supposed *to be living here in Hickory Hollow,* Katie thought, *let alone marrying a forty-year-old Amish bishop. I'm* supposed *to be Katherine Mayfield, whoever that is!*

But she didn't dare reveal Mam's secret—even to Mary. An unspoken pact had been made. Mam had suffered more than enough already. Now, faced with the opportunity to pour out her soul to her dearest friend, Katie had better sense than to add insult to injury.

She hid the numbness away, as deep inside as she could push it, just as Mam had pushed the baby dress deep into the white vase. If she did not suppress the pain, Katie feared it would surface to wound her mother yet again and tear savagely at her own future. And so she did what Mary would call "the right thing." She kept her secret safe—buried in her heart.

CHAPTER FOURTEEN

On her wedding day, Katie was up before four-thirty. It was so important for everything to go well that Dat had called a family meeting the night before to rehearse last-minute instructions. "A sloppy weddin' makes for a sloppy bride," he'd said.

Now, as Katie dressed in choring clothes by lantern light, she resisted the temptation to brush her hair down over her shoulders and play with it—arranging it this way and that—wondering how Katherine Mayfield might have looked on her wedding day.

Only in her mind, though, did she try on a satin wedding gown trimmed in lace . . . and discarded the kapp, replacing it with a shimmering white veil. So now she understood why she'd been drawn to lovely things her entire life. Understood—but didn't know what to do about it.

Katie's wedding would have none of the modern trappings such as flowers or wedding rings. The bride was to be content with her hand-sewn, homespun dress, apron, and cape. And since the day had turned out rather warm, she wouldn't have to fuss with a heavy shawl.

Won't Ella Mae be mighty glad about the weather? Katie thought, remembering how the Wise Woman had mentioned it on her most recent visit. And out of the blue came the thought that her great-aunt was probably one who suspected Katie's true origins—worldly Englishers, people outside the Amish community.

But the thought passed as quickly as it had presented itself, and Katie went about preparing for her wedding day, feeling neither pain nor joy. This numbing indifference to the shock of her mother's announcement carried her through the hours before she would answer "Jah" when Preacher Zook asked her if she would accept her brother in Christ, John Beiler, as her husband, and would not leave him until death separated them.

Delicious smells filled the house as each detail was checked off the list. At six-thirty, the assigned helpers began to arrive, and by seven o'clock, John, Katie, and their attendants were eating breakfast together in the summer kitchen, a long, sunny room off the main kitchen.

"What a heavenly day for a wedding," Mary Stoltzfus whispered in Katie's ear.

"You'll be the next one getting married . . . and soon," Katie predicted.

Overhearing the comment, John smiled. "It's a right fine day for our wedding," he said, stroking his beard. "May the Lord God bless His People."

Katie nodded, smiling back. For just an instant, a vision of Dan's face seemed to blot out John's, and she blinked in amazement. Then, rubbing her eyes, she glanced away. Would she never stop thinking of her first love?

"What's-a-matter?" John frowned, leaning toward her.

"Ach, it's nothing." She waved her hand the way her mother often did. "Nothing at all."

"Last-minute jitters often play tricks on people," John's brother Noah spoke up.

Katie opened her eyes wide, trying to erase the mirage. Mary had told her to forget about Dan Fisher, to put aside the past lest it poison the future. Mary was always right. But she'd failed to offer a suggestion as to how one did away with cherished memories.

Marrying John Beiler—putting him first—maybe that was the answer. Maybe that was why Mary had insisted that this marriage was *supposed* to be.

After breakfast, Katie went with John and the attendants through the kitchen, stopping to inspect dozens of pies that had been brought in. From the bounty harvested from their land, the good cooks of Hickory Hollow had baked up peach and apricot and cherry pies, apple and mincemeat and pumpkin.

Cakes, too. Five-pound fruitcakes and layer cakes of every variety. Later, after the wedding sermons and the actual ceremony, when Katie and John came back downstairs as husband and wife, they would see for the first time the two lovely wedding cakes decorated with nuts and candies. For Katie, who was known for her sweet tooth, there would be a wide array of other desserts to be sampled at her table—tapioca pudding, chocolate cornstarch pudding, and mouth-watering jellies, of course—Rebecca had seen to that.

In fact, the very best of all the foods was to be reserved for the *Eck*—the bride's table—a corner section placed so as to be most visible to the wedding guests. Ten twenty-foot-long tables, adequate for seating two hundred people, would be set with the best china in the house, including the dishes borrowed from Katie's sister-in-law, Annie, and others.

When it came time for members of the bridal party to change into their wedding clothes, the women—Katie, Mary, and Sarah Beiler, John's grand-niece—stepped into Katie's bedroom; the men, into Eli and Benjamin's room.

Outside, in the side yard, five teenage boys—cousins or nephews of the bride and groom—helped unhitch the horses as each carriage arrived and parked. It was an honor for a young man to be asked to be one of the Hostlers, who would care for the horses during the festivities.

Upstairs, Katie waited patiently as her mother fastened the white wedding apron and cape with straight pins at the waist, the bridesmaids looking on. When it appeared that Katie and Rebecca were ready to talk privately for the last time before the service began, Mary and Sarah discreetly left the room, waiting in the hallway as far from Benjamin's bedroom door as possible.

"I'll always love ya, Katie," Mam said, embracing her. "Always and forever."

"And I'll love you, too, Mamma."

"I wish we hadn't had to talk . . . things . . . over so close to your wedding day," Rebecca said as they drew apart, looking at each other fondly.

"Ach, it's over and done with." Katie brushed the painful thought aside.

"Over, jah."

"I'm just Plain Katie, ain't?" Even now, she was thinking of the satin baby dress, resisting the thought of its splendid feel beneath her fingers.

"Plain through and through" came the fervent response. Rebecca reached out and gripped Katie's wrists. "You do love John, now, don'tcha?"

"I love him . . . enough."

The words were hollow, and Rebecca pulled Katie to her. "You're not still thinkin' of someone else, are ya?"

Katie's voice sounded thin and desperate, even to her own ears, when she answered. "He was everything I ever wanted, Mam. Dan knew my heart. No one can ever take his place. No one."

Rebecca fluttered her lashes, and a deep worry line creased her forehead. "Himmel . . . you're in love with a memory!"

"I love Dan's memory, jah. I won't deny it. But there's more to it." She walked to the window, not wanting to hurt her mother by mentioning the music she and Dan had shared. Rebecca did not press the issue further, and Katie was relieved.

Below, gray-topped carriages were rolling down the long lane out front. Some of the young people were arriving in black open buggies. And there were a few cars—Mennonite relatives and friends, probably.

It was nearly seven-forty-five. At eight, the ushers would begin bringing guests indoors, seating them according to a prescribed order. First came the ministers, Preachers Yoder and Zook, followed by the parents of the bride and groom, and other close family and friends.

The haze that had carried Katie through the rituals of the past two days began to lift. She stared at Rebecca, not comprehending, and trembled. *Who am I, really?*

Planting a quick kiss on her mother's cheek, Katie hurried to meet Mary and Sarah in the hallway, in time for the bridal party to take their places downstairs on a long bench in the kitchen. The bench was set up near the stairway so that female guests could pass by and greet the bridal party on their way upstairs to deposit bonnets and shawls.

Bishop John sat between Katie's youngest brother, Benjamin, and John's own brother, Noah. He looked fit in his new *Multze*, a long frock coat with a split tail, and his black bow tie. He and his attendants wore high-topped shoes and wide black hats with a three-and-a-half-inch brim. His untrimmed beard was frosted with touches of gray, and although he needed reading glasses more often than not these days, he had come to his wedding without them.

Farther down the bench, Katie sat between Mary and Sarah, preparing to shake hands with the female guests. The men would assemble outside—in or around the barn—waiting until the ushers,

Forgehers, brought them inside to be seated—men in one section, the women in another—same as Sunday Preaching.

Katie felt her stomach knot. She felt as though she were sitting on the middle plank of the rickety old boat, rowing toward the island—her secret childhood escape. In her mind she rowed faster and faster, energized by the sweeping pace of the oars in the water, yet feeling trapped between the shore and the longed-for hideaway. Trapped between two worlds—her place with the People, and her hunger for the modern outside world, forbidden as it was. The world of her biological parents had always beckoned to her, the world of the young woman who had sewn a satin baby gown for her infant daughter, lovingly dressed her in it, then given her away.

You got a lot to be thankful for. . . .

Katie stole a glance at John. Only two hours separated them from spiritual union. Man and wife . . . forever to live among the People, carrying on the Old Ways. She remembered her promise to him, the one she had made last Saturday—now broken. How many promises did one dare to break?

Like a sudden wind chasing wispy clouds, her thoughts trailed away and she could not recapture them. She began to greet the women, many of whom she had known since early childhood. She shook hands with Mattie Beiler when the time came, and watched as Mattie went back to help her aging mother, Ella Mae, move down the line. Katie thought of her deceased grandparents and wished Dawdi David and Mammi Essie had lived to see this day.

When Ella Mae stopped to offer Katie her thin, wrinkled hand, she felt an urge to hug the old woman. *People always do what they wanna do*, Ella Mae had told Katie once. *Even if a person sits back and does nothing, well, not doing somethin' is a decision in the end.*

Next came several of Katie's first cousins—Nancy, Rachel, and Susie Zook—followed by Naomi, Mary, and Esther Beiler, and the girls' mothers, Becky and Mary—Ella Mae's married daughters.

Many more women came through the line. One of them was Lydia Miller—her mother's Mennonite cousin—the woman who talked to God as though He were really listening.

Lydia's handshake was warm. "May the Lord bless you today, dear," she said briefly, then went on to greet Mary Stoltzfus.

The Lord exalts those who humble themselves. . . .

If anyone was humble, it was Lydia Miller. She always dressed Plain—in long print dresses—and wore her hair tied back in a bun. Humility was written all over her round face. Love was there, too. You could see a singular compassion for the world in those eyes.

At that moment, Katie wished she knew more about Cousin Lydia, the woman targeted by the family as an example of how *not* to pray. Surely there was another side to this story.

In the short lull between guests, troublesome thoughts darted into her mind, stinging like nettles. *You looked just like a Katie . . . right from the start.*

Katie began to feel sorry for herself, though the sorrow was a mingling of anger and fear. Learning, on the eve of her wedding, that she was not truly a Lapp—a part of the fabric of the People—was like having finally learned how to sew the finest set of short, running quilt stitches and then, after criticism, deciding to rip them out.

She felt restless as the young people—the teenagers in the church district and surrounding areas—made their entrance into the house. Unmarried brothers and sisters of the bride and groom led the procession, followed by couples who were recently married or published.

I might've been passed over. . . .

A group of cousins, nephews, nieces, and friends came in next, followed by the young boys, who quickly took their seats. All the men except Preachers Yoder, Zook, and Bishop John—because he was also a minister—removed their hats and put them under their benches. The formality represented the belief that Samuel Lapp's dwelling place was now—at this moment and for the rest of the service—a house of worship.

After the guests were seated, another old custom was carried out: The three ministers continued to wear their hats until the first hymn.

On the third stanza, Preachers Yoder and Zook stood up and made their way, followed by John and Katie, to the guest bedroom upstairs. There, Preacher Yoder began giving instruction, encouraging John and Katie, reminding them of their duties to one another as married partners in the Lord. Katie knew what was to come and wondered how embarrassing it would be not to be able to truthfully answer yes when asked if she had remained pure.

John's eyes shone with devotion as he reached for her hand and descended the stairs, entering the crowded room holding hands with Katie publicly for the first time. They made their way along the narrow aisle with their attendants.

When Katie spotted little Jacob Beiler in the crowd, he flashed an angelic grin at her as the People sang the third verse of the *Lob Lied.*

I can hardly wait for ya to come be our mamma. . . .

The bridal party found the six matching cane chairs reserved for them, and they sat down exactly in unison. Katie, Mary, and Sarah sat on one side facing John, Benjamin, and Noah.

Everywhere she looked, Katie saw the kind, honest faces of loved ones and friends—dear Nancy Beiler and her sister Susie, soon to be Katie's young charges. And there was Levi, their sullen brother, sitting with arms crossed, staring curiously at Katie. The boy would keep her on her toes; that was for certain. His brother, Hickory John, sat tall on the bench, reminding her of his father.

But there was not one soul in the house who had any idea that Katie Lapp was a disobedient church member—one who had willfully disobeyed her bishop, her beau. Who had chosen to hide her guitar instead of destroying it.

She was, therefore, guilty of unconfessed sin. And worse, she was a hypocrite—a wolf in sheep's clothing. Not having been born Amish made her quite different from anyone else present today, or so it seemed. She wondered if being adopted and never being told might not even nullify her baptismal vow.

You don't like being Amish, but you're stuck. . . . Mary's commentary echoed in her ears as the People sang the sixth and seventh verses of the next hymn.

No matter what happens, remember I love you. . . .

Would that beloved voice never stop speaking to her from the grave? Would she have to settle for an obliging relationship with John Beiler when her heart craved so much more?

The congregational singing ceased, and Bishop John's uncle stood up to give the *Anfang*, the opening, which included biblical accounts of married couples—from Adam and Eve to Ruth and Boaz. When the speaker was finished, each person turned and knelt for a period of silent prayer. While the others closed their eyes, Katie peeked at a familiar wall hanging. *One who wastes time, wastes life itself.* The old Amish saying caught her eye; the message spoke to her heart.

I've been wasting the People's time, she thought. *Dat's, Mam's, Mary's . . . Bishop John's. And my own life—have I wasted it away? Haven't I tried hard enough to follow the Ordnung?*

As quickly as the questions came, they were pushed away. She took a deep breath, remembering her life oath before God. She had made her baptismal vow before all the People, the same folk assembled here in her parents' house, soon to witness her marriage vows. *What's done is done,* she thought. And when the silent prayer was finished, she stood with all the others.

She waited respectfully as one of the deacons read the first twelve verses of Matthew, chapter nineteen, before the People sat down again. The Old Way, das Alt Gebrauch. Church order and rules—the way things were.

All of it bore down on Katie as she waited for the inevitable moment when Preacher Zook would speak first to John and then to her. He would ask her if she promised to be loyal to him and care for him in adversity, sickness, and weakness.

Preacher Yoder stood very slowly to begin the main sermon. His shoulders were slumped, and his voice so hushed that his words were almost inaudible. With each phrase, his voice grew louder, and soon he slipped into the familiar singsong manner of exhortation. Wiping the sweat off his forehead, he continued. After about an hour, he arrived at the account of Jacob and Rachel.

With eyes glistening, he reached for a German Bible and read, "For the husband is the head of the wife, even as Christ is the head of the church: and he is the savior of the body. Therefore as the church is subject unto Christ, so let the wives be to their own husbands in everything."

In everything . . .

Katie's heart sank. *Here I am, not even married yet, and I've already broken the rules of submission.* Sadly, she glanced at her father. Not even his rigid parental training had broken her will, causing her to submit to authority.

If I can't obey my own dear Dat, how can I obey a firm, standhaft man like the bishop? She wondered how long before her guilt would overtake her, before she would have to confess her refusal to destroy the guitar. Days? Weeks? Ultimately, she would have to confess her sin to John. What a way to start a marriage!

You're like no girl I ever knowed. . . . Mammi Essie's strange words came back to Katie now like a specter, lurking in the corners of her mind.

Preacher Yoder sat down, and Preacher Zook took his place,

speaking from the book of Tobit. He quoted long passages from the account of a couple named Tobit and Sara, then veered from his text and began to address the congregation: "We have before us a brother and a sister who have agreed to enter the bonds of holy matrimony, John Beiler and Katie Lapp."

Leaning slightly against her best friend and bridesmaid, Katie was tempted to reach for Mary's hand, but knew it would be inappropriate. She would simply have to get through this on her own. She must.

"If there is a brother or sister present today who can give cause why these two should not be joined in marriage, let him make it manifest at this time, for after this moment not one complaint shall be heard," the preacher stated.

Katie stiffened, and she unconsciously held her breath. Dat's words rang in her ears. *Doth a fountain send forth at the same place sweet water and bitter?*

Preacher Zook paused, giving ample time for someone to speak up, then continued, "If there be no objections, and if our sister and brother are in agreement, you may now step forward in the Name of the Lord."

Katie stood, but instead of taking John's extended hand, she walked past him, toward the preacher. Then, feeling faint, she turned to face the People. "I have something to say to all of you here." She took a deep breath, looking down at the floor for a moment.

Slowly, she allowed her gaze to drift up and out into the congregation. One by one, her family and dear friends came sharply into focus. Her parents, her brothers, Ella Mae Zook, the bishop's children, first cousins aplenty, and Mattie the midwife, who'd held a grudge for not being allowed to help bring her into the world. And there was Lydia Miller, one of the few Mennonites in attendance.

Katie searched their familiar faces, wishing for a kinder way, one that would not bring anguish to her loved ones.

"I am so sorry to have to confess this," she began, "but I am not fit to marry your brother in Christ, Bishop John Beiler."

Purposely, she avoided John's eyes, knowing if she looked into them, she might break down, or worse—back away from what she knew she must do.

She made a single mistake, though. Her eyes lingered on her parents, and the pain in their faces wrenched at her heart. "I am so awful sorry," she heard herself whisper, "so sorry to hurt you like this, Dat . . . Mamma. . . ."

Rebecca gasped and stood up, her eyes bright with tears. She started to speak, but Katie didn't wait to hear her mother's pleas. She turned and fled down the narrow aisle, through the crowd of relatives and friends, to the kitchen, and past the startled cooks, her brother Elam, and Annie.

Katherine, called Katie, burst out the back door and ran from her childhood home—the temporary house of worship—away from the gaping mouths. Away from Rebecca's tear-stained face, far from the bishop she had shamed and disobeyed, from the People she had betrayed.

Far, far away.

CHAPTER FIFTEEN

"She's up and gone ferhoodled," Mattie Beiler whispered to one of her married daughters. "And my, oh my, ain't it odd? Why, I said this very thing at Katie's quilting just last week."

"Said what?"

"That when there's something important to do, Rebecca Lapp's daughter behaves poorly." Mattie shook her head, muttering. "Katie—running out on her own wedding. Well, if that don't beat all."

Several benches away, Rebecca whispered something to her husband, and while the baffled bishop stood at the front with Preacher Zook, she dashed toward the kitchen and proceeded to rush out the back door. "Katie! Katie, come back!"

John Beiler, eyes wide and hands shoved hard into his pockets—accompanied by his friend, Preacher Zook—headed for the now vacant chairs and sat with the rest of the bridal party, who appeared to be quite befuddled. He sat there for only a few awkward seconds, then stood up again and left the room, making his way into the enclosed front porch, which would have accommodated the guests during the wedding feast if Katie hadn't just run off.

"Well, what do ya make of it?" Preacher Zook asked.

John shook his head. "Something must be troubling her. She wasn't herself this morning."

"Well . . ." The Preacher paused, probably wondering how best to comfort his longtime friend. "Do you have any idea why she would have done such as this?" Before John could attempt a response, he continued, "It's not like the *Madel's* getting any younger. For all she knows, this might've been her last chance at marriage."

John nodded in agreement, but secretly suspected that Katie's rash act had something to do with the way he'd handled things at her confession last week. Had he failed to get over to her the seriousness of her offense? Treated the matter too lightly—seeing as how she was soon to be his bride? He scratched his beard and was mulling over the whole sorry mess when Samuel Lapp appeared in the doorway.

"What words can I offer ya?" Samuel inquired. "My daughter is gravely in the wrong." He bowed his head.

"Do not blame yourself for Katie's actions," Preacher Zook spoke up.

"I've done my best bringin' her up in the fear of the Lord, but this . . . this . . ."

Preacher Yoder came out of the front room to join them on the porch. " 'Tis a shameful thing witnessed here today."

"Jah, shameful," Samuel said, still hanging his head till his beard brushed his chest. "Our gut bishop . . . spurned by his own bride."

"Maybe she'll come to her senses . . . realize what she's done," Preacher Zook offered.

Samuel shook his head. "Ya don't know my Katie. The girl's

headstrong, she is. Has been, since the day she was born. Only her Mam could ever do anything with her."

"Such a reproach to the church," Preacher Yoder put in. "She must come clean of it, repent."

John remembered Katie's penitent attitude last Saturday—the sweet, innocent way she had approached him, coming into the room toward him, allowing him to hold her hands a bit longer than necessary. He remembered . . . and longed for her, even now.

At last he spoke. "As for confessing, let the subject be dropped. That's all that need be said." The men ceased their speculating and went back into the house.

Inside, John heard the low buzz of conversation. Katie Lapp, running out of her own wedding . . . well now, nothing like *this* had ever happened in Hickory Hollow.

The bridal party—what was left of it—was still seated together, shifting nervously. With no precedent for such a thing, apparently they weren't sure what to do next. One by one and in pairs, the other guests began to move about but did not leave, waiting for a decision to be made as to what should be done.

As for John himself, all he could feel was a throbbing ache in the area of his heart—an emptiness that only Katie could fill.

"What could've caused her to do such a horrid thing?" Sarah Beiler asked Mary Stoltzfus.

Mary, noticing Bishop John the instant he came back into the room, colored slightly. "I can't say, really," she replied evasively. Feeling the bishop's gaze on her, she dipped her head in humility. Poor man. What he must be going through!

"You must know *something* about her getting cold feet," Mattie's granddaughter persisted. "You've known her all your life!"

"No, no, I have no idea what Katie was thinking." She couldn't always read the older girl's actions, although heaven knows she'd tried these many years. *What'll happen now?* she wondered, feeling a little guilty about the urge to sneak glances at her best friend's former beau.

Actually, truth be told, she hoped John Beiler was through with the likes of Katie Lapp. The girl had pushed her limits, after all. Hadn't listened to a thing Mary had been trying to tell her all along. Yet, in spite of her frustration, she couldn't help feeling compassion for her friend. "I best be looking for Katie," Mary told Sarah, excusing herself as she sailed past Benjamin Lapp, who was scowling fiercely.

Mary proceeded to search the house for Rebecca Lapp. Surely, if she could find Katie's mother, the two of them could talk some sense into the bishop's bride-to-be. What on earth had Katie meant by saying she was unfit to marry their brother in Christ? Didn't she consider John Beiler *her* Christian brother, too?

Ella Mae looked on as Katie's best friend scurried about the house, going from room to room. The Wise Woman knew that Mary would ultimately catch up with Rebecca—but no matter. Neither Mary Stoltzfus nor Rebecca Lapp would be able to talk Katie into returning to the house. Not now . . . maybe not for hours.

Ella Mae knew things about Katie. Intimate, sorrowful things. Over the years, she'd listened as the young girl had come to her, spilling out her woes—her fickle growing-up years, her heartache over Daniel Fisher . . . and here lately, something about an English baby dress and a promise she couldn't keep.

What the promise was, Ella Mae couldn't tell. But one thing was for sure and for certain: The broken promise—whatever it was—had some bearing on why Katie had left her groom so disgraced and alone.

She sighed, wondering what she might have said or done

differently to change the way things were turning out for the poor, lost lamb.

"She was gonna be my mamma," little Jacob Beiler wailed to his sister Nancy, sitting near the bridal party. "She was, honest she was. . . ."

"Now, now. Try not to cry." Putting a big-sisterly hand on his shoulder, Nancy patted him, ending with a firm shake. "You're a big boy now." She sure hoped her youngest brother wouldn't cause a spectacle—the way Katie had.

Ach—embarrassing her father like that! Nancy felt her face redden. It was a disgraceful thing. Surely God himself would rain down judgment.

Maybe it was just as well that Katie Lapp was not coming home to be their mother. Besides, no one could take their own Mam's place. . . .

Levi Beiler uncrossed his long arms and glanced about, his gaze falling on the old woman several rows behind him. Ella Mae Zook appeared to be as baffled as everyone else, although he thought he spotted a glimmer of hope in her eyes and wondered what it meant. He could almost taste the hot cocoa the Wise Woman had ordered up for him last Thursday, exactly one week ago.

Katie was making ready last week, he thought. *She was making ready to do this very thing today. Planning to leave Daed without marrying him.*

Usually timid and aloof, Levi suddenly felt bold. He was thinking of the lost English stranger with reddish hair and the long black car. Somehow or other, the fancy woman just might be connected to what happened here today. He stood up and sauntered back to say "Hullo" to the Wise Woman.

About that time, though, Samuel Lapp asked for everyone's attention. Levi listened carefully, hoping that the food for the wedding feast would be put to good use.

Samuel cleared his throat. "You're all welcome to stay on and eat the noon meal with us. We will break bread together in spite of what has just taken place."

Levi was sorely disappointed when Daed called his five children to him and prepared to leave the house. He'd sure hoped they'd at least stay long enough to eat.

When all six of them passed the tables, laden with pies and cakes and all kinds of mouth-watering goodies, his stomach growled. And just when it seemed all hope was gone, Annie Lapp came to the rescue, calling on her husband to fill some baskets for "Bishop John's family."

In spite of Daed's forlorn look, Levi and the rest of them headed outdoors for the newly painted carriage—intended to carry home a new Mam—happy with their tasty treasures. He could hardly wait to get home and dig in.

In fact, he *didn't* wait. The preaching service had lasted over two and a half hours, and he was hungry. He pinched off a hunk of warm bread and stuffed it into his mouth.

His baby sister spied him. "Levi's snitchin'," Susie piped up.

Their father did not reply until the girl repeated herself. At last, John Beiler waved his hand distractedly. "Leave your brother be."

Levi grinned, and Susie pursed her lips at him. Simultaneously, Nancy and Hickory John each put a hand on Levi's shoulder. Daed was in no mood for their pranks, it was clear to see.

"Where's Katie, Daed?" little Jacob asked, looking a bit worried. "Ain't she comin' home with us?"

John shook his head. "Not today."

"Did she take sick, maybe?"

It took a long time for Daed to make up his mind, it seemed. "Can't say she's sick exactly. She didn't seem to be feeling poorly earlier today. But about now, I'd be guessin' she's feeling a bit sickly—same as I do."

Levi felt sorry for his father, and if they hadn't been out in broad open daylight, he'd have put his basket of food down and climbed up front to sit beside him. *Poor Daed. First, Mamma has to die . . . and now this. . . .*

———————

Rebecca made a beeline for the haymow, where Katie often escaped to be alone. She scrambled up the ladder leading to the soft bed of hay high above the lower level and called, "Katie? Are you up here?"

She checked behind several bales of hay, hoping to find Katie hiding there, sulking. She found only the barn cats and plenty of dust. When she was satisfied that the place was unoccupied, except for six or seven mouse-catchers, Rebecca turned to leave, heading outside again. This time she walked on the mule roads, choosing one that led toward the woods.

Discouraged, she trudged along the vacant clearing, willing away tears of regret and disappointment. If she expected to help her daughter through this crisis, she'd have to remain sober and dry-eyed. Yet she felt resentment growing in her. What had possessed Katie to abandon the bishop on her day of days? What on earth could have been more important than marrying such a fine Amishman?

A frightening notion struck her. Laura Mayfield-Bennett might even now be driving around the area, hoping for a glimpse of her long-lost child. She was dying, she'd written. That much Rebecca remembered, although there were times since she'd burned the letter that she wished she could remember more of its contents.

What would it be like to be dying . . . never knowing your only child? Rebecca sighed, pushing on. Much as she hated to admit it, she really couldn't blame the woman. Any mother would do the same.

The stillness was almost eerie. The sun seemed to have forgotten it was mid-November and shone as hard and hot as though summer had returned, beating against Rebecca's back. Her strides were short and swift as she made her way to the woods and beyond, then into the clearing and toward the pond with its secluded island.

She stood on the shoreline, searching the area with hungry eyes. The old boat was nowhere to be seen—Rebecca's first clue that her daughter may have chosen the childhood fortress as her refuge.

"Katie!" she called, cupping her hands around her lips. "Katie, it's Mamma!"

She waited, hearing nothing.

"Katie, are you all right?" she called again, studying the island where tall willow trees tangled with thick dry under-brush, creating a private cove unseen from this side.

Her heart beat faster, and she called again and again, feeling the sorrow and the rejection gouge as deep as the silence.

Would Katie answer if her flesh-and-blood mother were calling to her now? The thought left her weary.

"You don't have to tell me what's-a-matter, Katie, honest ya don't. Just let me be with you, girl."

She waited, longing for the voice she loved so dearly. But nothing could be heard except the sound of crows flitting back and forth across the placid water.

Then she knew what must be said—the one thing that might make things easier for Katie. She said it with great sincerity, her voice cracking as she aimed her plea again in the direction of the island. "You don't have to go back to the house just now. Don't even have to marry the bishop if ya don't want."

The waiting could have been likened to the travail of child-birth, so intense was it. Yet, just as her stillborn baby had never been given breath to voice its life cry, neither did Katie utter a sound.

Torn between the impulse to leap into the pond and swim to Katie, and her obligation to the People gathered in her home, Rebecca sadly turned away and headed for the wooded trail.

Under a willow tree nearest the center of the island, Katie sat with knees pulled up tightly under her chin. She had removed her devotional kapp and unpinned her bun, allowing the long auburn tresses to flow down over the front of her dress. Singing her favorite tunes, she ran her fingers through the traditional middle hair part, separating the strands, and swept it to one side, then plaited it into a thick braid.

She played with her hair to her heart's content, wishing for a small hand mirror to view the new look. The fancy new woman.

She began to sing louder as she unraveled her hair and rebraided it, weaving in dried wisps of willow leaves, wishing they were gold cords or silken hair ribbons.

"I'm Katherine now," she called to the sky. "My name is Katherine Mayfield." She forced images of her parents' sad faces from her mind.

Looking out toward the pond, she decided to have a peek at herself and would have made it to the small pier, except that she heard her mother's voice at that very moment. Quickly, she crouched in the shelter of the brownish willow curtain. Despite the absence of lush greenery, she was certain she was well hidden.

Several times Mam called out to her, probably hoping to lure her from her hiding place. But Katie didn't budge. This was *her* day. A day to sort out the questions and haunting fears. A day to let the fancy side of her go unbridled, with no one to call her to account.

She waited until she saw her mother turn and, with shoulders slouched, plod back to the wooded trail and home to face their guests. Katie allowed herself just the tiniest twinge of regret for placing her parents in this embarrassing position. Still, they'd most likely go on with the feast as planned, eating and visiting and wondering what had possessed her. There would be no light-hearted celebration under the circumstances, but the atmosphere would be sweet with the bond of peace and the kindred spirit of the People.

No matter. This was her time, and she planned to make the most of it. Katie crept toward the pier and flattened herself against it, staring into the pond water below.

Her hair. How different it looked. In place of the familiar center part, her shiny hair lifted at the top before dipping slightly over one eye, the silky cascade caught up in an intricate design. She pulled at the willow leaves twining through the thick strand and flicked pieces into the water, making ripples on the glassy surface. She watched the ripples widen until they washed up on the far shore. Somewhere deep within, she recognized the symbolism of her own life.

Who am I, really? she wondered. *If I'm Katherine Mayfield underneath my skin, then who is this Katie Lapp dressed in dull, homespun clothing?* She dangled her kapp over the pier, staring at its reflection.

She was on to something, but she didn't know exactly what. Pensive, she watched a leaf float lazily out of sight. A good Plain woman obeyed the Ordnung, was totally submissive. How could she have failed so miserably? In trying to be good, she had become weak. How had the teachings of the People turned her into someone she was not? Someone who could disobey the very bishop who had administered her life oath—her kneeling baptism? Someone who could hurt that same bishop beyond words, and in the presence of the entire church district, too?

But she must not dwell on that. Truth be told, she had been wounded the most.

Getting to her feet, she walked to the shore and pulled the old boat out from under the pier and turned it right side up. Then, stabbing the pond's surface with the oars, she rowed to the other side.

Within minutes, Mary Stoltzfus met up with her on the mule road leading back to the farm. "Where've you been? Your Mam's worried sick." Mary's eyebrows shot up as she took a closer look at Katie. "And what's happened to your hair?" She reached up and touched the wide braid, still adorned with the willow leaves. "Where's your kapp?"

Katie rumpled her head covering into a ball. "I'm not coming back to marry John, if that's what you're thinking. So don't be asking me what happened. Besides, I think you already know."

"But aren't you the least bit concerned about the bishop's feelings? And his children . . . what about them?"

Katie wished Mary hadn't mentioned John's family. Dear little Jacob's face would be forever emblazoned on her memory. She had let the lad down. She'd let all of them down.

"It was never meant to be—the bishop and I," she said. "And hard as I tried, I was not meant to be Amish, either."

Mary shook her head. "Ach, not this again. I thought you had all that business behind ya."

"Well, I don't."

"But the right thing to do is—"

"I'm not interested in doing the right thing anymore," she retorted. "I've been trying to do the right thing all my life, and it never worked."

Mary's blue eyes widened in horror. "But Katie, what on earth are you talkin' about?"

"Just what I said. It's not working out for me to be Amish. I wish it hadn't taken so long for me to see it, but I know now what's the matter with me . . . why I can't seem to measure up around here." Katie cast a woeful glance at the farmhouse just below the sloping grade. She would not reveal the truth of her so-called adoption—such things should be left to Dat and Mam to decide. For now, she was simply eager to play her new role as Katherine Mayfield.

"I'm going into town for a bit, so if you don't mind—"

"You're going . . . where?" Mary's eyes were becoming lighter and lighter, surprisingly luminous as though Katie's odd behavior were robbing them of their color. "What you *need* to do is go in there and apologize to everyone."

"No, I won't be doing any such thing."

Mary's voice came soft. "Aren't you sorry for what you did?"

"Sorry? I did the bishop a favor by running out of his wedding. Those sweet children, too." Katie felt a lump rise in her throat.

Mary frowned and bit her lip. "What did you mean when ya said John wasn't your brother in Christ?"

"You heard me right, Mary." The braid swung around as Katie headed for the barn. "Satin Boy and I are taking a ride."

"Satin Boy? When did you give him such a curious name?"

"A while back."

Before Mary could question her further, Katie hitched up her pony to the cart. "I'll be back 'fore dark. Tell Mam I'm all right."

"But you're *not*. I can see it clear as day, you're not all right, Katie Lapp!"

CHAPTER SIXTEEN

The road was crowded with cars and trucks—buses, too—some honking their horns impatiently as they sped past, leaving Katie in their dust. But she persevered, riding in the pony cart, perched high for the whole English world to see.

At last she turned into a small strip mall, tied Satin Boy to a fireplug, and unhitched the cart. "I'll get you some water in a bit," she promised. "Be back soon."

Eager to see all she could, Katie glanced up and down the row of shops, her eyes coming to rest on an elegantly furnished display window. Squaring her shoulders, she marched toward the boutique, intent on trying on some fancy, worldly clothes.

"May I help you, miss?" The saleslady was obviously trying not to stare, Katie thought. Still, she must look a sight in her rumpled long dress and apron, her braid, woven with willow, tumbling over one shoulder.

"I'd like to try on the fanciest satin dress you have."

"Satin?"

"Jah. You do have it, don't you?"

"Well, no, we don't normally carry satin until later in the season." The woman picked up her glasses, which had been dangling from a chain around her neck, and placed them on the bridge of her nose. "Is the garment for yourself . . . or someone else?"

Katie chuckled under her breath. "Oh, it's for me, all right. It's time I get to see what I've been missing."

Blinking rapidly, the woman turned to the counter. "If you'd like, I can check with one of the other stores, say in York or Harrisburg. They carry a larger inventory."

"No, no," Katie interrupted, "it's important that I see something *today.*" Spotting a rack of exquisite dresses with brocade bodices and lace detailing, she left the lady gaping at the counter and hurried over. "What about one of these?"

She lifted a soft chiffon gown off the rack and held it up to herself in front of a wide three-way mirror. Turning this way and that, she admired her reflection from several angles, humming one of the songs she loved the best. Dan's song.

"What size are you looking for, miss?"

"I don't know, really," Katie replied, thinking of all the sewing she had done for herself over the years. Still, it was a bit overwhelming—seeing all these garments in a dazzling variety of colors, styles, and fabrics, just waiting to be worn. "I've never been asked that question before, but I 'spose I ought to find out. Why don't I just try it on and see for myself?"

The clerk seemed at a loss for words. "Uh . . . yes. Of course. Right this way."

Without bothering to inspect the price tag, Katie followed her to a small dressing room at the back of the shop. At the touch of the saleslady's hand, a velvet pull curtain draped her in privacy, just Katie and the sheer golden dress—fragile as a butterfly's wing.

When she turned, she let out a little gasp, catching her reflection unexpectedly. The tiny space was covered with mirrors on all sides—from floor to ceiling. "Am I dreaming?" she whispered as she touched the glass with her finger.

Relishing every second, Katie removed her clothing. First, her apron, then her Plain—very plain—wedding dress. With great care and near reverence, she lifted up the fanciest gown ever created. It slipped easily over her head and dropped lightly onto her shoulders, coming to rest at an astonishing mid-calf.

She loved the swishing song of the fabric, the silky feel of it against her skin. And, oh glory, the open neckline, free and unrestrictive!

Katie stepped back to admire herself, inching away from the mirror to grasp her full reflection. This was no Katie! This had to be Katherine. But even while reveling in the moment, she was feeling robbed, cheated of the years when she'd been deprived of her rightful heritage. Would she ever be able to wear the rich, vibrant colors of the English without having to do so in secret?

She wondered, too, about the woman who had named her Katherine. What kind of woman would allow herself to bring a child into the world without nurturing that life? Would give the baby a fancy name and then hand her off to some stranger? What kind of person did such things?

Her joy tainted, Katie stepped out of the filmy dress and retrieved her own clothes. "Someday I'll wear a dress like this out in public," she promised herself. "Someday I will." With tears filling her eyes, she slipped the hanger gently into each puffed sleeve and hung the dress on a two-pronged hook.

"Do come again," the salesclerk called to her.

Katie did not reply. She hurried outside to Satin Boy and the old wooden cart, never looking back.

On the way home, Satin Boy began to labor under his load. "Aw, poor thing . . . can you keep going a bit longer?" Katie coaxed him from her seat. "We'll stop by Elam's and Annie's and get some water for you. All right?"

Satin Boy struggled as Katie reined him toward the long dirt drive leading to her big brother's farmhouse, two miles east of the sandstone house on Hickory Lane.

"Look, Elam! Look who's come!" Annie called to her husband from the front porch of their white clapboard house. Annie waved at Katie as though she hadn't just seen her that morning.

"I didn't think my pony was going to make it here," Katie called to them, forgetting how peculiar she must look with her hair in the forbidden braid—and without her kapp. "My pony's dry to the bone. Can I water and feed him?"

Elam marched down the steps and promptly removed the harness from the tired animal. Her brother eyed Katie sternly. His look of reproach reminded her of Dat, but Elam didn't voice a single word of rebuke. Katie stood there watching as he led Satin Boy around to the barn behind the house.

He's put out with me, Katie thought. *And rightly so. I've caused everyone so much trouble.* She knew the pressure was bound to build up sooner or later, until her brother spouted off about the wedding.

Reluctantly, she headed up the steps where Annie stood waiting, her hands folded over her protruding stomach. "You should have seen the way Satin Boy was acting up on the road," Katie told her.

"I thought his name was Tobias." Annie eyed Katie's hairstyle and quickly looked away.

"Things change."

"Oh." Annie opened the screen door and went inside. "Come in and have something to drink for yourself," she called over her shoulder.

It wasn't until Annie had offered her a tall glass of iced tea and she'd sat down at her brother's table that Katie realized how thirsty and tired she was. "It was a pretty foolish thing to go so far with just a pony," she mused aloud.

Annie lowered herself carefully onto the bench beside the table. "Where'd you end up going?"

"Out to Bird-in-Hand." Katie would have gladly said more but feared she would be letting herself in for all kinds of questions. Besides, Annie Lapp knew nothing about ladies' dress shops and boutiques. She was a good, upstanding Amishwoman. Women like Annie were never tempted to peek into worldly English shops.

Annie's eyes seemed fixed on her now, Katie thought, probably because she was trying to figure out why she wasn't wearing her kapp. "Well, my goodness, what were you doing way over there?" Annie blurted.

Katie flinched. Should she tell? Should she divulge the secret pleasure of a few hours away from home, trying on the fanciest chiffon party dress in all of Lancaster County?

She took a good look at Annie—Daniel's beloved sister. She looked so like the boy with blueberry eyes! And oh, dear Lord, her baby would probably look like him, too. Katie shuddered to think of being haunted by Dan's expression on the faces of her own nephews and nieces. Of course, Elam's offspring would carry some of his traits, as well. But as spirited and attractive as Daniel Fisher had always been, Katie suspected that her big brother's children would bear a strong resemblance to her one true love. *Just as I must look something like my real mamma. . . .*

The notion startled her and she shrugged it off, trying to remember what it was that Annie had asked her. She was relieved when her sister-in-law brought it up again.

"Were you distraught today, Katie? Is that why you left the wedding ceremony?" Annie asked softly. "Because if ya need to talk, well . . . I'm here for you. Anytime."

Touched by the offer, Katie reached across the table to squeeze her sister-in-law's hand. "I just might be taking you up on that," she whispered as the guilt crept back, threatening to spoil her moment of freedom. She stiffened her back, determined to make every minute count.

Elam came in noisily, bumping around in the utility room and shutting the door with a resounding bang before making his way into the kitchen. One glance at Katie, and he began to shake his head. "You need to be findin' your kapp and wearin' it, don'tcha think?"

Katie tilted her head and surveyed her oldest brother. "I don't have to *find* it," she stated. "I know exactly where it is."

"Then why isn't it on your head where it belongs? And what're those knots all the way down your hair?"

Annie's eyes caught her husband's in a meaningful stare, much the way Mam and Dat often exchanged glances. Katie almost expected to hear Annie speaking up on her behalf, but when she didn't, Katie knew she was on her own. Rebecca Lapp was the one and only woman who had ever taken her side against a man.

Elam was close to scolding her now. Katie could see the telltale signs—his twitching eyes, the flaring nostrils. She didn't want to risk humiliation, not in front of Annie.

"I got a bit ferhoodled, maybe."

"Ferhoodled? Jah! And when Dat gets ahold of ya, you'll be wishin' you'd walked up to the preacher with John Beiler at your side and gone through with your weddin' vows!"

"Don't speak to me that way, Elam Lapp!"

"It's about time *someone* did," he said, barely able to check his anger. "Dat never could, that's for sure."

"Leave him out of this!" Katie demanded. "Dat's done just fine raising me and you know it."

"I'm tellin' ya right now," Elam went on, "if you go home

with your hair lookin' like that, you'll be regretting it long before mornin'."

Her brother was right. Tonight there would be a tongue-lashing from Dat, and first thing tomorrow, either Elam or Dat would report her multiple transgressions to Preacher Yoder or Bishop John.

"I'm ashamed of ya, Katie. You must try and stay in Jesus," he said. "You must try."

Katie stood and headed for the back door. "I'll be going now. And don't call me Katie anymore. My name is Katherine."

"Since when?" Elam sneered.

"Since the day I was born," she said over her shoulder as she reached for the doorknob. Suddenly she felt uneasy, fearful that she had stepped into forbidden territory, a place that could only lead to betrayal.

"You're talkin' nonsense. Better get your hair done up in a bun. And don't say ya weren't warned," Elam called after her. "Sinning against the church is no laughing matter . . . it's sinning against God." Elam sat beside his wife at the table, his head bowed now.

"Good-bye, Annie," said Katie, completely ignoring her brother.

Annie's farewell was a whispered "Da Herr sei mit du."

The afternoon was still hot, and the sun shone heavy on the round, full hills south of the road.

You must try and stay in Jesus. Elam's words echoed in her mind. But the logical side of her brain argued back: Did staying in Jesus require her to wear the kapp at all times? Must she wear her hair long and forever parted down the middle—squeezed into a bun? Was this the only way?

Daniel Fisher had not thought so. Salvation came, he'd often told her, through faith in Jesus Christ—not by works, not by following man-made rules.

She sighed, letting Satin Boy plod along at his own pace. If need be, she would get out and walk the rest of the way home.

Why hadn't she paid more attention to Daniel back then? Why had she gone along with the teachings of her parents' Meinding church without question, ruling out the other Christian churches outside of Hickory Hollow?

Katie knew why, of course. She was young, too unsure of herself to leave the Old Ways and embrace the New. Too ignorant of the Scriptures to debate them. Dan, on the other hand, had secretly joined a Bible study group somewhere. Not only had he memorized several chapters of the Bible, but he was learning what they meant and how their truths could change a life committed to Christ. Wisely, he'd kept his activities hidden from the rest of the People. Only Katie had been aware of his secret. Of this she was fairly certain.

If Dan had lived, she knew he could help her now. He could lead her to the truth—wherever it was to be found.

An ominous feeling settled over her as the red sandstone house came into view. The truth, she was almost assured, was not found in wearing a head covering or denying oneself an occasional braid now and then.

In defiance of it all, she sang—a vigorous rendition of "What a Friend We Have in Jesus." Satin Boy, apparently inspired by the rhythm of the melody, began to pick up speed.

"Gut boy!" Katie called to him and promised a long brushing and some fresh hay and water when they got to the barn. They passed the wide front yard and turned into the dirt lane leading to the barnyard.

She put off going into the house as long as possible. Finally, when she heard Mam call to the men, she slipped out of the pony stall and headed for the kitchen door.

Tiptoeing into the utility room, she remembered the festive

atmosphere of the house just hours before—the multitude of wedding guests, the greeting lines, the sermons, and the cooks preparing for a feast. Its present somber appearance convicted her.

Quickly, she began to wind her hair around her hand, ready to put it up into the usual bun, but changed her mind and let the tresses fall down her back. It was too late now to make amends. What was done was done.

"Katie, you're back!" Mam cried, spotting her. She hurried over and wrapped her arms around the prodigal, appearing not to notice Katie's unruly hair springing free of the confining kapp. "I came looking for you after ya ran out of the house," she babbled. "I went out to the pond and called and called. Where on earth did you go?"

Katie shook her head. This wasn't the time. "Maybe you won't understand this, Mamma," she said, looking at the woman who had cared for her from infancy, "but I can't talk about it just yet."

"Well . . . it'll keep 'til after supper, then."

Katie held her breath as she entered the kitchen with Mam at her side. Even with Elam's warning, she was not prepared for Dat's display of righteous indignation. "Where's your head covering, daughter? Don't you have any respect at all for God's laws—not to mention the poor bishop's feelin's tonight—without a wife to warm his bed or a Mam for his children!" He ranted on for minutes that seemed like hours while, at her side, tiny gasps of emotion escaped Rebecca's lips.

"I know for a fact that Preacher Yoder'll be comin' to talk to you in a couple of days," Dat went on as the Lapp family sat down around the supper table.

"I'll speak to him," Katie agreed quietly.

"Gut, I'm glad you're coming to your senses."

Katie breathed deeply. "I don't mean that I'll be confessing, though, if that's what you're thinking. It's just that I want to ask him some questions—about the Scriptures."

There was no audible response. But when Dat bowed his head for the silent prayer over the meal, the ritual lasted at least twice as long as usual.

Eli gave her a long, cold glare and would not accept any of the serving plates she passed him.

He's treating me like I'm a shunned woman, Katie thought.

Benjamin, however, was kinder, passing the bowls of buttered potatoes, carrots, and onions, and the ham platter to his brother on behalf of Katie.

Halfway through the meal, Dat exploded. "I will not eat another bite until ya go put up your hair the right and holy way!"

Startled at this outburst, Katie got up from the table and ran upstairs to her room. With trembling hands, she brushed her hair and wound it into a bun, without even checking the straightness of the part in her hand mirror. Then, finding a clean, pressed kapp, she placed it on her head and scurried back downstairs like a frightened mouse.

Meanwhile, Dat had pushed his chair away from the table, still muttering about the disgrace she'd brought on the Lapp family.

Katie said nothing. She was wounded to the depths of her spirit. But she would not allow her father the satisfaction of witnessing the pain he had caused. In fact, his reaction—though not unexpected—only fueled her resolve to speak to the preacher when the time came.

Later that night, after the kitchen was cleaned up, but before evening prayers, Benjamin whispered to Katie that she must come outside with him. Katie, unwilling that Dat be aware of some vague conspiracy, agreed. They waited for the best time to slip out—during one of his longer snoozing sessions in front of the woodstove.

Once outside, Benjamin headed for the milk house at a brisk stride.

"What's so important?" Katie wanted to know, doing her best to keep up.

"I have to tell ya—Dat's not just encouraging you to confess," he said, his breath pluming in the frosty air. "He's madder'n a hornet at whatcha did today."

"Well . . . he's got every right."

"Jah, and he's not the only one who's plenty angry." Benjamin opened the heavy door and held it for his sister. It was warmer there in the milk house. "You spurned the *bishop* in front of all the People, for goodness' sake! Such a shameful, awful thing ya did."

Katie nodded but resisted the guilt that inched nearer. "I didn't expect John to be angry, really," she thought aloud. "Hurt or disappointed, maybe . . . but not angry."

"Jah, and here's what I wanted to tell ya before tomorrow. If you don't go ahead and promise to confess in front of the whole church come Sunday, you'll be in danger of the Ban, Katie. *The Ban!*"

She felt a sliver of fear—like an icicle—cold and tingly. Still, she shouldn't have been surprised to hear it. After all, she'd as much as announced publicly that John Beiler was not her brother in Christ.

In the eyes of the People, she was a sinner. She deserved to be excommunicated.

"Better be thinkin' things over, Katie. I'd hate to see ya put through die Meinding, really I would."

Die Meinding—the shunning. The mere thought of it sent another tremor rippling down her spine.

"There's been talk already. . . ." Ben paused and scratched his head, as if wondering if he should have kept his mouth shut.

"What're you tellin' me, Ben?"

"Well"—he glanced around, looking toward the house—"Mam asked Eli and me to go over to the bishop's and get your cedar chest and suitcases and things and bring 'em back home."

"Jah?" She felt her throat constrict.

"While we was there, Eli heard Bishop John talkin' things over with his friend, Preacher Zook." He paused, his eyes growing soft. "I'm tellin' ya, Katie, things could get real bad for ya. And awful quick, too."

"I can't confess. I just can't."

Benjamin stared at her in disbelief. "You can't *not* confess."

"But it would be a lie." She reached up and plucked off the kapp again, pulling out the hairpins that held her bun in place. "Look at me! I'm not the person you think I am, Ben. I'm not Amish."

He frowned, shaking his head.

"I ain't Plain. The kneeling baptism never happened to me—not the me you see standing before you here."

Ben was obviously puzzled. "You're talkin' in riddles."

"Jah, I am. But my whole life has been a riddle." She shook her head sadly. "I wish I could, but I honestly can't say any more about this now. Someday I'll be able to tell you, promise I will."

"Someday will never come if you're shunned, Katie. And ya don't want to wait and see, I guarantee!"

Ben's prophecy bore deep, plunging a shaft of terror into the very recesses of her soul.

CHAPTER SEVENTEEN

The next day the weather turned chilly again with needlelike pellets of rain pounding the frozen ground. Plumes of vapor from the horses' warm breath hung in the air, mingling with thready fog, as the People made their way to quiltings or weddings and an occasional farm sale around Hickory Hollow.

Katie still had no answers to the questions that plagued her like a swarm of mosquitoes on a summer day. Preacher Yoder would surely be able to set her mind at ease over the biggest question of all—the one she was hoping might solve all her problems and put an end to the talk of the Ban and shunning. But in order to inquire about it, she would have to tell Preacher Yoder her parents' secret.

Would Dat consent to it? After the blowup last night, would he allow her to reveal such a thing?

She decided to approach her mother instead. And while the two of them were working together, unpacking Katie's suitcase and rearranging her linens in the cedar chest, she brought up the idea.

"No, no, no!" Rebecca was adamant. "There'll be no telling it around that you're adopted!"

"But I have to tell Preacher Yoder."

"You'll do no such thing." The look in the hazel eyes was almost fierce.

"But don't you see?" Katie went on. "If Preacher knew the truth—that I'm not Amish by birth—then everything else would make sense to him."

Mam shot her a curious glance. "*What* would make sense?"

"My troubles with being Plain," Katie mumbled under her breath, so softly she wasn't certain she'd been heard.

The silence hovered between them for the longest time, and Katie wondered if she should repeat herself. She touched her braid, feeling the series of ripples up and down the length of it, and wondered if her father would force her to put her hair up again today.

Finally, Mam spoke up. "Your troubles don't come from being adopted, Katie," she admonished. "Your troubles come from a disobedient spirit."

Katie shrugged. "Still, I should be telling the truth about my birth mother, don't you think? My English background?"

The next outburst was such a shock that Katie could only gape in amazement. Was this the sweet-tempered mamma who'd never raised her voice in anger in her life? "No! You can't tell, Katie"—she was actually shouting now—"because I forbid it!"

Turning away, Katie hid her face in her hands and tried to calm herself. When she looked up, Rebecca was gone.

Katie tossed the remaining items of clothing into the only dresser in the room, and eyes filling with angry tears, she located the rose baby dress in a compartment of the suitcase. Then, stuffing the dress into a pocket of her apron, she hurried downstairs and out of the house, letting the storm door slap hard against the frame.

She would not wait around for Preacher Yoder to come to her; she'd go to him. What she was about to do would bring hurt to her mother, she knew. But her own agony was so raw, so deep, she simply could not bring herself to care.

The preacher was helping a customer when Katie arrived at the General Store. "I'll be right with ya," he called, glancing over to see who had come in, jangling the bell above the door. His friendly smile vanished when he spotted her hair—done up fancy in a long braid—and the missing head covering.

Stepping away from the counter, Katie waited for him to finish making his sale, wondering how she should begin the conversation with the elderly man now that she was here.

The making of change and the final ding of the cash register signaled the end of business. It was her turn. "Preacher," she began, a bit sheepish now that the sting of Rebecca's words had abated somewhat, "I heard you wanted to speak to me."

Preacher Yoder, wearing a purple shirt and heavy homespun trousers, cut wide and full in the legs, scanned the store for prospective customers, then pointed Katie in the direction of a small back room behind the counter.

The place was sparsely furnished, except for rows of shelving that occupied one entire side of the room. The wide shelves stored odd bolts of fabric, arranged in an orderly fashion.

Preacher Yoder's countenance registered concern as he pulled out a chair for Katie, and the two of them sat facing each other. "Well now, I must say I'm glad to see ya comin' forward to confess. Will it be this Sunday?"

"No, no, I'm not here about confessing."

He frowned, creating deep furrows in his already wrinkled forehead.

"I have something to tell you in confidence," she added softly. "It's something that nobody else must ever know."

223

He waited to hear her out, his expression unchanging.

Katie held herself erect. "Will you promise before God that you'll never tell a soul what I'm about to say?" The request was a mighty bold one, she realized, coming from a young woman who just yesterday had humiliated the bishop in front of all the People.

Preacher Yoder rested both hands on his knees. "Well, I guess I'll have to be hearin' what you have to say before I can make any promises."

She drew in a deep breath. As far as she could tell, this was her one and only chance to clear herself without actually confessing sin. She began to spill everything: how she had been told of her non-Amish heritage just days before her wedding; how her parents had kept the secret from her these many years.

"Now that certainly *does* explain some things." He shook his head in amazement, pulling on his gray beard. "You say you're not Amish by birth, then?"

"My real name is Katherine Mayfield. I have proof right here." She pulled out the satin gown. "This was my first baby dress, and you're the only person in Hickory Hollow besides Ella Mae and my parents to lay eyes on it."

"Ella Mae?" He leaned back in his chair. "Does she know your secret?"

"Ach, no. I never told her anything about the dress or where it came from."

"But she has seen it?"

"Jah."

"And why would you be tellin' *me* all this?"

She took in another deep breath and held it a moment. "Because . . . well, because I was wondering if it might change things in some way . . . cancel out my baptism. Me being adopted and all, wouldn't it do away with my vow to the church?" She paused, waiting, but her questions were followed only by silence.

She spoke again. "Don't you see? I was tricked, Preacher . . . I wasn't who I thought I was back then."

The old man pushed up his glasses and peered through them critically as though he'd never heard such strange talk. "The promise you made to God and the church will stand forever, whether ya call yourself Katherine or something else altogether." His eyes tunneled into hers. "Forever and always, you'll be held accountable to the church for the way ya walk—for the life ya lead before God. And if you choose not to confess come Sunday, you'll be in danger of the Ban at the meeting of the membership."

She knew better than to argue. To talk back meant instant shunning. The man of God had spoken. There was no recourse, no hope. English or not, she was bound to her baptismal oath for the rest of her life.

As for promising to keep her family secret, the preacher had vowed he would do so, but mentioned before she left that he truly hoped his brother and sister in the Lord, Samuel and Rebecca Lapp, would come to him voluntarily to confess their years of deceit.

Before Katie left, he gave her one more chance to confess her faults and ask the forgiveness of the church, "lest ya fall into Satan's snare."

Once again, she declined. So the decision to be shunned had been made. The probationary restriction hinged on her refusal to repent, and since she was determined not to confess, not to marry the bishop, and not to behave in keeping with the Ordnung, the wheels of the Meinding had already been set in motion.

On the way home, she thought of stopping by for a quick visit with Ella Mae but decided against it. Why prolong the inevitable? She knew she was in for a tongue-lashing from her parents just as sure as she knew she was the daughter of an English family some-where out in the modern world.

Katie was late getting up on Sunday.

Frustrated and sorrowful over the girl's deplorable conduct during the past week, Rebecca knocked on her daughter's door. "Mustn't be late for Preaching today," she sang out.

"I won't be going" came the terse reply.

"Not going? Katie, don't be this way," Rebecca scolded. Even though she was reluctant to incite another exchange of words with her rebellious offspring—in spite of that—she hurried downstairs to find Samuel and the boys.

Within minutes, the three men were standing outside Katie's room. Samuel was the first to speak. "Katie, don't be letting stub-bornness hinder ya from going to church on the Lord's Day."

No answer.

"Come on, sister," Benjamin implored. "They'll be talking about shunning you for sure if ya don't go. At least come and act like you're sorry—a little humility would help a lot."

Katie groaned. "I told you already. I can't be confessing. Now leave me be."

"Then you'll burn in hell," Eli offered, since all else had failed. "You'll—"

"Eli, hush." His father pointed to the stairs. Samuel leaned forward, his beard touching the door. "If you choose to stay home, daughter, the bishop will have no recourse but the shunning!"

"I know," Katie replied. "But I won't go to church and pretend to confess—not after the way I've been lied to all these years."

Rebecca breathed in quickly, her heart pumping hard at the accusation. Still, she had to speak her piece. "Don't go blaming *us*, Katie," she said, her voice breaking. "We did the best we could."

Why wouldn't the girl listen to reason? Why wouldn't she heed her family's advice? If only there was something else she or Samuel or the boys could say or do to prevent what was coming. . . .

Sorrowful, Rebecca turned away and descended the stairs. She couldn't bear it. Dared not ponder what Preacher Yoder would be thinking of them—her and Samuel—now that Katie had gone and told him everything. Katie said he'd promised not to breathe a word to a soul. But the truth was . . . now Rebecca herself and Samuel were in need of confessing. Most probably, they'd have to meet the preacher out in the barnyard behind David and Mattie Beiler's house after church service. Best they do it soon, too, before he had to approach *them*.

One thing was for sure and for certain. They'd be doing their confessing in private—before the situation spread out of control, like a cancer that could not be cured.

Katie ate the noon meal alone. She thought of the People and what was going on over at the Beiler house—Bishop John's relatives; hers, too—Mattie being her mother's first cousin.

She could see it now—Mattie flapping her tongue every which way long before Preaching ever got started. She would be all ears, too, especially when the preacher began his discussion before the membership after the church service. He would mention Katie's unwillingness to come to Preaching on this the Lord's Day to humble herself before God and these many witnesses. He would say that she had been properly warned but would not refrain from her transgression and rebellion.

Each church member would be allowed to voice opinions about the wayward one in question. Ella Mae might speak up, remind the People of the hardships that had already befallen the poor lamb. Rebecca, too, might even put in a few good words on her daughter's behalf. At least, she'd think about it. But in the end, she wouldn't go through with it, because she was in need of repentance herself, and the preacher knew it!

Mary Stoltzfus might be brave enough to say something nice about her best friend—that is, if she'd been able to forgive Katie for the harsh words she'd spoken to her on the mule road the last time they'd seen each other.

At some point, the bishop would be called to the front. John's place was to decide what to do about the situation, and knowing how things were usually carried out, Katie was pretty sure the People would be warned not to eat at the same table with her, do business with her, and so on, for the probationary period of six weeks. After that, if she did not come to church and offer a kneeling confession, she—Katie Lapp—would be shunned "even unto death."

CHAPTER EIGHTEEN

Mary Stoltzfus was not at preaching, either. A few minutes before the service started, Rachel told Rebecca that her daughter was suffering from a severe headache. But Rebecca's mind was not on such a small botheration; it was on the membership meeting to come.

Rachel, however, wanted to discuss Mary's problem, whispering behind her hand that one of Mary's beaus—Chicken Joe—had taken Sarah, Mattie Beiler's granddaughter, home from a supper with their buddy group last night. "Mary's terrible upset about it—and awful worried, too."

"Why's that?" Rebecca asked, hardly able to pay attention when her heart was breaking for Katie.

"Mary's . . . afraid she'll never get married."

"Ach, she will, she will," Rebecca said, waving her hand.

"Too bad Katie won't be able to help Mary with her disappointment," said Rachel, glancing at the preacher and the bishop already conferring. "The girls have been so close for so long. They seem to know how to comfort one another."

"Jah. But things are about to change, I fear," Rebecca said.

"Unless the bishop's heart is softened somehow, there will be a Meinding amongst the People."

The verdict was harsh.

Rebecca sat stiff and straight on the hard wooden bench, wishing with all her strength that something might happen to turn the tide. Her Katie—poor, dear, stubborn Katie—being the topic of all this awful shunning talk, well, it was more than she could endure. To keep from crying out, she clamped a hankie over her lips.

Mattie must have heard the muffled sob, because she glanced cockeyed at Rebecca from a few benches away. Rebecca felt anew the familiar twinge of conflict between them. Her cousin's look spoke volumes: *You didn't call on me to help deliver your daughter long ago, but look at me . . . my grown children are better than yours. My children never would think of goin' and gettin' themselves shunned.*

Rebecca closed her eyes, blocking out Mattie's haughty gaze and the distressing scene on all sides.

Preacher Yoder and Bishop John were both presiding over the membership meeting now. Rebecca heard the voices but kept her eyes shut.

The room was filled with confusing talk. "Love the wayward one back to the fold," someone suggested. "Impose severe restrictions so she'll know what's comin' if she don't repent," said another.

Then Bishop John spoke up. "The bride of Christ must not tolerate arrogance. Katie Lapp has shown rebellion and insolence repeatedly."

The Scriptures and theology behind the practice of shunning were familiar enough to Rebecca, but today the Meinding took on a heartbreaking new dimension. Today it had struck at her very heart—her beloved Katie. And with everything in her, Rebecca wished there was another way.

Katie heard the news first from John Beiler himself. It came just before her parents and brothers arrived home in time for afternoon milking. She saw the bishop step out of his carriage and walk, rather awkwardly, toward the back door.

The thought of stealing away to the Dawdi Haus presented itself, but she knew, sooner or later, she must hear the truth from John Beiler's own lips.

He gave a firm knock. Then, standing tall as though braced for battle, he stepped into the house when Katie opened the door. He came only as far as the utility room, took off his felt hat, and faced her with a stern expression in his steel gray eyes.

Katie said nothing, did not even greet him or bid him welcome in her father's home.

When he spoke, it was with icy control. "I urge ya to attend church during the next six weeks. Come as a non-member and meet with the ministers"—by this, she gathered he meant himself—"but you'll have to leave before the fellowship of members and the common meal each Sunday. Not one of us in the Hollow will be speaking to you now. You may not eat at the same table as church members or do business with any of us until such time as ya return and offer a kneeling confession."

Katie listened, limp with disbelief. The swiftness with which the discipline had been issued left her reeling.

"The punishment is suitable for all those who have surrendered themselves to the Lord," he explained, then quoted Ezekiel, chapter thirty-three, verse nine. " 'Nevertheless, if thou warn the wicked of his way to turn from it; if he does not turn from his way, he shall die in his iniquity.' "

Die in iniquity. . . .

She kept quiet, eager for him to leave. *I nearly married this cruel man*, she thought with disdain. *How could I have considered such a thing?*

"Do you understand that this chastening is so that the weeds will not continue to grow while you wait for the judgment of Christ?" John asked solemnly. "To bring you back to the loving heavenly Father?"

She felt the fury welling up inside her. She began to shake her head. "No, no . . . I *don't* understand anything about my life here with the People. Not one little bit of it."

A frown, mingled with concern, flashed across his face, and for a moment, Katie feared that he might be thinking of addressing her in a more personal manner. But his jawline hardened, and he turned and let himself out the back door without another word.

When Dat arrived, he came directly inside and set to work, putting up a small, square folding table across the kitchen a good distance from where the rest of the family ate their meals. He did not speak to Katie as he worked, not even to offer a smidgen of sympathy, and she knew the Meinding had officially begun.

Mamma came in not long after, her eyes swollen and red. The sight stirred Katie's compassion, and she wanted to run to her mother and comfort her. But she forced herself to sit stone still as Rebecca shuffled past her and went upstairs.

Eli and Benjamin appeared in the doorway and steered clear of Katie, moving almost mechanically as they headed toward the woodstove to warm themselves before the afternoon milking. Their faces were sullen, eyes cast down, as though they might be contaminated if they made any contact with their wayward sister.

Already, the rejection was unbearable. Unable to put up with it any longer, Katie went next door to the Dawdi Haus. The place was bitter cold, so she hurried outdoors and filled her apron with chopped wood to start a fire.

Inside, with teeth chattering and fingers shaking, she struck a match, ignited the kindling, and blew on the feeble flame. She had never felt so cold in all her life.

———

Rebecca stood at the top of the second-floor landing, glancing at the bedroom she and Samuel shared, the numbness creeping through every fiber, every tissue of her being. This wasn't like her. Not at all. Not being sure of her next move. Not knowing what to do. . . .

With great hesitancy, she turned and forced her legs to carry her down the hallway to Katie's room.

The door was open. Dazed, Rebecca entered. Private and feminine—so like her dear daughter—this bedroom had belonged to Katie for over twenty-two years. Her belongings seemed to draw Rebecca, compelling her to go about the room, her fingertips trailing across the dresser doilies, the headboard, the scattered bed pillows.

Why did Katie have to be so willful in spirit? Why couldn't she be more yielding, more submissive . . . more *Amish*?

Rebecca winced, thinking of the events of the day—the church members' meeting and the pronouncement of the Meinding by Bishop John—and went to sit on the straight-backed chair near Katie's bed. Life with her dear girl wasn't supposed to turn out this way. Things had been much better, she told herself, before Daniel Fisher had come into Katie's life.

Rebecca turned and stared out the window, remembering. Daniel's mother had told her—in strictest confidence—years back that he'd gotten himself invited to a Bible study somewhere outside the Hollow. Nancy Fisher had been mighty concerned for her son at the time and had decided not to tell a soul—not even Annie, her youngest daughter, anything about it.

Rebecca had agreed. It was wiser not to talk it around, and she'd kept her word, not even telling Katie. It was the one thing about Daniel that she'd never shared with her daughter. And now . . . now with this great burden hovering over her loved ones, Rebecca wondered if Daniel had somehow played a part in all of this, influencing Katie to think for herself, maybe. . . .

The more she pondered, though, the more she began to question her suspicions. Hadn't Katie gone ahead and followed the Lord in baptism into the church just eighteen months after Daniel's drowning? Didn't that prove he'd had no evil influence on her, after all?

Rebecca stood up again and breathed in the lovely lilac fragrance permeating the room. Katie's room had always had a breezy freshness about it. Her daughter enjoyed drying lilac clumps and mixing them with various herbs and spices, placing the homemade potpourri into netting purchased at the General Store. She often concealed the sachet squares inside her dresser drawers.

Without thinking, Rebecca opened the top drawer of Katie's dresser and leaned over to sniff the sweet scent. "Oh, Katie, what I wouldn't give to make your troubles disappear," she said aloud. Then, reaching inside, she tried to locate one of the little sachets. Instead, her fingers closed over the satin baby gown.

She began to cry. Softly, at first. Then, holding the little dress to her bosom, she wept great, sorrowful tears.

And then she heard it—the delicate, almost timid strains of a guitar. Who was playing? And where?

She went to the hallway and pressed her ear against the wall. It was a solid foundational wall, shared by both the Dawdi Haus and her own home. As she listened, holding her breath, the sounds became more clear. Katie's voice—mellow and sweet—singing the saddest melody she'd ever heard.

So the girl had disobeyed yet again. Katie had not destroyed the guitar as the bishop would surely have ordered her to do at the private confession.

It was difficult to make out the words, but the mournful tune caught Rebecca's attention, suiting her own mood. Good thing Samuel and the boys were outside now, tending to milking chores. Best *they* not hear the guitar music or the singing coming from next door.

Reluctant to forsake the haunting music, she went back to Katie's room, returned the baby dress to the gaping drawer, and headed downstairs to make supper.

In the painful hours that followed, not only did Katie's entire family nix any conversation with her, they also refused to accept written notes from her. Katie had come up with the idea of writing when she found herself wanting more information about Mary Stoltzfus, who had taken ill—best Katie could tell. During supper preparation, she had overheard her parents talking about her friend.

"Rachel said she's got some awful pain in her head," Rebecca told Samuel as he was washing up. "Ain't contagious, though. Sounds like something's up with Chicken Joe quitting her."

"Well, why don't you go over and offer some of your gut chicken corn soup tomorrow?" he suggested.

Katie dashed across the kitchen, eager to communicate with them. She scribbled a note on a piece of paper—*How long has Mary been ill?*—and held it up for her mother to read.

Both Samuel and Rebecca turned their backs. Katie, not about to give up, ran around in front of them, pointing to the words on the paper and holding out a pencil for them to write a reply.

Samuel shook his head, refusing to respond. Rebecca's eyes grew sad and moist, but she, too, remained silent.

Katie wrote once more: *Why didn't anyone tell me? Mary's my dearest friend!*

She pushed the paper under Rebecca's nose.

Silence.

"Well, I'll not be staying around here when my friend is in need," she announced. "I'll go where I'm wanted!" It was then that she decided to see for herself how Mary was doing, even though it was already near dusk. Surely her best friend would be glad to see her. Surely she would.

Desperate for someone to talk to, she grabbed her shawl and left the house with Molasses and the family carriage, startled at the emotions the shunning had begun to rouse in her. Angrily, she urged the old horse on.

Along the way, she passed several buggies. Instead of the usual cheerful hellos from other Amish folk, Katie's greetings were met with downcast eyes.

When another buggy approached her on the left, she could see that it was Elam and Annie, probably going visiting. Eager to greet them, even from a distance, she called out to them, "Hullo! S'good to see ya!"

They responded with the same blank stares as all the others. Tears sprang to Katie's eyes, and approximately a mile from the sandstone house, she turned the carriage around and headed home.

Heartsick and lonely, she suffered through her first meal—five feet or so away from the family table, stuck off in the corner of the kitchen by herself. She overheard the chatter of beloved voices and the friendly clink of silverware on plates, yet was not included in the conversation. Sadly, she decided that she might as well be five thousand miles away.

Later in the evening a choking heaviness settled in, and she put her dowry money—the eighteen-hundred-dollar gift from her parents—in an envelope and shoved it under their bedroom door. The money did not belong to such a sinful, rebellious soul, and she penned a note on the outside of the envelope to tell them so.

No "good-nights" were exchanged, and Katie went off to her cold, dark bedroom, undressing there while her family shared in evening prayers downstairs in the warmth of the kitchen. With a lump in her throat, she climbed into bed without offering her usual silent prayer.

CHAPTER NINETEEN

One by one, the empty days dragged by, each more dismal than the last, now that winter had come early, shrouding the barren land with bleakness.

Four days had passed since Katie's first attempt to visit Mary. She longed for her friend's bright smile, the joyful countenance. Was Mary improving? No one seemed to know. At least, if they did, they weren't saying. Even Benjamin had clammed up, though he'd had plenty of chances to steal a moment away from either Eli's or Samuel's watchful gaze to speak to her privately. And Katie knew why. Benjamin, Eli—all of them—were afraid of getting caught, of being shunned themselves.

She could take it no longer. Twenty-four hours seemed like an eternity. So many eternities without Mary—lonely, friendless days. Katie sighed, wishing she and her friend had not exchanged cross words on the mule road last Thursday. It was time to make amends.

Rachel Stoltzfus met Katie at her kitchen door. But seeing who was there, she proceeded to shake her head and back away, putting both hands out in front of her.

"I've come to see Mary," pleaded Katie, wrapped up in her warmest shawl. "Is she feeling any better?"

The door was completely closed—not slammed in her face, but soundly shut—by the time the last word left her lips.

Cut to the heart, Katie turned to go. Suddenly she knew the meaning of the word *alone*. Knew it more powerfully than she'd ever known anything. She shot the word into the crisp, cold air as she coaxed Molasses out of the lane. "Alone. I'm all alone." The sound of it throbbed in her head.

In the past—when Dan died—she had experienced what it meant to be separated from someone she loved. But she'd been surrounded then by caring friends and relatives to help her over the worst days. And, on the whole, her life had never been a lonely one. There was always something to do and someone to do it with in Hickory Hollow. Some work frolic—a rug braiding or a quilting; weddings and Singings; games such as "The Needle's Eye" and "Fox and Geese," and in the wintertime, ice-skating marathons on Dat's pond under a vast, black canopy of sky, studded with a thousand stars shining down on them all.

No, she had never been truly alone in her life. But she was beginning to understand what it meant. Worse, she knew *what* she was missing—a whole community of People, lost to a bishop's decree. She couldn't help but wonder if the probationary shunning hadn't been a retaliation of sorts—John Beiler getting back at her for not marrying him!

Maybe John thinks he can win me back this way. Make me repent—then marry him on top of it. She forced a laugh that ended in a fit of coughing.

It was then she decided to turn around and go back to Mary's house. She halted Molasses on the dirt drive next to Mary's bedroom window and tied him to a tree.

"I'll throw stones," she told her horse. "That'll bring her running."

Katie went to the dried-up flower bed near the tree, avoiding the rise in the earth where tree roots had pushed up random hard lumps. Reaching down, she gathered a few small pebbles and tossed them gently, hoping not to attract Rachel's or Abe Stoltzfus's attention. She waited a moment, then tried again, aiming for the second-story window. To her great relief, Mary came to see what the commotion was about.

"I miss you, Mary," Katie called lightly, hands cupped around her mouth. "I want to talk to you." She gestured for her friend to raise the window, but Mary didn't seem to get the idea. She just stood there, looking down with a forlorn expression on her face.

"Are you all right?" Katie mouthed.

Mary didn't say a word, nor did she use sign language to make herself understood. But what happened next was more eloquent and heart wrenching than anything she could have said. She simply placed her hand on the window and held it there—as if to make contact through the cold glass—then slid it down and inched away until she was out of sight.

It would do no good to plead with her to stay, Katie knew. So she turned and trudged back toward the carriage. She climbed in with a sigh of resignation, then made a circular swing around the side yard before driving Molasses out onto Hickory Lane.

There was no song in her now, no desire to hum. She was an outcast among the People. What would Daniel think of her if he knew? Would he be ashamed?

She craned her neck to look up at the sky, wondering if the dead had any idea what was happening down here on earth.

"I best be making some plans," she announced aloud. It probably wouldn't take much to get her old housecleaning job back. But if she was going to make it on her own, she would eventually have to learn to drive a car, most likely. Maybe even go to school somewhere. One thing was certain, though, she had made up her mind that she would not confess after the six weeks were up. As difficult as it was, she might as well admit that she was as good as shunned for life.

A quarter of a mile ahead, she spied David and Mattie's place. Impulsively, she pulled into the main drive, then parked her buggy directly behind Ella Mae's Dawdi Haus. If there was anyone left on the face of the earth who would speak to her, it would be the Wise Woman.

Hesitantly, Katie approached the door and knocked.

"It's open" came the reply.

Katie stepped through the door and into the warm kitchen. "It's me, Ella Mae. Katie," she called, feeling something like a leper—as though she should sound a warning. "I might not be welcome. . . ."

The Wise Woman appeared, carrying her needlework. "Nonsense, lamb. *Kumm yuscht rei un hock dich anne*—come right in and sit down. Warm yourself by the fire. It's right nippy out there, ain't?"

At the sound of another human voice—especially Ella Mae's thin, quavery one—Katie all but hugged her. "Oh my, it's so wonderful-gut to see you! No one else will talk to me."

"Jah." Ella Mae nodded thoughtfully. "And it just don't seem right, insulting a body the way they are."

"Don't you believe in the Meinding?" Katie pulled her braid over her left shoulder, wondering if Ella Mae had noticed that she wasn't wearing her kapp.

The Wise Woman only waved her hand in the air—the way Rebecca often did when she didn't want to discuss something. So Katie sat at the table and let the matter drop.

She watched, comforted by the familiar ritual of Ella Mae making tea—putting a kettle on to boil, getting out the teacups, pinching off two sprigs of mint. . . ."I hear Mary Stoltzfus is under the weather."

"Jah, but she'll live, I 'spect."

"It's all because of Chicken Joe and Sarah Beiler, ain't?" Katie said, careful how she phrased the question since Sarah was closely related to Ella Mae.

"Love plays cruel tricks on its victims now and again."

Katie wondered if the bishop felt she'd played a cruel trick on him. "John'll find someone else someday, won't he?" she asked, hoping to justify herself. "Someone much better suited for him."

Ella Mae shook her head. "Don't be downin' yourself now. You're as fine a woman as any, with or without your kapp."

They laughed together, the old woman coming around to inspect Katie's irreverent braid. It was a shining moment they shared, a moment of triumph.

"My goodness me, it's nice to have somebody come for tea," Ella Mae said, heading over to fold up her counted cross-stitch linen. She placed it on the arm of the sofa behind her before joining Katie at the table. "You're like me, I'm a-thinkin'. Not many folk drop by to visit anymore—and the nights get long and lonesome."

"Maybe it's the weather . . . the cold and all."

"No, no, no. I know better."

"Why, then? Why don't they come?"

"Well, I'm thinkin' the church leaders got wind of my string of visitors—the ones who look to me for a bit of advice, ya know."

"That's too bad, really. I would have thought they'd know you're doing people a big favor, the way you listen to all of us talk out our sorrows and such."

"Ach, it's just that Preacher Yoder wants the People to look to *him*, I do believe. Maybe he figures I'm *Dummkopp*—touched in the head, ya know." She patted her kapp and began to laugh that warm, wonderful chuckle that started deep inside and rumbled out, on good days, when her voice was stronger.

It was pure heaven to hear her go on so. Sitting there in Ella Mae's toasty kitchen, Katie felt her spirits lift. She was happy for herself, of course. Glad, too, to be company for the poor old soul who had welcomed her—shunning or no.

"I 'spose word got out that young Levi and I had a cup of hot cocoa together down at the General Store one morning a few weeks back," Ella Mae put in.

"Why would *that* matter?" Katie was truly astonished. How could such a small thing cause the People to turn their backs on an old woman?

"Ach, it's hard to say, really. But it's my guess that Levi Beiler went home and told his Daed that old Ella Mae Zook was saying this and that, and thus and so." She reached over the table and patted Katie's hand. "We do need one another, child. The People just ain't enough, I fear."

Now Katie was beginning to worry. Was her great-aunt's mind truly failing her? She wasn't making sense. "Well, the bishop and Preacher Yoder are only doing what they believe is best for both of us now," Katie spoke up. "It's das Alt Gebrauch, the Old Way, the way we've always done things here in the Hollow."

Startled at her own words, Katie realized what she had just said. Had she spoken out of habit—defending the People that way—or was she beginning to believe that she deserved the temporary Ban? Was the weight of guilt beginning to press in on her? Was this how the Meinding ultimately worked to bring sinners to repentance?

Ella Mae sat up straighter, releasing Katie's hand. "No, no, I ain't talkin' about your predicament with the church just now. You're payin' for your sin, that's true, and you'll probably be confessing here sooner or later. We all do. A body can't go around forever without communing with friends." She paused to catch her breath. "No, no, what I'm talkin' about is far different. Something to do with eternity—where one life ends and another begins."

Katie gasped. "Oh, Ella Mae, you're not dying on me, are you?"

"We're all dying in one way or t'other." She got up to take the teakettle off the stove and pour the boiling hot water into two cups. Next came the sprigs of mint leaves. "You're young, and you may be thinkin' you have all the time in the world. But I hope ya don't go wasting your allotted time—any of it."

"Don't go worrying about me," Katie reassured her, still confused. What *was* the old woman trying to say?

Then, out of the blue, the Wise Woman spoke, her words reaching deep into the private corners of Katie's soul, where no one else had ever dared to go. "I was born Amish, and I'll die the same. The Plain life is the only life I'll ever know. But you, Katie, you have a chance to see what's out there, what's on the other side of things."

"You mean . . . the modern world?"

"It's what you're looking for, ain't?"

The question struck Katie like a blast of cold air. Was it? Was she searching for the boundary line, the proverbial fence around the People? Hoping someday to break through, to find her true self? "Why are ya saying all this?"

"Because you seem out of place somehow," Ella Mae said in a raspy whisper. "Always have."

Katie felt a tingle of discovery. "I've been coming over here since I was little, telling you my troubles, trying to be a gut Plain girl—and here lately, an even better grown woman, worthy of the bishop's . . . trust. I tried . . . but I failed. . . ." Her voice trailed away.

"You're a thinker," said Ella Mae, shaking her head. "Thinkin' and submittin' to the Old Ways don't mix."

Katie caressed her braid. "You're probably right." She stared off into space, remembering that Dan Fisher had said the same thing once.

Ella Mae placed a cup of mint tea in front of her visitor, struggling with her own conscience. Should she tell Katie what she and young Levi had seen a week ago? The black limousine and the worldly woman . . . with hair the color of Katie's own? And the letter the lady was so eager to hand over?

She watched the poor girl hold the cup to her lips and sip her tea. When she set the cup in its saucer, she began to pour out her troubles in a steady stream—like the mint brew in the old teakettle.

"It wonders me about the strange thing Mam told me before my wedding day," Katie began. "And I'm more puzzled by it now than ever."

Ella Mae sipped, then sighed. "Ach, was it about that little dress you brought over to show me?"

Katie nodded. "That dress has changed everything. It's turned my whole life upside down. The family's, too."

Ella Mae appeared not to notice Katie's distress. "I believe I know what your mamma may've told ya, Katie. I wouldn't sit here and lie to ya, pretending I didn't."

Katie was elated. At last, someone else—someone she could trust—knew the secret! Of all the People she could have chosen to speak with about it . . .

Ella Mae continued. "I saw her, Katie. I saw your birth mother, clear as day."

Katie nearly choked on her tea. "My birth mother? Where? In Hickory Hollow?"

Ella Mae nodded thoughtfully.

"I can't believe it! Why was she here?"

"She's a-lookin' for ya, Katie. Isn't that what your mamma told ya?"

Katie fought back tears. "No, no, you must be mistaken somehow. Mamma never told me any such a thing."

"Himmel," Ella Mae whispered.

"Mamma told me that my real name was Katherine Mayfield—that I was given as an infant to her and Dat to raise after

their fourth baby was stillborn. But she never said anything—"
Her breath caught on a sob.

Ella Mae shook her head woefully. "Ach, I've spoken out of turn, I'm afeared. Forgive an old woman for heapin' more pain on your head, child." She set her cup down and removed her glasses to wipe her eyes. The startling truth, although she had suspected as much, tore at her heart.

"When did you see her . . . my real mother?"

"There was a letter over a week ago," Ella Mae began, telling Katie how the fancy lady had approached her carriage at the General Store. "She pleaded with me to help her find a woman named Rebecca. Told her there were lotsa Rebeccas in the Hollow, but she seemed in an awful big hurry to get her fancy letter into the right hands."

Without warning, Katie leaped out of her chair.

Following the direction of her gaze, Ella Mae peered into the shadows across the room. "Ach, Mattie, is that *you* standin' over there?" she muttered.

Her daughter stepped into the lantern light, revealing herself without a word, while Katie steadied herself, leaning hard on the back of the chair.

"What in the world?" Ella Mae spun around, nearly knocking over her cup of tea. "Land a-mighty, don'tcha ever knock, woman?" she scolded.

"I heard voices," Mattie said, refusing to look at Katie. "And, Mam, you know better than to be talking to a shunned person . . . and sharing your table, too!" She marched toward them. "Katie best be leaving or I'll have to report this to Preacher."

"What'll he do?" Ella Mae scoffed. "Meide a feeble old soul like me?"

"Mam! You best be reverent when ya speak of the shunning."

Ella Mae turned to see Katie sitting forward in her chair,

reaching for the tea. The cup trembled in her hand. *What wretched thing has happened here?* she wondered. She ached clear to the bottom of her soul, for being the reason Mattie had overheard Katie's family secret. *We should've been more careful.* That busybody had heard every bit of their intimate conversation. Now *that* was a worry.

"How long ya been hidin' over there?" Ella Mae confronted her daughter.

"Just came in."

But the Wise Woman knew. So did Katie. And by nightfall, so did most everyone else in Hickory Hollow—including Bishop John.

CHAPTER TWENTY

"Katie Lapp's adopted, and her real mamma's out lookin' for her. Now what do ya make of *that*?" Nancy Beiler asked her big brother as they swept out the barn.

"How do *you* know such a thing?"

"Heard it today at recess."

Hickory John stopped for a moment and leaned on his push broom, eyeing his sister doubtfully. "Are ya sure 'bout this?"

Nancy grinned. "Came near straight from the horse's mouth."

"Whose?"

"One of our cousins."

"A girl?" he teased.

"Jah, our second cousin, Sally Mae." She sneezed in the wake of the dust they'd stirred up. "The way I see it, if it came from one of Aunt Mattie's grandchildren, it's gotta be true. Because Aunt Mattie was the one who overheard *her* mamma tell about meetin' Katie's birth mamma face to face."

"Well, we all know how Aunt Mattie is, don't we?" Hickory John laughed. "Can't always go by whatcha hear."

Out of the haze of dust and straw, Levi stepped forward, much to the surprise of Nancy and her brother. "Didja just say Katie's *real* mamma's lookin' for her? Is that what I heard ya say?"

"You were eavesdropping, Levi Beiler!" Nancy scolded. "That's a *greislich* thing for the bishop's son to do! Now go in and get washed up for supper."

Levi marched himself off to the house, mumbling about getting caught. "Guess maybe Daed might start payin' attention to me from now on . . . 'specially when I tell him about red-haired strangers comin' to our front door!" she heard him say.

———

Katie waited until her father and brothers left the house for a barn raising near White Horse before deciding to speak to her mother. Rebecca had not been feeling well—an upset stomach, or so Katie thought.

Rebecca remained silent, leaning her arm against the table and sighing audibly.

"I'll bring some tea up later," Katie offered, hoping to hear *something* out of her mother. But there was not another sound.

How long would it take before Mam would start talking when there was no one around to overhear? She hadn't purposely set out to trick her mother, but Katie was desperate for answers. Answers to the questions that Ella Mae had brought to her attention only yesterday.

Mute as a fence post, Rebecca seemed bent on forcing herself through the household chores. She did allow Katie to assist with the baking—bread and six dozen each of molasses cookies and apple muffins—to take to a quilting frolic planned for tomorrow. But along about ten-thirty, her mother collapsed into Dat's big rocking chair.

Katie finished wiping off the counters and washed her hands. Then, stepping around to the small table that was hers alone, she paused and observed her mother. "It's all over Hickory Hollow about my birth mother trying to find me," she said. "Mattie got it all started, the nosy thing."

Rebecca's head seemed to bob in agreement, but Katie couldn't be sure that it wasn't caused by the motion of the rocker. "I never would've wanted to spread your secret around like this, Mamma," she went on. "You know I'm telling the truth, too, because I had Preacher Yoder promise not to tell anyone." She watched and waited, hoping Rebecca would say something—*anything.*

No comment came.

"Ella Mae said there was a letter. Do you know anything about that?"

The tiniest squeak passed Mam's lips. Was that a reply?

Katie went over and knelt down, resting her head on her mother's knees. "I'd give anything to know, Mam," she said softly.

Rebecca's hand found its way to her daughter's slender back. She began to rub in soothing, circular motions—the way she always had when Katie was a little girl.

Cautiously, the words began to slip out. "I did a wretched thing with the letter," she admitted. "I threw it in the stove—out of fear, mostly—but it got burned up all the same."

"You burned it?" Katie lifted her head and the back rub ceased, but only for a moment. "Why did you burn it?"

"Just listen," Rebecca whispered. And Katie, apparently basking in the sound of her mother's voice, did as she was told. Rebecca put her hand on Katie's head and could feel her daughter relaxing against her lap again.

"I was so awful worried and upset that day," she went on, her voice breaking occasionally. "I thought the woman—your natural mother—was gonna come and take you away from us. But looking back on all that's happened, I wish I'd kept her letter so you could be readin' it for yourself right now."

"Why does she want to find me, do you think?" Katie asked, not lifting her head this time.

"The doctor's told her . . . she's dying." Rebecca's hand paused momentarily before continuing its healing journey.

After a heart-stopping silence, Katie looked up. Rebecca could see the tears brimming in the girl's eyes.

"What's her name?"

"It's . . . Laura. Laura Mayfield-Bennett. She must've kept her maiden name—and added it onto her married name. I've heard they do such things out in the modern world."

Katie whispered the peculiar name into the air. "Laura Mayfield-Bennett."

"Wait here." Rebecca got up and found a pencil and a scrap of paper in a kitchen drawer. "I'll spell it out for you the way I remember it."

Katie studied the name on the paper—the strange English name. The letters squinted up at her, telling her—in some disconnected way—important things about herself. Things she did not fully understand.

"Did she . . . did Laura write her address down in the letter?"

"Honest, I don't remember now." Her mamma's glistening eyes were proof she was telling the truth. "She lives somewhere in New York, I think."

"New York City?" Katie gasped. "Ach, I hope not!"

"No, no, it's somewhere else in the state."

"Well, I'll just have to get me a map, I suppose," Katie said. "A map of New York State, since I've never been outside Lancaster County."

"So . . . will you be tryin' to find her, then?" Mam's voice now sounded thin and pathetic—almost childlike as she sat back down in the rocker.

Even though Katie was momentarily distracted by the compassion she felt for her mother, a startling surge of resolve followed, surprising her with its power. "I have to look for her, Mamma, you know I do. I can't just forget about her now." She rose and took Rebecca's hands in hers, gently pulling her up and out of the rocking chair. "I don't mean to hurt you with all this. You do understand . . . don't ya?"

Her mother couldn't speak for the tears, and Katie hurried on before she weakened. "I can't stay here much longer anyway, not with the shunning and all. I thought about going next door to the Dawdi Haus, but it's no use. I can't see confessing now . . . or later. It's time I think about leaving."

"Aw, girl, no!" Then, more softly—"Where will you go?"

Katie took a deep breath. "Lydia Miller has a room for rent. I saw the sign yesterday on my way home from Ella Mae's."

Her mamma shook her head and fumbled for a handkerchief. "You're not going to leave Hickory Hollow, are you?"

"Laura Mayfield-Bennett doesn't live anywhere near Lancaster, now does she?" Katie hugged her weeping mother. "Oh, Mamma, I'm so happy you finally talked to me today. So very happy."

"It must not happen again," Rebecca declared, giving way to a coughing fit before clearing her throat. "I can . . . not speak to you again . . . not until you repent."

"I know, Mamma," Katie replied. "You're a good Amishwoman, and I understand."

When Rebecca's desperate hacking subsided, the two women clung to each other as though it was to be the last embrace of their lives.

Mattie was thrilled when Elam Lapp called her to deliver Annie's first baby, a full six weeks before the due date.

About time I catch a Lapp baby again! she thought as she rode back with Elam to the young couple's farmhouse. Silly how she'd carried on over not being asked to assist with Katie Lapp's birth. But now she knew the truth and felt quite ashamed of herself for making such a mountain out of a smidgen of a molehill.

Still, it was hard to believe that Samuel and Rebecca had been able to keep such a secret. But when she tried to draw Elam out about it, it was obvious from his intense frown and pursed lips that he had more important things on his mind—like becoming a father in the next few hours.

When the horse pulled the carriage into the lane, Elam jumped out and dashed into the house ahead of her, leaving Mattie to attend to the unhitching of the horse. "These new papas," she clucked. "I do declare!"

By the time Annie's contractions were less than two minutes apart, word had spread to several Amish farmhouses, including Rebecca Lapp's—thanks to Lydia Miller's telephone and her fancy car.

Katie could hear the cries of the newest little Lapp as she helped her mother out of the carriage. "Sounds like a hefty set of lungs to me. Must be a boy." She smiled at her mother even though by this time, she didn't expect a reply.

Rebecca said nothing, lips tight.

They hurried up the front porch steps, meeting Elam as he burst through the door to greet them. "Mam, Wilkom!" he said, without so much as a glance in Katie's direction. "You have yourself a fine, healthy grandson!"

He ushered them into the downstairs bedroom, where Annie lay, perspiring and exhausted, holding the tiny bundle.

"He's mighty pretty," Katie whispered as her sister-in-law handed the baby to Elam.

"Mamma, I want ya to meet my first son . . . Daniel Lapp." Elam held the infant up for Rebecca and the others to see. "The name's for Annie's brother, ya know."

The reference to Dan pierced Katie's heart. But she was drawn to her new nephew like a bee to honeysuckle. "May I hold him?"

Elam ignored her request, placing the baby in Rebecca's arms instead. "He may be a bit premature, but he's a fine, sturdy boy, ain't?"

"Jah, he's strong, all right." Rebecca began to coo in Pennsylvania Dutch. "Won't Dawdi Samuel and your uncles be surprised when they get home?"

Mattie, now standing next to Rebecca, began to stroke Daniel's soft cheek. "I think it's time for me to be speakin' to ya about something, Rebecca," the woman said, looking her cousin full in the face.

Not wanting to stand there and witness the busybody trying to patch things up with her mother—not after the way Mattie had spread the word all over the Hollow about the adoption and all—Katie slipped out of the room, unnoticed. She wondered about Annie's early delivery. What had made her sister-in-law go into labor so early? Had she counted wrong . . . or what?

Katie walked into the front room, stopping to examine the pretty pieces displayed in the corner cupboard. Seeing the fancy china reminded her of the gay wedding plans she and Bishop John had made. She'd let him down terribly. All the People, really. Now Elam had taken it upon himself to go a step further and punish her by not allowing her to hold his son. Whoever heard of such a thing? Not letting your own sister hold your baby? That wasn't part of the shunning!

Out of the silence, she heard her name spoken and tiptoed back toward the bedroom, within earshot. It was Mattie, saying something about Katie's horrible behavior at the wedding. "I think it's this whole shameful thing with Katie that upset Annie so awful much."

Elam had a few choice comments of his own. "I think die Meinding upset Annie much more than any of us thought," he agreed. "Started up her labor too soon, probably. A sensitive one, she is."

Katie backed away silently and hurried to the front door. *They're blaming me!* She was shaking—whether with fear or rage, she wasn't quite sure. *Who knows—I might've killed the poor little thing!*

She refused to cry, but took in a deep breath and ran to the carriage to hitch up ol' Molasses.

Daniel . . . they named my nephew Daniel. How could they?

For a moment she gave in to her sobs, reliving the pain of losing her beloved. Didn't they understand? No one could ever take his place!

She slapped the reins and the horse trotted away. Her haughty big brother would just have to take time away from his precious new baby and drive their mother home later on.

Meanwhile, now was as good a time as any to stop in and chat with Lydia Miller about the room she had for rent.

CHAPTER TWENTY-ONE

A spill of late autumn sunshine—like molten gold—poured into a glass-walled sun-room overlooking acres of rolling lawn and lavish gardens, now frosted with snow. Well-manicured walkways lined the area directly south of the old English-style mansion, shaded in summer by a canopy of regal trees.

From this vantage point, Laura Mayfield-Bennett could see the waterfall splashing into a lily pond two stories below. Floating lily pads shimmered silver-green in the morning light.

Laura reached for her sunglasses just as her maid came into the sun-drenched room, green with ferns and ivy and spreading ficus trees.

Rosie adjusted the chaise lounge to accommodate her mistress. "If it's sunshine you want, Mrs. Bennett, then it's sunshine you get," she remarked cheerfully.

"This is delightful. Thank you for coming up again, Rosie." Laura wiggled her toes inside her velvet house slippers, enjoying the warmth of the sun's rays on her feet and lower legs.

"Will there be anything else, ma'am?"

"Thank you, but no."

Laura sighed heavily, hearing the rapidly fading footsteps on the marble stairs. Below her, on the circular driveway, one of the chauffeurs pulled up, waiting for her husband. She watched as Dylan Bennett folded his lanky frame into the backseat.

The car sped away—down the long, tree-lined lane—leaving Laura alone with her thoughts. "Well, Lord, it's just the two of us again," she began to pray, her eyes open to take in the sweeping view. "I come to you today, grateful for life"—she paused to look up through the skylight—"and for the sky so clear and open, wearing its pale blue gown. I thank you for all that you have provided, especially for your Son, Jesus Christ.

"Please touch each of my loved ones with your tender care this day, especially Katherine, wherever she may be. And, dear Lord, although I fail to understand why her Amish family has not contacted me, I give Katherine to you, knowing that you do all things well."

Drawing a deep yet faltering breath, she continued. "Perhaps it is not in your will that my daughter see me this way. But if it is . . . please allow her to contact me while I'm alert enough to know it's my darling girl who's come to me. Grant this, I pray before . . . before you call me home. In Christ's name, amen."

What a compassionate gesture if her heavenly Father should grant her last wish, her dying wish. But to fully trust in her Lord and Savior, Laura had learned through the years that she must relinquish selfish desires and wishes.

She reached for a glass of water on the marble-topped table and sipped slowly, retracing in her mind the recent journey she had taken to Pennsylvania—to Hickory Hollow—and the encounter with the elderly Amishwoman sitting in a carriage in front of a general store. The woman had seemed highly reluctant to share information, Laura recalled—had seemed almost offended to be approached. But her acceptance of the letter was tacit agreement, Laura sincerely hoped, that the woman would assist her in delivering it to the proper Rebecca—the one and only Rebecca who would understand the urgency.

Of course, she couldn't be certain that the letter had been passed around in the Plain community at all. And time was against her now. It was out of the question to think of making another such trip, a five-hour drive from the Finger Lakes region of New York to the farmlands of Lancaster County. She was not up to it—not in her present condition—and worsening by the day. Her physician would never hear of it, even if she were stubborn enough to attempt it.

So there she sat on the top of a hill, within the noble estate of her childhood, passed on to her when her mother, Charlotte Mayfield, had died twelve years before. Breathing in the tranquility, Laura longed to recapture the atmosphere of the Amish community. Something had drawn her to the Pennsylvania Dutch country— something more than her mother's fondness for the area. She had never forgotten her introduction to Lancaster County, nor the events surrounding the day of Katherine's birth. . . .

Her mother had coaxed her to take a trip by car that June day. At seventeen and in the latter stages of pregnancy, Laura had been struggling with frequent panic attacks and, in general, needed a change of scene—away from the questions of high school friends who could not understand why she was being tutored at home.

Young and petite as she was, she'd undergone an ultrasound—at her doctor's insistence—to determine her ability to deliver naturally. In the process, they had discovered that the baby in her womb was most likely a girl. So, to occupy Laura's time, her mother had suggested a sewing project—a satin baby gown.

For weeks, though, she'd been lonely and sick with grief over the loss of her first real boyfriend, unable to control her tears most of the time. A deep depression had left her restless, and she slept fitfully, if at all. When she closed her eyes at night, she could think only of her humiliating condition and her anger and guilt in having given up her innocence to a boy who'd never truly loved her.

Fearing her daughter was on the verge of an emotional collapse, Charlotte Mayfield had consulted a therapist, who'd recommended the short trip to Pennsylvania, despite the advanced stage of the pregnancy.

In their chauffeur-driven car, they had followed the Susquehanna River south to Harrisburg, turning east to Lancaster.

Soon, there were no more residential districts, no machine shops, factories, or shopping centers. The landscape had opened up, revealing the wide blue skies, fringed with trees—as if seen through a camera lens. The fields were patchwork perfect, like the handmade quilts made by the Amish who lived here. Under a benign sun, farmers were busy working the land, using the simple tools of centuries past. It was a scene straight out of a picture book.

Miraculously, Laura began to unwind. Perhaps it was the way the ribbon of road dipped and curved past fertile fields on every hand. Or the nostalgic sight of horse-drawn carriages. Or the gentle creaking of a covered bridge, flanked by groves of willows—their long fronds stirring in a lazy breeze.

Whatever it was, her mother noticed a change in Laura's mood and asked the driver to slow the car so they could watch a group of barefoot Amish girls picking strawberries. The girls laughed as they worked, making a game of the backbreaking task.

Laura abandoned the handwork she'd brought along—the satin baby gown—to watch. There was something about these strangely ordinary people. Something that tugged at her heart. Was it their innocent ways? The peaceful surroundings?

Months earlier, she had gone back and forth about giving up the baby for adoption—one day deciding it was best for the precious life within her, and the next, certain she could never part with the baby she'd carried all these months.

Observing the simple delight of these young women, gathering ripe fruit on a dirt road in the heart of the Amish country, Laura had known what she must do. She'd heard her own heart-voice speaking to her, that faithful, confident voice she knew she could trust. She would give her baby up for adoption.

When the contractions came unexpectedly, the driver had sped away to the hospital. There, Laura had given birth to the baby daughter she'd promptly named Katherine. After holding her, with Charlotte hovering near, she'd relinquished the bundle to the nurse who insisted she get some rest.

It was then, while dozing in and out, that she'd overheard one of the nurses speak to the attending physician outside her door. "The young Amish couple down the hall just lost their baby. Stillborn . . . full term—a perfect baby girl."

She'd heard the doctor's hurried footsteps, and later, the sober whisperings of other nurses. The loss wrenched Laura's heart, and she'd wondered what it would be like to grow up Amish—a question she had voiced to her mother earlier in the day.

Here she was, unmarried, and with no father or no real home to offer her baby. Yet this couple—who had just lost their own child—could give Katherine everything good and simple and honest. It was an easy decision.

When she told her mother, her voice was surprisingly calm. "I know what I want to do about Katherine. . . ."

A gust of wind shook the bare trees, and, instinctively, Laura wrapped her frail arms about herself, shivering in the November sunshine that had suddenly lost the power to warm her. She should call for Rosie to bring a wrap.

She longed to be able to move about without constant help,

wondering if her days of complete mobility were behind her. But she decided to put off ringing for Rosie again. She would sit here a little longer.

A foreboding sense of loneliness overshadowed the brightness of the day, and she recalled the thought that had insinuated itself into her consciousness so many times during the years. *What if Katherine, my precious child, never lived to adulthood? What if something has happened to her?*

Shaking off the dreadful idea, Laura directed her thoughts to her most recent trip to Lancaster, destined to be her last, she was certain. The memory of her time there, although disappointing in its findings, served to lighten her mood—at least for the moment.

She recalled the darling young boy of eight or nine—all shining eyes and golden hair and a spattering of freckles on his nose—who had come to the farmhouse door. In answer to her question, he had pointed out the way back to the main road, giving excellent directions for one so young.

The children . . . They kept popping up, groups of them, in their quaint, black felt hats and winter bonnets, crowded into the back of a market wagon or walking along the road to school. Mostly blond-headed children, she recalled, although there were older ones with darker hair. She had specifically looked for a lone redhead among them; had even driven past an Amish school yard during recess, searching for an auburn-haired girl, before sadly remembering that her baby was a grown woman now, not a child at play.

Where had the years flown? Lost years. Years she could never regain. Years filled with emptiness and anguish. Yet, at the time—as a distraught teenager—she'd done what she'd believed was the best thing for little Katherine. The best thing . . .

Laura lifted her sunglasses and brushed away the tears. *Katherine, my dear girl. How I long to know you.*

She leaned back on the chaise, allowing the sun to bathe her face with light and heat, and wondered how many other women had felt such pangs after relinquishing a baby—pangs as real as the birth itself.

"If I had known what I know now," she said aloud, "I would never, *never* have given you away." She spoke into the air, daydreaming in the stillness of the morning, hoping that the Lord's angels might carry the words from a mother's broken heart directly south—to the place where Katherine might be living. If she was indeed alive. . . .

CHAPTER TWENTY-TWO

Everyone in Hickory Hollow was preparing to attend the wedding on Tuesday. There would be nearly three hundred guests at this wedding; Mattie herself had seen to *that*. She'd made a long guest list for her granddaughter—had even offered to have the wedding at her house.

She was stocking up on white sugar at the General Store on Saturday morning when Rachel Stoltzfus and Rebecca Lapp came in together. Mattie waited until Rebecca was out of earshot before she wandered over to chat with Rachel. "It'll be a mighty fine wedding—my granddaughter's and the King boy's."

"Jah, right fine."

"Hickory John and Levi Beiler are gonna be two of the Hostlers. And I think Bishop John agreed to be one of the ministers."

"That's nice." Rachel headed for the aisle filled with shelves of sewing notions, her back turned to Mattie.

"You'll be comin', won't ya?" Mattie inquired.

"Maybe . . . if Mary's feeling better."

Mattie nodded. "Oh my, I forgot to ask. How is your girl these days?"

"Well, I don't think it's serious what she's got." Rachel pushed on, eager to avoid any more questions. The truth was, Mary had taken to her bed ever since Chicken Joe had asked Sarah Beiler to go to Singing with him. It was the worry about never getting married that had given her daughter a bad case of dysentery. That—and Katie Lapp's shunning.

Just then Rebecca turned the corner and Rachel hushed up. No sense in Rebecca finding them buzzing like bees.

"Well, hullo, Mattie," Rebecca greeted her.

"Mornin', Rebecca."

Seeing the two women together like this—Rebecca and Mattie Beiler—it was clear to Rachel that their old feud had cooled down. Things were actually quite different between them, and she supposed it had something to do with the news of a stillborn baby and an unwed mother so long ago. It seemed that Rebecca's secret had mellowed Mattie remarkably, even though she, and she alone, had broadcast that particular juicy bit of gossip.

Relieved to see Rebecca—knowing her presence would put an end to Mattie's wedding jabber—Rachel offered to hold her friend's basket while she checked off her list. It would do Rebecca Lapp no good to get an earful. Not with her still reeling from her own daughter's recent disgrace.

Just as she suspected, though, Mattie wasn't about to mind her own business but trailed after them in the store, trying her best to draw them into conversation about her granddaughter's wedding.

Several times she mentioned Katie, wondering how the "dear girl" was doing. "Is she any closer to confessin', do ya think?"

That did it. Rachel stepped up and looked Mattie squarely in the eye. "Just be in prayer for Katie, will ya?"

"That I certainly will do." Mattie smiled a little sheepishly and darted to the counter to pay for her items.

It was safe now for Rachel and Rebecca to go their separate

ways again—Rachel, heading for the fresh coffee grounds; Rebecca, to the piece goods counter.

Mattie was just leaving the store when Bishop John strolled in with his son Jacob. Seeing the two pass each other at the door, Rachel feared the nosy one might decide to stick around. But much to her relief, the woman kept going, straight for her carriage.

Bishop John removed his hat and approached Rachel with a pastoral smile. "We missed having your Mary at church last Sunday."

"She's been having quite a bout lately."

"Sorry to hear of it." John rumpled his young son's hair.

Jacob grinned, looking up at Rachel. "Mary cooks gut, jah?"

Rachel nodded. "That she does. And I hope she'll be feelin' well enough to go to the next wedding in the Hollow—come Tuesday." Thinking of what she'd just said, Rachel could have bitten her tongue. Poor Bishop John, what must he be feeling, having to stand up and deliver a wedding sermon right on the heels of his own sad wedding day!

"So it's not Mary who's gettin' married?" Jacob asked, his eyes shining.

"No. Not Mary." Rachel chuckled at the eager look in the child's eyes. "I'm thinkin' you're a tad young for my Mary. But I'll tell her you asked about her."

Jacob scratched his head and glanced up at his father, then hurried off toward the candy counter.

The bishop wiped his forehead. "Well now, it seems they start payin' attention to the girls mighty early these days, don't they?"

Rachel laughed again, said her good-byes, and went to find Rebecca. But she had the oddest feeling that young Jacob had had another reason for asking about Mary. Could it be . . . that if Katie Lapp wasn't going to be his new Mam, he was hoping it'd be Mary?

Hmmm. Best not to say anything about *that* speculation. And if she did, Rebecca Lapp would be the *last* person she'd tell.

Katie waited until she was absolutely sure Abe and Rachel Stoltzfus were sound asleep before she entered the front door of their house. She had left Molasses and the carriage out on the road, the horse tied to a tree nearby, so as not to cause any commotion. *It has to be this way*, she decided. *This way or no way at all.*

The next to the top stair creaked, and Katie froze in place for a second, then crept down the hall to Mary's bedroom.

There was a small gasp of surprise from Mary when Katie appeared in the doorway, lit for a moment by the pale moon, and she hurried in and closed the door softly behind her.

"Shh, don't be afraid. It's only me. I have a flashlight right here, so don't bother with a lantern." She stood at the foot of the bed, feeling awkward for having intruded on her friend's privacy this way. "I know you shouldn't be talking to me, but I couldn't leave without seeing you one last time."

Mary sat up suddenly and reached for Katie's arm, then fumbled for the flashlight. She took it from her and shone the light on herself, shaking her head. Her eyes were huge in her white face.

"If you talk to me tonight—right now—I won't ever tell a soul. Ya won't have to worry about the Meinding, Mary. You can trust me on that, I promise."

Mary stared back at her, eyes ever widening. "Don't go, Katie," she pleaded softly. "I won't ever forgive you if ya leave here."

"How can I stay? I'll be shunned forever, don't you see? As good as dead. And my family won't be allowed to take communion if I stay on without confessing."

In the uncomfortable silence that followed, Katie twisted her long braid.

"You'll *never* confess, is that whatcha mean?"

Katie sighed. "Never."

"Then where will ya go?"

"To Mamma's Mennonite cousins down the lane—Peter and Lydia Miller." She handed Mary a slip of paper. "This is my new address, at least for the time being. When I save enough money, I'll be heading to New York."

"No, Katie, please don't!"

"I have to find . . . my real mother," Katie explained. "She's dying, and I might never see her alive if I don't hurry."

There was a long silence before Mary whispered, "I heard a rumor—people saying you were adopted—but I didn't want to believe it. Now you're saying you have to search for another Mam?" Mary wrinkled her nose. "Oh, Katie, I wish ya could just stay here where ya belong."

Katie took her friend's hand and squeezed it between both of hers. "I don't belong here. I never did, really."

"Ach, Katie, you're wrong, you're so wrong about that."

"And you're right?" She chuckled softly. "You've always been right about me, Mary. Always. Until now. But it doesn't change the way I love ya and always will."

"I'll probably up and die if you go away," Mary insisted.

Katie smiled at her friend's theatrics. "You're not going to die. I promise you that."

"But look at me now. I'm sick, ain't?"

"You're young and strong. I'm sure you'll pull through. Besides, I'll be off finding my true family, so don't go worrying about me. I'll be just fine." Katie sighed. "And before long some gut fellow'll come along, and you'll be married and having all the babies you ever wanted."

The stillness prevailed. Then Mary spoke again. "You'll never forget me, will ya?"

"How could I?" Katie's eyes had grown accustomed to the dim room, and she didn't miss the quiver in Mary's lower lip. "You're like my own sister." They hugged fiercely; the flashlight flickered and nearly went out.

"When will ya go?" Mary whispered.

"Next Tuesday, while everybody's down at the Zooks' house . . . for the wedding." Katie stood to leave.

"Will I ever see you again?"

"Someday, Mary. Someday I'll come again." Katie backed out of the room, memorizing the plump silhouette sitting with her blankets and quilt wrapped around her. Then she tiptoed down the stairs and slipped quietly out of the Stoltzfus house.

Hard as it was, she did not look back to see if Mary, who knew her heart better than all others, had left her warm bed to peer through the window and whisper one last good-bye.

Annie was nursing baby Daniel when a horse and buggy passed the house along about midnight. She rose from her rocking chair to burp the little one and was standing in front of the window in the living room, watching the moon rise, when she spotted the lone figure in the carriage.

It was impossible to see who was hurrying down the lane at such a late hour. But when she looked more closely, she recognized the horse from his slight limp. It was ol' Molasses, the Lapps' driving horse.

The next morning at breakfast, she mentioned to Elam what she'd seen. "Your sister was out all hours last night. At least, I'm pretty sure it was Katie I saw."

Elam poured himself a second cup of coffee. "You'd think she'd be trying to settle down and behave herself—with the shunning and all. But not pigheaded Katie." He sipped his coffee, making a slurping sound. "I guess I should'a known all these years the girl wasn't my blood kin."

What a horrible thing to say! Annie thought, but kept it to herself.

Meanwhile, Daniel began to howl in his cradle near the wood-stove. Annie got up quickly. "There, there, little one," she crooned, kissing his fuzzy head as she picked him up. She sat down at the table again and began nursing him. "Do you think we might've done wrong by not letting Katie hold her new nephew?"

"The girl's shunned, for pity's sake!" Elam spouted. "I don't want her holding our baby when she's in rebellion to the church. The harder the shunnin', the sooner she'll be repentin'."

"Maybe," Annie said, "but you just said she was pigheaded."

"She's stubborn, all right. Who knows how long she'll hold out?"

"What if she doesn't repent? Then what?"

Elam shook his head, evidently disgusted at her question. "Well, that would be a mighty awful mistake."

Katie won't make that mistake, Annie fervently hoped. And for a moment, she thought of her deceased brother, wishing Daniel were alive to see her firstborn son and to help Katie—bless her dear, stubborn soul—find her way through the shunning.

Tuesday came, and before Samuel, Rebecca, and the boys left for the Zook-King wedding, Katie turned to speak to them from her isolated table in the corner of the kitchen. "I'll be packed and gone by the time you get home," she said as they finished eating breakfast.

No one turned to acknowledge her remark. But Katie knew they were listening, and she continued. "You already have the Millers' address—Peter and Lydia. I'll be renting a spare room from them if anyone needs to contact me by mail." Her brothers were staring at her, mouths agape.

"I know you aren't allowed to speak a word to me because of the Meinding," she went on, "and I understand all that. But if you *could* say something, if you could speak to me and tell me good-bye—*The Lord be with ya, Katie*—well, I know you'd mean it . . . you'd mean it with all your hearts."

She turned away so they wouldn't see her sudden tears and began to clear off her little table. The tears dripped into the rinse water as she stood over the sink, realizing it was to be the last time she would wash dishes for her family. She was truly leaving, and the process of bidding farewell was more painful than she'd ever imagined it would be.

When the rest of the family had finished, she offered to clean up the kitchen so they could be on their way. Of course, no one said anything. And minutes later, after Katie had assumed she was alone, she was surprised to see her mother, scurrying back into the kitchen as if she'd forgotten something.

"Here, Katie," she said, all out of breath. "I want ya to have this." She pushed an envelope into her daughter's wet hand.

When Katie looked down, she knew instantly that it was the dowry money. "Ach, no, Mamma, I can't take this. It wouldn't be right."

"Nonsense. You'll be needin' to buy some different clothes if you're going up to New York to find your . . . your first Mam. Now, take it and don't breathe a word to anyone, promise?"

Before Katie could refuse again or thank her mother, Rebecca had spun around and rushed toward the back door.

"Mamma . . . wait!" Katie ran to her, flung her arms wide, catching her mother in a warm embrace. "I love ya, Mam. Honest I do. And . . . no matter what you may think, I'll always be missing you."

Rebecca nodded, tears filling her eyes. "You can't stay on here, Katie . . . I know that."

"Oh, thank you," she whispered as her mother turned to go. "Thank you for loving me so."

Katie was determined to leave her bedroom tidy—the kitchen, too. So a good portion of the morning was spent mopping, washing up, and dusting. When she was packed to her satisfaction— leaving several old dresses and capes hanging on their wooden pegs—she located the satin infant gown in her dresser drawer and carried it to the window. There she inspected it carefully, lovingly, once more.

With her fingers she lightly traced the tiny stitches spelling out *Katherine Mayfield,* and in the sunlight, she noticed a tiny spot on the dress. A closer look—and she decided that Mam must have come into the room, found the little dress, and wept. The spot looked, for all the world, like a teardrop.

Waves of emotion washed over her, carrying her along on an undulating tide—sadness . . . joy; confidence . . . uncertainty. Was she doing the right thing? Mary had drilled the question into her so often during their growing-up years. But now? Was leaving Hickory Hollow "the right thing"?

Hours later, with suitcase packed, guitar case in hand, and the contents of her cedar chest stored away neatly in attic boxes, Katie went out to the barn. Her pony seemed restless as she stood beside him. "I wish I could take you with me, Satin Boy, really I do. But you'll be much happier here with the other animals."

She set the guitar down and went to get his brush. She talked to him as she brushed his mane with long, sweeping strokes. Then she let her tears fall unchecked as she began to hum one of her favorite songs. "Maybe someday I'll come back for you, boy, and take you home to live with me—wherever home ends up to be."

She hand-fed him some hay and patted his nose. "Don't grow

up too fast, and don't look so sad. It's not such a bad thing, really. Eli and Benjamin will take good care of you . . . Dat, too." Speaking her brothers' names and her father's familiar nickname aloud brought a lump that seemed to stick in her throat. She knew she should walk away without looking back—the way she had at Mary's. Maybe then she wouldn't break down completely.

She took a deep breath and kissed the white marking below Satin Boy's right eye. Then, picking up her guitar case, she hurried straight to the door and out into the barnyard.

The house seemed much too quiet to Rebecca when she stepped into her kitchen after the wedding. And while the men prepared the cows for milking, she headed upstairs to Katie's room, hoping she'd find a final note from her. Some keepsake to read over and over again.

Katie's room looked the same as always. The only items missing were a few dresses; she hadn't taken many of them. All the old choring clothes still hung on their wooden pegs, along with the organdy head coverings.

Searching the top of the dresser, Rebecca saw that the hand mirror was gone, along with Katie's brush and comb. The lilac sachets were also missing from the drawers.

Lydia's spare room will soon smell wonderful-gut, I'm thinkin'. The notion brought a pain to her chest, and she put her hand to her heart and held it there as she made her way down the hall to the bedroom she shared with Samuel.

There on the bed, she spied the little satin dress lying on her pillow. *Oh, Katie, you did leave me something. You left the little dress.*

Her heart swelled with love for her daughter, her precious but unyielding Katie. She leaned down and picked up the small garment, lifting it to her face and noticing, as she did, the faint scent of lilac.

Lydia Miller slowed the car as she approached the shady cemetery. "I'll be glad to take you all the way," she offered. "No need for you to walk so far."

Katie shook her head. "Thanks, but it's not that far from here, really. And I need the exercise." She got out of the car on the passenger's side and walked up the slight incline, the sloping area that led to Dan Fisher's wooden grave marking.

What do ya see when ya look into your future? he'd asked her years ago.

"Not this," she muttered to herself. "Never this."

Dan had gone to heaven, she could only hope. And soon she, too, would be leaving Hickory Hollow for good. *Things just never seem to work out the way you plan*, she thought.

Katie approached the flat area reserved for Dan's body. The spot lay cold and empty now as she stared down at the dry, dead grass. "I'm going away," she whispered. "Can't stay Amish. But maybe you already know about that." She glanced up at the blustery, gray clouds high overhead. "You see, I'm fancy inside—and soon will be on the outside, too. And the music—our music . . . well, I'll be able to sing and play as much as I want to from now on."

She didn't cry on this visit, but bent down and knelt on the spot where Dan's body would've been buried if they'd ever found it. "I'll take good care of your guitar for you," she said, leaning her head close to the ground. "I promise you that."

CHAPTER TWENTY-THREE

Katie rode into town with Lydia the next morning to make a deposit in her checking account, then accompanied Lydia to market. Because of her mother's generous gift, Katie had decided to postpone her housekeeping jobs in hopes of finding some good leads on her birth mother's whereabouts.

"Before I do anything, there's one more place I must go," Katie told Lydia. "Will it be too much bother?"

"You say the word." Lydia was smiling. "Happy to help out a relative in a pinch."

Katie nodded. Her situation was more desperate than a "pinch," but she said nothing and kept watching for the turn-off to Mattie's place.

The fancy blue car stopped in the barnyard behind the main house, and Katie got out. This time to bid farewell to the Wise Woman.

When Ella Mae appeared at the window, there was no cheerful greeting, no welcoming smile. Only a glassy blank stare.

Katie's heart sank. The Meinding and its practices had caught up with Ella Mae, too. Either that or the old woman had gone daft for sure.

A shadowy motion alerted her to the real reason for the vacant look in the faded hazel eyes. Behind her stood Mattie Beiler, shaking her head solemnly.

"I just came to say good-bye," Katie called loudly enough to be heard through the door. "I'm leaving Hickory Hollow." She turned and pointed toward the car. "That's my Mam's cousin, Lydia Miller. You probably remember her. . . ." Her voice trailed off when she looked back at the window and saw that Mattie was still standing there, glaring at her through the windowpane.

But it was the single tear tracking a path down the wrinkled lines of Ella Mae's face that broke Katie's heart. Reassured her, too. She was not alone in the world, after all.

"I'll miss ya forever," Katie blurted, choking back the blinding tears.

The Wise Woman blinked slowly, deliberately, then smiled the faintest smile, creating the familiar dimples. One of the family traits Katie had always loved.

One last, long look, and Katie turned and walked toward the waiting car.

Samuel pulled up his rocking chair near the cookstove, removed his socks and wiggled his toes, warming them as he waited for the noon meal. Rebecca felt the emptiness anew without Katie to help with the table setting, and she glanced over at her husband, who seemed to be settling easily into his daily routine.

Wonder how's he managing, really? she thought, turning her gaze to Samuel several times before announcing that dinner was ready.

The spot that had always been Katie's at the big table seemed exceptionally bare in the light of day, even in spite of the fact that she had not sat there for the past ten days—since the shunning began. Still, Rebecca could not get used to it. She never would.

Casting a quick look over her shoulder, she fully expected to see the small table in the corner and was disturbed that she had not remembered seeing Samuel remove it—sometime last evening, maybe. Had she been so caught up in her own despair that she'd blocked it out of her mind?

"When did ya put away Katie's table?" she asked Samuel, who was busy forking up the beef stew.

"Didn't do anything with it," he answered, stretching his neck to have a look at the vacant space.

Rebecca pondered the situation while she cut the meat on her plate. Was she losing her mind?

Then the answer came to her, and she knew precisely what had happened. Katie herself had taken on the chore of folding up the table and putting it away in the cellar. A loving gesture for sure—one that Katie knew might soften the blow for her mother.

Rebecca started to tell Samuel what she was thinking, but her husband stopped her abruptly. "From this day on, there is not to be one word spoken about Katie in this house. We will not be speaking her name—not ever again!"

Startled and hurt, Rebecca jerked her head down. Her hands flew up over her eyes, hiding the quick tears. It was then that she felt Samuel's warm hand on her arm. His hand remained there long after she'd regained her composure. And because of it, she felt comforted.

———

Annie was tending to baby Daniel on a frigid January morning when there was a knock at the front door. She tucked the baby into his cradle in the warm kitchen and hurried to the front room to open the door.

A round-faced postman was standing on the porch. "I have

a letter here for Annie Lapp," he said, reading the name off the envelope marked Priority Mail.

"*I'm* Annie Lapp," she said hesitantly, wondering who on earth would pay so much money for a piece of mail—and why they felt they needed to send it so fast.

"Here you are, ma'am." He handed her the envelope. "Have a good day."

She closed the door against the biting wind and sat down in the living room, turning her attention to the large, cardboard envelope. A small arrow pointed to a perforated strip, and when she pulled on it, she was surprised at how easily it opened.

Before reaching inside, she turned the envelope over and searched for a return address, but there was none. "That's odd," she said aloud.

The idea that it might be a belated New Year's greeting from Katie excited her, and quickly she pulled out the smaller envelope inside, hoping she was right. Dropping the outer covering, Annie read her name on the front of the small envelope. This didn't look like Katie's handwriting, but then again, she could be wrong; after all, she hadn't had reason to see her sister-in-law's handwriting all that often. But this . . . this writing seemed strangely familiar. Where had she seen it before?

She opened the envelope and pulled out a letter written on lined paper, much like the paper she'd learned to write on at the one-room Amish school, many years ago.

Curious, she began to read:

My dear Annie,

For several years now, I have wanted to contact you secretly. I trust this letter will not startle you unduly. If you are not sitting down, maybe you should be, because, you see, I, your brother Daniel, am alive.

Annie leaped out of her chair, trembling, still holding the letter. "Ach, how can this be?" She paced frantically, going to stand in front of the window, staring out but seeing nothing, then sat down again to read the next line.

> *Indeed, there was an accident at sea, but I did not drown on my nineteenth birthday, as you may have believed all these years.*

She rushed into the kitchen, past the cradle holding her sleeping son, and out the kitchen door to find her husband. "Elam! Come quick!"

When she did not find him in the barn, she hurried to the milk house. "Elam, where are you?"

She felt her heart thumping hard and her breath coming in short, panicky gasps. When her husband was nowhere to be found, she stood there in the barnyard, shivering from the cold and her inner confusion, reading the letter from her long-deceased brother.

> *Now, however, I wish to come to Hickory Hollow for a visit. I must do the Christian thing and make amends, starting with Father, because it is he who I have most surely wronged.*
>
> *If it is not too presumptuous, I will contact you again by mail in a few days, and later, if you agree, I want to speak with you—face-to-face—about approaching our father with this news.*
>
> *And Katie Lapp. I am wondering how she is, and hoping that she has not already married, although I cannot imagine that she has waited for a dead man all these years.*
>
> *If I am to be allowed to come to the Hollow, it is Katie I want to see first of all. . . .*

Annie's head was swimming with her brother's brief explanation. So much had been left unsaid. Still, her heart was breaking— for Katie. Poor, dear girl. Even if someone wanted to risk being shunned to tell her about this unexpected turn of events—even so, Katie had already left for New York.

She shook her head mournfully as she walked toward the house. Feelings of anticipation—the possibility of a reunion with her darling brother—stirred within.

When her little one began to squirm and fuss, she picked him up and walked around the kitchen. Thoughtfully, she began to tell him the story of a handsome uncle who had been dead and now was alive, and a stubborn aunt who was as good as dead because of the shunning—and how they had loved each other.

She put her lips to the top of his sweet head and kissed the warm, pulsing soft spot. Such a frightening thing to ponder—this sad love story—its end so unlike its simple beginning.

"Some things just ain't very simple, really," she heard herself saying. "Some things just ain't."

She turned toward the kitchen window, facing west. And holding baby Daniel close, she looked out over the wide stretch of pastureland that bordered the woods. The sun had slipped below the horizon, leaving long, trailing tendrils of red in the sky—like a woman's hair floating out over the trees, free and unrestrained.

EPILOGUE

How swiftly my life has changed, though I 'spect things in the Hollow plod along, same as always. Tongues are forever wagging these days, but all I *really* know is hearsay.

Talk is cheap, but rumor has it that Mam has stopped her storytelling. My heart is awful pained over what she must surely be going through. Still, I don't know how I could've stayed on, not with the Meinding and all. I'd have become a yoke around my family's neck. Eventually, the People would've ousted me anyway. Bidding a sorrowful farewell was my only hope.

They say Mary Stoltzfus's uncle—her father's youngest brother—is interested in moving out to Indiana somewhere. Most likely to look for available farmland. I only hope my leaving hasn't stirred up unrest among the People.

One thing is for sure and for certain. I am free now. No more Ordnung hanging over my head. No more bishop telling me how to dress, how to pin up my bun, how *not* to sing or hum.

But freedom's come with a terrible high price tag—leaving my family and turning my back on the only life I've ever known. Honestly, sometimes I have to reassure myself, and it's at those times that I stop and pray: *O God, help me to be of good courage.*

Still, I remember the shunning, and if the truth be known, I realize it's a grievous blessing—a springboard to freedom. Freedom to experience what the dear Wise Woman could only begin to imagine. Freedom to search, and hopefully, find my roots.

Yet more than any of that, I've been cut loose to discover who I truly am . . . who I was meant to be. And for the part of me that is Katherine Mayfield, it is a wonderful-good thing.

ACKNOWLEDGMENTS

It is a myth that writers work alone. In the matter of this particular book, I wish to thank the following people:

The Lancaster County Historical Society, The Mennonite Information Center, The Lancaster Public Library, and The People's Place; Fay Landis, John and Ada Reba Bachman, Kathy Torley, and Dorothy Brosey.

During the course of my research, as well as my growing-up years in Lancaster County, I have been blessed with Amish friends and contacts, most of whom choose to remain anonymous. A heartfelt *Denki!* for your warm hospitality and many kindnesses.

Deepest gratitude to Anne Severance, my editor and friend, who graced these pages with her expertise and enthusiasm.

Special thanks to Carol Johnson and Barbara Lilland, who believed in this story from its inception, and to the entire BHP editorial and marketing staff.

For ongoing encouragement, I am grateful to Judy Angle, Barbara Birch, Bob and Carole Billingsley, Bob and Aleta Hirschberg, and Herb and Jane Jones.

I forever appreciate my husband's keen interest in my work, and his willingness to talk out plot angles and ideas with me. Thank you, Dave . . . for always being there.